Wicked Love

Wicked Mind

Monica Robinson-Gay

iUniverse, Inc.
Bloomington

Wicked Love Wicked Mind

iUniverse books may be ordered through booksellers or by contacting:

iUniverse
1663 Liberty Drive
Bloomington, IN 47403
www.iuniverse.com
1-800-Authors (1-800-288-4677)

ISBN: 978-1-4620-2391-2 (sc)
ISBN: 978-1-4620-2392-9 (e)

Printed in the United States of America

iUniverse rev. date: 5/24/2011

This book is dedicated to:

	Sunrise	Sunset
Amanda Robinson (Mandy)	October 18, 1919	October 21, 2010
Christopher Jones	July 19, 1977	May 6, 2010
Sherlynn Brooks	March 17, 1977	May 11, 2010
Gloria Smith	May 12, 1964	October 14, 2010
Sherry White	March 19, 1977	December 25, 2010

I will miss you guys so much…
When you left you took a part of me, but the part you let me keep
is the memories that's within my heart and soul…
To my grandmother, cousins and close friend
I will love you until the end…

My mother Mildred Robinson, if it weren't for you I'd be lost or in jail, but you kept me sane and out of trouble and I love and thank you for that. You're such a wonderful person and a great mother who would do anything for anyone and for that they should be blessed to know you and be in your present. This book is for you mom and I love you for being you, and all your help and support.

Marvin Gay Sr. my husband and my rock, thank you for your support and patients and standing behind me as I worked on my first novel. Behind every good woman there's a man and your the perfect example. Kadejah, Shymil, Neajah, Marvin Jr. and Jah'Metri mommy loves you guys so much.

LaTeisha Jones-Meekins my baby sister, whom stood and still is standing behind me, pushing me to make this happen. You get your 5%. (ha ha ha) But on the real thanks for listening to me when I call in the middle of the night you when you just had my niece and taking care of my other niece and nephew love you sis.

To Mrs. Paula Brown my mom best friend and twin, you believed in me when I didn't believe in myself and I just want to thank you and love you auntie.

Barbara Robinson, yo you was the first one to read my BABY, and you like it so much that you took it to work and for that I'm really glad you took the time to read it and call me and let me know what mistakes I've made. Good looking out cuz. Hope you're ready for the next one…

A'Rhonda Gay my sis and a true rude girl, thanks for hooking me up with all the toughest reggae songs, all the hottest spots in the area and all the updates on the events.

I would also like to thank Nikolai Ronalds, Mara Rockey, and Jesse Loudenbarger at iUniverse for their patient, understanding and most importantly time. You've made this experience for me a wonderful one, thanks for all the phone calls and e-mails to keep me updated. Wonderful job the three of you have done…

Thank you God and Jesus for everything I have and for this talent.

Chapter 1

Sasha

Sasha Jones was born in a world with no love. Her father Chamber Jones were murdered when she was three months old and her mother Susan Jones left her when she was two years old with her grandmother Betty Fill, who is a mean cold-hearted woman, she only kept Sasha for the extra income and assistance she was collecting from the state. Her grandmother has a thick Caribbean accent that Sasha didn't understand, so when she got old enough her grandmother taught her to understand everything about the language. She made Sasha life a living hell while doing so and didn't hide the fact that she was doing it. When Sasha turned seven years old her grandmother taught her how to cook and clean, telling her that if she wanted to eat then she had to cook for herself because she wasn't her maid to be cooking and cleaning up behind her. So every morning Sasha would wake up at five in the morning to clean her room and the rest of the house, and then she had to prepare breakfast for the both of them, all this before she left to go to school, Sasha guess she turned out to be the maid. When Sasha turned fifteen her grandmother told her it was time for her to get a job and help pay the bills even though Sasha wasn't allowed to use the phone or watch television but for an hour her grandmother told her that if she lived there she had to pay, because nobody was living rent-free in her house, she act like Sasha didn't know she was getting a fat check for her every month. So just so Sasha wouldn't hear her mouth she got a job working at McDonald's every afternoon when she got home from school. Sasha best friend Janet Day mother Marcy opened a bank account in her name for Sasha so she could deposit her money when she got paid, and her grandmother never knew anything about it. Sasha was on the honor roll at school and got no more then a B- on her report card, when it came to school her grandmother didn't play around, and she made sure Sasha never failed a class, plus Sasha learned along time ago that if she brought anything under a D she would get a beating of a lifetime with no question asked. Sasha loved school and was good with every subject, it came to a point where she would used school as an escape from her grandmother, so she attended everyday not missing one day unless she was sick to a point that the school nurse had to send her home. When Sasha turned seventeen she graduated from Warwick High School with honors and a scholarship. Her grandmother never showed up for her graduation and even though she was really hurt she would never let her emotions show or tell her grandmother how she felt. Sasha cried one time when she was ten because she wanted to know who her mother was, and why she left her, and her grandmother slapped her so hard on the face, to give her something to really cry for. As she was beating her she'd say to Sasha. "Yuh madda left yuh because she didn't want or luv yuh, yuh was a pain in di ass, now shut di hell up for mi give yuh someting ta really cry bout." After that Sasha cried for nothing and showed no emotion for anything no matter how bad it was. When Sasha turned eighteen she went to the poster office and got a P.O. box in her name, and then she went and applied for a couple of apartments. Her grandmother was hinting about her living there and she knew soon or later her grandmother was going to kick her out or asked for her for more money so Sasha was getting prepared to get her own place. Her mother had two sisters Helen and Clara they never claimed Sasha as their niece and never acknowledge her unless they wanted to borrow some money or for her to baby-sit for them, and then she became their niece. Her mother has three brothers also and they were pretty cool with her. Daniel and Danny was twins and Daniel was the quietest and more normal one out of all of them, he moved to Chicago and married a woman name Nelly and they had two kids a boy and girl name Nathan and Natalie and then he open his own garage shop fixing cars. He would send money every month to Betty and she was happy with that unless it didn't come and then she would call and curse him out until it came and then he became her favorite child again. Now Danny and Hue are totally different, and Sasha know when not to be around any of them when they smoked crack or laced weed or drank anything stronger then a Pepsi. Sasha saw her uncle Hue shoot a man for looking at him wrong, and her other uncle Danny choked his girlfriend out because he said she was eye balling another guy all the while her grandmother just sat there and didn't do anything, if she did do anything was to raise her hand to smoke her blunt or drank whatever she's drinking at that moment. Most of the time when they're high or drunk Betty make Sasha cook them all something to eat and than clean up behind them. Sasha uncles never told her but they showed her their thank you by buying her things or giving her money for all the cleaning she's done behind them, of course without Betty knowing it. Sasha was sitting on her bed when her grandmother busts in the door, as usual she was dress to kill hair and nail freshly done, but her eyes were always red. Sasha didn't know how her mother look, but she thought her grandmother was beautiful. She stood about 5'7 and weight 185 with auburn complexion, and with reddish brown dreadlocks that came to her shoulders. Her eyes were as far as the eyes could see was dark brown and for fifty-five she didn't look it. "Mi knows damn well yuh heard mi calling yuh ass, yuh just like yuh madda," said Betty. Sasha jumped off her small twin sized bed and her CD player and paper fell to the floor. "I'm sorry Momma Fill I was listening to some music," said Sasha, she never called Betty grandma or NaNa like most kids do, she did once and was smacked so hard that she had a hand print on the side of her face for a whole week, so she decided to called her Momma Fill instead. "I need mi money gurl, hurry up and get it." Sasha already knew what time it was; she just gave her grandmother two hundred dollars two days ago and she wasn't about to give her a dime more. "I don't have it Momma Fill, I owed my friends and had to pay them back," lied Sasha. At time like this Sasha was glad Marcy opened an bank account for her, all her bank statement was going to Janet's mom house, but they switched all the information recently when she turned eighteen so all her bank statement goes to her P.O. box, but she made sure that she destroyed all of the paper work and if it was important she would let Janet keep it for her. The only money she kept in the house was ten dollars and she kept that in her drawers;

she knew her grandmother saw it when she came into her room plundering through her things and thirty dollars she kept in her book bag purse she knew her grandmother never goes into. Sasha grandmother sucked her teeth and looked at her. "Mi better not find out yo ass lying ta mi," said Betty. "All I have is ten dollars to catch the bus to work; I don't get paid for another week." "Well give mi dat and I get Zoe ta take yuh ta work," said Betty smiling. Sasha shiver with the mention of Zoe Ashland name and she differently didn't want to ride to work with Zoe, he was worst then her uncles, he didn't scare her but he brought out a mean side she always tried to hide or she would end up tongue tied, so she made sure she always stayed away from him and his crew. "That's okay I'll get Brittney to pick me up for the rest of this week," said Sasha as she walked over to her dresser drawer and took out the ten dollars. "Dat girl Red Eye, take mi word for it, but yuh know Z asked about yuh right, wonna know if yuh got a man, mi tell him no, he's gonna come by later and holla at yuh take yuh out, be nice or yuh have mi ta answer ta," said Betty as she grabs the money out of Sasha hands and walked out the room. Sasha couldn't believe with her grandmother had just said, Zoe the male Hoe was asking about her, she diffidently had to leave and fast. Sasha hurried and picks up her CD player and paper and shoves them in her book bag purse and headed out the door, when she was on the porch she saw Zoe talking to one of the girls who lived in the house on the corner, when he saw her he just stared at her like he wanted to eat her up something. It wasn't as if Sasha wasn't attracted to Zoe who wouldn't be after all he was breathe taking handsome. He was about 6'1 and weighted about 240 with nothing but muscles on his chest and forearm as far as she could see; he was brown skin with a low hair cut and a goatee on his smooth brown face. He's every female dream catch. He dress good and carried himself with respect, but it was the meanest about him that scared her. She knew he had girlfriends yes with an s and that was something she would never do is talk to someone who's already involved, plus she knew for a fact that he was controlling and she didn't want another Betty in her life. When she got to the store, Sasha almost turned around when she saw Zoe, parked in the parking lot. As he got out of his car Sasha heart skip a beat, he was handsome, with dimples. Holding her head down Sasha walked towards the store and stop when she felt his hands on her arms. Looking around she saw a couple of females looking there way and one even got on the phone and called someone she only heard "gurl you want believe what yo man is doing" after that her attention was lost when Zoe said her name. "Sasha, wat's good wid yuh, Shorty?" asked Zoe as he looked Sasha over from head to toe. He thought she was beautiful, untouched and he planed to be the only one to touch her if he had anything to say about it. He already knew she didn't have a man, and she wasn't sleeping around which was another bonus for him, plus he always get what he want and he wanted Sasha. "Um, nothing," Sasha said still looking at the ground. "Yuh want ta hang wid mi for awhile? Yo granni called and said yuh needed a ride ta work later on," said Zoe in his thick accent. "I don't work today, and I'm catching my friend to work when I do." Sasha felt him squeeze her arm a little tight and tried to pull away. "Who's ya friend? Mi hope tis a female," said Zoe through clenched teeth. Sasha pulled her arm free and finally looked into his eyes, which was a big mistake. He had the most beautiful light brown eyes. It took Sasha's breath away. "Look, Zoe, I gotta go, but thanks for the offer." Sasha rushed towards the store, to get away from Zoe. His thuggish ways were nothing new to her, but she was just looking for something different. That's why she was sending off college applications so she wouldn't have to be in Newport News anymore. When she walked in the store the owner greeted her with a big smile. Stella Gray was in her mid fifty, brown skin, with reddish brown hair. She was about 5'5 and weight 150. She's original from South Carolina but moved to Virginia when she was twenty five and opened a store and lived in Newport News, Virginia area for the last twenty years. Sasha like her the first time she came in to buy a pack of cigarettes for Betty. "Hey Sasha, where you been hiding, I haven't seen you in weeks I thought you done moved without telling me," said Stella. "Hey Stella I been working, how are you and your family," asked Sasha. "We good, my sister just had her baby and they doing good, she wants to move back down here to be close to the family, so she should be down this way in another month or so." "Tell her I said congratulation, so are you guys ready for the parade," asked Sasha. "Yep, were marching this year, you can join us if you want I know how you like the parades," said Stella. "I let you know if I'm off on that day." "Sure, I don't want to hold you up, so what can I get for you," asked Stella. "My usual ham, turkey and roast beef cold club on white bread and a Mountain Dew," said Sasha looking at the potato chips. "That'll be five thirty-five," said Stella. As Sasha reached inside her book bag purse she froze when she heard Zoe saying he got it. Sasha looked up at him and smiled a thank you while cursing under her breath because she knew it was pointless then argue with him about paying for her things so she waited for Stella to fix her sandwich so she could go visit her friend Janet while she was in town. When Stella handed her, her sandwich she looked at Zoe and then back at Sasha shaking her head. Sasha already knew what she was saying without any words, she was warning her to stay the hell away from Zoe. "Thanks Stella, I'll let you know by Friday if I can join you or not," said Sasha taking her bag and leaving out the store. "Wat's up Sasha, why yuh playing games, I don't like games, but wid yuh mi play, mi don't mind chasing yuh," smiled Zoe in his broken English. "Yeah me and every other female who has legs to spread," mumbled Sasha. "Wat yuh say," asked Zoe looking at her. "Nothing," said Sasha. "Anyway mi knows ya granni told yuh mi asked bout yuh, she just called and told mi herself." "Yeah she told me, but I'm not interested, plus I'm in a relationship and I don't want to disrespect him by going out with you," lied Sasha. She wished at that moment that she did have a boyfriend to get out of this situation; it wasn't as if she didn't have the opportunity because a lot of guys tried to holla at her. Standing 5'6 and weighting 140 Sasha was caramel complexion with shoulder length hair that she always kept down and she had the body every female dreamt of having, but she wasn't trying to get involved with no one in Newport News, because when she moved she wasn't coming back to this area for nothing. "How yuh gaan ta stand in front of mi and lie, Shorty I know all about yuh, and I know for a fact dat yuh don't have no man, and even if yuh did mi wouldn't give a fuck, plus yo granni owe mi some money and she said we can work someting out ta clear her shit," said Zoe in his broke English. "She what," shouted Sasha pausing in the middle of the sidewalk. "She owes mi five." "I'll pay you the money; just give me an hour, but as far as us going out NO." "Dis is noting ta negotiate about, we're going out and dat's final, so be ready in two hours or ya granni will have ta pay and I don't tink ya gaan ta like di way she's gonna have ta pay," said Zoe and walked off. Sasha was furious when she walked into the house, she was suppose to meet Janet since she was in town, but now she had to miss her best friend to confront her grandmother. She found her grandmother in the living room sitting on the sofa smoking a blunt listening to a reggae song on the Internet on the computer while bobbing her head to the beat. "How dare you, how could you sale me like you're my pimp," shouted Sasha. Her grandmother sat the blunt easily on the ashtray and walked up to her and just as easily she smacked Sasha in the face. "Who di hell do yuh tink yuh talking ta, mi own dis house and mi want have some stuck up ungrateful bitch yell at mi in mi own shit," said Betty. Sasha put her hands to her face and stared at her grandmother. "I will not go out with him, if you needed money I would've given it to you, but for you to make a decision for me, no it want happen," said Sasha standing her grounds. "So yuh let him beat mi or kill mi for di money, yuh said yuh didn't have any remember, mi took yuh in mi house and raised yuh ass even when ya own madda didn't wat yuh ass, yuh gonna do wat mi say or pack yo shit and get di hell out of mi house," said Betty glaring at Sasha. Sasha turned and headed in her bedroom and began to pack her things, she didn't have much so when she was finished she walked in the living room thirty minutes later only to find her grandmother and Zoe sitting on the sofa talking, when they saw her they both stop and looked at her. "Yo B, leave us for a min, mi need ta holla at shorty," said Zoe. When Sasha grandmother was gone Zoe looked at Sasha. "Sit Shorty we need ta talk," said Zoe as he stretches his long legs out. Sasha took a seat at the end of the sofa. "Look mi like yuh and wants ta take yuh out, get ta know yuh better." Sasha was quiet looking at the coffee table. "Come now say someting." "Look rude or not your not my type, and if I'm not mistaking you already have a girlfriend or should I say girlfriends." "So mi have many girlfriends, wat dat got ta do wid anyting." Zoe leaned in and took Sasha face in his hand. "Yuh really beautaful yuh know dat, one date and see wat happens," said Zoe looking in Sasha eyes. Sasha was either hypnotized from his sexy eyes or voice, but she was shocked when she heard her own responds. "Okay." "Good now go put yuh stuff back and get ready." Thirty minutes later they were pulling out of her grandmother's driveway, and when Sasha looked back at the house she saw her grandmother peek out the window as Zoe speed off down the road. When they pulled inside a Caribbean restaurant Sasha was shocked when Zoe leaned over and kissed her on her mouth. She never been kissed and it made her stomach do a flip-flop. When they were getting out the car, Sasha saw Brittney coming out of the restaurant heading their way. "Zoe will you excuse me I'd like to speak to my friend for a moment," said Sasha as she grabs Brittney arm and pulled her towards her car. "Spill, what the hell you're doing here with Zoe," asked Brittney. "I really don't know, he asked me out and besides saying no I said yes and here we are, so don't go thinking were dating because we're no, it's just one date nothing more." "How the hell did you manage to get him to take you out on a date, hell I've been trying to get with Zoe for months now, but then again he do choose his flavor of the month, and then dumps them when he's finished, if I were you I'd run, Zoe is to much male for you," said Brittney turning around looking Zoe up and down. Sasha didn't miss the way Brittney was looking at Zoe, she always knew Brittney like Zoe, but now she could see the lust in her eyes. "Maybe I should introduce you to him, since he's to male for me," said Sasha pulling Brittney towards Zoe. "Zoe I'd like you to meet my friend Brittney, Brittney, Zoe." "Oh we already know each other, but it's always a pleasure seeing you again Z," said Brittney flirtatiously. "Wat's up," said Zoe looking only at Sasha. "Are yuh ready ta go inside, "asked Zoe getting irritated with Brittney. " I'll see you tomorrow," said Sasha as Zoe ushered her inside the restaurant. Sasha looked over her shoulder, and saw the hurt and disappointment on Brittney face as Zoe ushered her inside the restaurant. "Look Sha, I don't like yuh passing yuh friends on ta mi, mi know wat mi likes and wat mi wants," said Zoe helping Sasha in her seat. "Thank you, but I don't know what you're talking about." "Mi hope yuh don't tink mi fool, yuh tried ta pass yuh friend on mi, she's not mi type, now yuh are on di other hand is," said Zoe as he took his seat. "I'm sorry and your right, it's that she's really more of your type than me, and she even likes you." "So wat yuh telling mi, is dat yuh don't like mi." "Um, um, what I'm saying is that I don't know you, all I know is what I hear and what I hear I don't like," explained Sasha. Zoe sat back in his seat and stared at Sasha. "Mi likes honesty, mi like yuh even more, now tell mi more of wat yuh like, and don't like Sha." "Sasha." "Wat yuh saying yuh name for," said Zoe. "You called me Sha, my name is Sasha." "Mi know wat yuh name is, mi like Sha mi call yuh Sha, now tell mi wat yuh like ta do for fun," asked Zoe. Before Sasha could respond a waitress came over to their table to take their order. " Hi, I'll have the curry chicken special with extra rice with a glass of water," said Sasha "Ya mon, mi have di same, but mi want Gray Goose on ice," said Zoe. Ten minutes later their food came and they were sitting and talking when a dark skin waitress came to the table eye balling Sasha as she approached Zoe. When they started speaking in their Jamaica Patois Language, for once Sasha was happy that her grandmother taught her the language because what she was hearing made her mad, angry, and upset. Apparently this was one of Zoe many girlfriends or as Brittney said earlier his flavor of the month, and she didn't like the fact that he was fucking her last night and was out with another bitch the next day. Sasha got fed-up when the girl asked Zoe was she going to be another one of his bitches. Sasha was ready to stand up and leave when Zoe stood up before her. "Sha excuse mi for a minute, mi have ta handle someting mi be right back," said Zoe getting up from his seat. Sasha caught them both and herself off guard as she used her Patois language for the first time in years. "Easy nuh, yuh cyan hab him, he has nuff ooman as it is and mi want be anedda. Mi don't do montel dont dat serious. So don't vex mi now, plus dis not mi pattan mi not panqoote like him. Yuh can take all di time yuh need mi gaan." (Chill out, you can have him, he has enough women as it is and I want be another. I don't do playboy it is not that serious. So don't anger me now, plus this not my style I'm not low class like him. You can take all the time you need I'm gone) Said Sasha getting up from the table and then walked out of the restaurant. She was flagging down a cab when Zoe grabs her hand and pulled her towards his car. "Take your hands off me," said Sasha as she snatched her hands from Zoe and looked him in the eyes, the same eyes that made her breath catch in her throat earlier. "Wat's di problem, no one leaves unless mi tells dem ta," said Zoe glaring at Sasha. "Are you crazy, you bring me to a restaurant where one of your many whores work at and you ask me what's the problem, I knew I never should've went out with you what hell was I thinking, your nothing but a ram goat and a male whore in my book," said Sasha as she turned to walk away. Zoe, was heated as he watch her leave. "Get di fuck in di car Sha, don't make mi tell yuh again or yuh gaan ta regret it," shouted Zoe as he reached in his jacket. Sasha paused in her steps when she heard a click sound then she slowly turned to look at Zoe, and then she saw his gun in his hand and she backed away. "What you're going to shot me if I don't get in your car are you serious," asked Sasha. "Yes, and if yuh tink mi playing try mi," said Zoe as he glared at her. Sasha got in the car and didn't say another word to Zoe as he took her back to her grandmother's house. When they pulled up she noticed a lot of cars parked in front and knew her grandmother was throwing a party. "Look Sha, I don't apologies ta anyone, but mi fucked up, I just wanted us ta get ta know each other," said Zoe. "I only went out with you because my grandmother owed you money, now since I did my part, leave us alone plus I have to go," said Sasha opening the door. Zoe pulled her back in, and with one quick moved Zoe had his mouth over her in a kiss that knocked the wind out her chest. Sucking on her tongue slowly Zoe deepen the kiss and when he heard her moan he released her as he looks into her eyes. "Mi will have yuh Sha, remember, mi always get wat mi want, but mi let yuh play yuh game for now," said Zoe letting Sasha go. Rushing out the car and not looking back Sasha ran to the house, if she had looked back she would've seen the wicked smile on Zoe face. When she opened the door clouds of smoke welcomed her with the loudness of the music that played in the living room. Sasha saw her grandmother sitting on the sofa getting rub on by a man who look half her age with about ten to fifteen other people sitting around smoking blunts and drinking so Sasha kept on walking until she was in her bedroom. She locked her door and then threw her purse on the bed and pulled out her cell phone, the one her grandmother didn't know anything about and called her best friend Janet since it was only going on nine o'clock. She answered on the second ring. "Talk because it has to be an emergency if your using your phone and for you to ditch me for lunch when you knew I was leaving tonight," said Janet. "My grandmother pimp me off today, and you want believe to whom," said Sasha as she lay across the small bed. "Tell and hold nothing back," laughed Janet. "Zoe Ashland." Janet stops laughing and started cursing. "I felt the same way, and you want believe what happen when we got to the restaurant?" "You actually went out with him are you crazy." "Momma Fill owed him some money, and she told him I would go out with him, but let me tell you, when we get there a waitress started talking in Patois language and she was asking him how could he be with me when he was just fucking her the night before, and then she had the nerves to ask him was I his new bitch, because if I wasn't then what the hell was he doing with me," said Sasha. "I hope you put their asses in place SaSa." "Did more then that, Zoe was about to get up and excuse him self when I spoke in Patois Jay," Sasha said excitedly. "You spoke patois, I thought you said you'll never speak it again after the hell your grandma put you through," asked Janet. "Yeah, but I had to, I had to tell them off, and I told her she can have him, and then I said he was a playboy and low class, and that they could have all the time they needed and walked off." "No you didn't." "Yes and when I was flagging down the cab he comes and pulls me to his car and has the nerves to asking me what's my problem." "I hope you slap him," said Janet sitting up in her own king size bed. "Are you crazy, when I walked away a second time he pulled his gun out and told me to try him, so I got in the car and he drove me home and when he parked he leaned over and kissed me. Girl I actually saw stars," said Sasha with a smile on her face. "Hold on Zoe Ashland kissed you, are YOU crazy, everyone knows that when Zoe kisses someone he claims them and that their his ooman as he calls them, oh boy SaSa your in trouble big trouble," said Janet. "What are you talking about, it was just a kiss, it meant nothing, and as far as he's claiming me, please, I think he has enough ooman that one kiss wouldn't mean anything to him, and I only went on the call so say date because my grandmother owed him money." "You're not hearing me SaSa he claimed you when he kissed you, he went out with you because he wants you, and Zoe don't date anyone unless he have an interest in her." "That's crazy why would he be interested in me?" "Are you blind you're beautiful, smart and you're to fucking nice if you ask me, you can't say no to anyone and if someone needs a favor you're always willing to help someone out and that's where people like your grandmother and aunts take advantage of you because they know you want say no to them?" "I don't always say yes, I say no sometimes." "Bullshit SaSa when you found out that your grandma owed that money what was the first thing you said." "I said I would pay it for her." "See, and she knew you would either pay her debt or go along with whatever plan she thought of, and that's what pisses me off." "Okay your right, but that's was a one time thing, I want be going out with Zoe any more after today," said Sasha as she touched her lips. "SaSa, stay the hell away from Zoe; he's not the type to play kissing games unless it's something in it for him." "Can I ask you something?" "Sure." "How you know so much about Zoe, I mean you been gone for four years, how you know so much about him, when I lived here my whole life and don't know crap about him, but what I hear on the street," asked Sasha. "Girl don't forget my family is still down there, and my cousin Katrina sister Stacey was going out with him, had her strung out and I'm not talking about no drugs, said he provide for everything all she had to do is follow his rules, and don't cause a problem, he would buy her whatever she want, and she said his sex game is crazy, but he ended it with her I don't know exactly why, but she was crushed for months," said Janet. "Well am not interested no matter what, and the only one who's going to be sexing me up will be my husband," said Sasha laughing. "Yeah, but you better stay clear of Zoe," said Janet. "I will, when do your flight leaves," asked Sasha. "In about ten minutes, call me tomorrow." "Alright bye," said Sasha as she closed her phone. Sasha off the bed and went to got her night clothes out and went and took her shower. When she was finished she got in bed and soon as her head hit the pillow and she closed her eyes, Zoe face was the only thing she saw before sleep claimed her.

Chapter 2

Sasha and Brittney

The next morning Sasha got up before everyone as usual and cleaned her room and the rest of the house. At ten o'clock when she was fixing breakfast her uncle Hue and Danny walked into the living room and sat down lighting a blunt. "Mawning Sasha, we didn't keep yuh up last night did we," asked Hue. "Naw, you know I sleep with my headphones on," said Sasha as she cracked the eggs and put them in the frying pan. "Mi was just making sure." "Want some eggs and bacon." Sasha asked her uncles. "Sure, mi belly is on E," laughed Hue. "Mi know wat yuh mean mon, fix mi up a plate ta, yuh need ta teach mi ooman how ta cook, mi tink she tries ta poison mi sometimes when she cook mi food," laughed Danny. "You two are wild, can I ask you a question," said Sasha. She knew if anyone knew anything about Zoe her uncles would. "Ask anyting," said Hue as he pulled up a chair. "Zoe Ashland, what do you know about him?" Both brothers looked at each other and than back at Sasha. "He's not giving yuh a hard time is he," asked Hue. "Not really, I went out with him last night for Momma Fills, but I don't know anything about him." "Keep it that way, he's bad news Sasha, and why would madda let yuh go on a date wid him, mi just don't understand her sometimes," said Danny. 'Maybe no one did,' thought Sasha as she handed her uncles their plate. "Well it want be happening again, so you don't have to worry about it," said Sasha easing her uncles mind. When she was sitting down to eat her grandmother walked into the kitchen in her robe and sat at the table and glared at her sons. "Where's mi food gurl," said Betty as she now turned to look at Sasha. Getting up Sasha went and fixed her a plate handed it to her and sat down and continued to eat. "So mi heard yuh finally using our language," said Betty as she got up and fixed her a cup of coffee. Sasha didn't respond. "Damn shame yuh only use it ta curse out dat poor boy, when yuh gwan ta learn dat men like Z needs an ooman on his arm, not a baby," said Betty. "Why don't you, date him than." Sasha heard herself say out loud. Betty glared at her as she walked back to the table. "Yuh nineteen, yuh young and mi must say beautaful, but yuh so smart dat yuh dumb," said Betty. "How I'm dumb for not wanting to talk or date someone who's a known drug dealer and who already has enough girlfriend to occupy his time," said Sasha not believing what she was hearing. "Z, has money, he has respect." "And he sells drugs," said Sasha as she lost her appetite and got up to clear her plate. "Madda, dats enough, she's not interested in Zoe, so let it be," said Hue also standing up from the table. He knew how his mother could be, and for the most part he stayed out of her plans and plots, and he knew what she wanted from Sasha and he didn't agree. To him Sasha was a smart girl who would soon be out from under his mother roof, knowing her as he did, she probably move somewhere far, but he also knew that if she ended up with Zoe she was doom. "When mi want yuh input, mi will ask, now shut di hell up and mind ya own bizniz," said to Betty. "Mi just." Before Hue could finish what he was saying, Betty threw her cup of coffee towards him. Missing him by an inch Hue wiped the coffee that did hit him and walked out the door not saying anything else. Danny got up taking his plate with him and followed behind his brother, he wanted no part of the situation. "Now like mi was saying, yuh want be young forever, and yuh should be lucky dat someone like Z is interested in yuh, mi see dem other gurls running behind him trying ta catch his attention, but for some unknown reason he wants yuh," said Betty. Sasha thought about what Zoe said and was going to ask her grandmother what untouched meant, than decided against it. "Well I'm not interested in him, and do you need to do anything else before I get ready to go to work," asked Sasha. "Clean up dis mess," said Betty as she got up leaving her untouched food on the table. Sasha re-cleaned the kitchen and walked outside where her uncles was and sat on the porch with them. "Thanks," was all Sasha said as she looked around her surrounding. Her grandmother lived in a four bedroom house on 19th street down town Newport News. Sasha remember riding her bike down the sidewalk to get away from her grandmother fusing and end up at Janet's house. There she would stay for hours playing games or listening to music. She missed those days. "Yuh work taday," asked Hue. "Yep, bout to get ready in a few, you want me to bring you guys something back when I get home?" "Naw we good, we going ta other party tanight," said Hue as he stood up. "Well have fun and thanks again," said Sasha as she also got up and headed back into the house. When she got in her room she locked her door and took out her cell. Sitting on the bed she dialed Brittney number and she answered on the third ring. "Hey, can I catch you to work." "Yeah I'll be there in thirty minutes so be ready," said Brittney as she hung up the phone. When Sasha was finished getting dress her grandmother called her into her bedroom. "Yes," Sasha asked from the door. "When yuh see Z, tell him mi needs ta holla at him," said Betty. Sasha couldn't believe her grandmother. "I'm on my way to work, so I want be seeing him," said Sasha. "Oh you'll be seeing him, and when yuh do tell him wat mi said, now close mi door," said Betty. Thirty minutes later Sasha was standing in front of the house when Zoe pulled up. "Wat ya still standing there for, get in di car," said Zoe. "Not now Zoe, my ride will be here in a few minutes, I'm on my way to work." "Dat's why mi here, ta take yuh." "Look I don't like to be rude but no thanks, my friend is picking me up now if you'll excuse me." "Sha don't make mi get out of dis car, now get in or mi get." "Look I don't care what you do, my ride is pulling up and I'm going to work, but since you're here my grandmother said she needed to see you, and I don't care what the two of you have going on but I want be a part of it this time," said Sasha as she walked over and got in Brittney car. Soon as they turned the corner Brittney was asking a thousand and one questions. "Look Brittney he came to see my grandmother, not me," lied Sasha. "Yeah right, the look on his face when we drove by said he wanted to light my car up, you better be careful when it comes to Z, he's not known to be turned down because he always end up getting what he wants," said Brittney as she made her way down Jefferson Avenue. "Look there's nothing going on between Zoe and I, so he can't get someone if they're not interested and believe me I'm not interested in Zoe," said Sasha. "Shit I wish that nigga would holla at me, hell one chance is all I need to let him realize what he been missing, shit he's tracing female who's not worth his time," said Brittney. Sasha ignore the insult and didn't say anything because as far as she was concern Brittney could have Zoe as long as it meant he's leave her the hell alone. When they pulled in the parking lot Sasha saw the same car parked in the back in its same spot with the same man sitting there talking on his phone as usual, the only reason she noticed him because she really liked his car, he was pushing a lime green Benz. When she got in she punched in and started work. She liked working at McDonald's but she wasn't trying to make this her life long job, she was going to ask Janet if she could see if her mom had any opening at her business, Your Dream Design was a place where you could fix and design your computer and laptop, and they installs what you would use more then less of, and they even did web site for business. It was everything Sasha wanted but she was going to wait until she moved out of her grandmother house before she worked there and it's a good distance from Newport News, and it was just what she wanted and needed. "So what are your going to do when you get off, you know Tay is having an party tonight, you want to ride with me over there," asked Brittney. "If you had told me earlier when I talked to you I would've brought some changeable clothes," said Sasha as she dropped the fries in the grease. "Girl please I'll take you home so you can change, and then I can change at your crib." "Alright I'll go with you, where is he having his party at this year?" "Girl he got his own house now, yep, broke up with his girlfriend and been doing well for himself." "Oh, let me go see if I'm off this weekend before I forget, Stella wants me to join her and her team at the parade and I told her if I'm off I'd let her know." "Tell her I want to come, you see how many nigga go to the parade to scope out the female," said Brittney. "I'll let her know, let's get back to work for Mr. Heel gets on our backs about talking." Sasha walked towards the back to the office and checked the schedule and saw that she was off on the following Friday and walked back and took the fries out and seasoned them. Four hours later Sasha was ready to take her break when Zoe walked in the doors, without thinking she touched her lips and cursed when Zoe smiled her way. "Welcome to McDonald's my I take your order," asked Sasha as she put on a big smile. "Mi thought it was yuh lunch break," said Zoe. "What can I get for you today sir?" "Why yuh not say yuh spoke Patois," said Zoe in his Native language. A shiver went down her spine as he spoke. "Because I didn't think I had to, and why wouldn't I know the language my grandmother and whole family is Jamaican," Sasha said. "But mi like how yuh sound, so for now on speak our language, when yuh speaking ta mi," said Zoe. "Welcome ta McDonald's may mi take yuh orda," said Sasha in her Caribbean accent. "Don't play game Sha, I come ta take yuh out for yuh break, go clock out and let's go," said Zoe. "Mi don't tink so mon, mi don't take breaks," said Sasha. "There yuh go lying again, like mi said before I knows everyting about yuh, and wat mi know is dat yuh take yuh break everyday at this time for thirty minutes." "And how yuh know dat mon?" "Mi have eyes everywhere, so stop playing games, and let's go," said Zoe. "Look I'm at work and I don't want you here, if you want to order something then order it or better yet, hey Brit, can you take over for me I have to go in the office for a minutes," said Sasha walking off going towards the back. "I'll be here ta pick yuh up when yuh get off, so be ready," said Zoe. Sasha turned around and stared at him. "Well when yuh get here mi want be here, like mi said earlier mi have a ride, so stop bothering me, for you being a man with so many ooooman, how do you have time to come bother me anyway," asked Sasha in her Caribbean language and then easily back in English. Zoe smiled a wicked smile. "Yuh will find out real soon, I only let tings go so far Sha, mi trace no female, I be by yuh house tamorrow morning at noon, be dress and ready when mi get there," said Zoe and left out the restaurant. Brittney looked at Sasha. "I didn't know you spoke Caribbean." "Why is everyone so shocked that I speak the language my whole family is Jamaican," Sasha said a second time that day. "It's a shock because no one ever heard you speak the language until now, hell you English is so clear, shit I thought you was adopted." "That's because I hate using it, and it makes Momma Fill mad when I talk English and not Caribbean, plus I know plenty other language like Spanish, a little French, and Italian, and I don't speak those either," said Sasha. "Okay good point, anyway I talked to Mr. Heel and he said if it's slow we can leave at ten thirty, that way we can make it to the party at eleven thirty or twelve," said Brittney sitting down across from Sasha. "Okay, that's what's up," said Sasha. The rest of the night went by with thoughts of Zoe on her mind; she couldn't forget the kiss and how she felt after wards, or the tingling feeling that stay long after he removed his lips from hers. When she got home she went and took a shower in her bathroom while Brittney took one down the hall. When they were finished it was fifteen minutes to twelve. Sasha was wearing a blue jean Baby Phat skirt outfit with an all white Baby Phat shoes she put her hair in a ponytail with light make-up and lip gloss. Where Brittney was wearing a red an white Polo dress outfit with her all white Polo shoes, she also put her hair in a ponytail, but she prefer the bright colors so she put on red lipstick red eye shadow, and she added white eyeliner on her eyes. When they got to the party it was packed. Standing outside, Sasha liked the surrounding. She like how Tay had his crib set up. The driveway paved with rocks instead of concrete with small lights that shined so you could see where you was going. His lawn was in diamonds design and his trees was trimmed nice and evenly. Inside the house Sasha notice the open space for the dance floor, and the huge entertainment system that sat in the far side of his living room and she couldn't wait until she got her own place to be able to decorate it anyway she wanted to. As Sasha got further inside she saw guys and girls who attended school with her and spoke and talked to them for a few and then her and Brittney went to get something to drink. At the bar Brittney saw a guy she been trying to holla at, and went to talk to him telling Sasha that she'd be right back. When she was turning around to check out the rest of the house the lights went down and then someone pulled her to him and kissed her dead on the mouth.

Chapter 3

Sasha and Zoe

Zoe was sitting in the back when he got the call letting him know that Sasha was heading to the party. Zoe was pissed because she always put up walls when he was around her, and she surprised him when she spoke their native language. He hated to admit it but his dick got so hard when she was speaking that all he could do was stand still and not move, and watch as she got up and left. He had to admit again that she was the only female who ever did that to him and he knew he had to have her and soon. Nancy was sitting on his lap when he saw Sasha and that bitch Brittney walk into the party. Every time he saw her she always flirted with him, he knew he could fuck her but she wasn't his type as Sasha said, and he didn't know how someone like Sasha could be a friend with someone like her. To him Brittney was Red Eye, and Sasha just didn't see it. "Get up," said Zoe to Nancy. "Where are you going, we just got here and I know you're not ready to go yet," said Nancy. "Mi be back, and don't question mi again or mi get Gunny ta take yuh home," said Zoe as he made his way to the dance floor. Zoe walked up to Sasha just as the light went down and kissed her on the lips. "What the hell," Sasha started but her words died on her lips as she looked to find Zoe smiling at her. "What the hell are you following or me something," asked Sasha as Zoe pulled her to a bedroom and closed and locked it behind them. "Take your damn hands off of me, and open the door," shouted Sasha. "Wat yuh scared ta be wid mi in a room," said Zoe as he looks into her eyes. "Scared of what, why you keep bothering me," said Sasha as she pulled away from Zoe and walked further in the room. "Come here, don't be like dat." Said Zoe as he followed behind her. "No, whatever you think is going to happen isn't, like I said before you're not my type." "But yuh my type, look at how ya make mi feel," said Zoe looking down at his erection through his pants. Sasha eyes grew big from the size. "Look um, I gotta go," said Sasha walking towards the door. Zoe was in front of her and before she could say anything else, he had her pressed against the door making her feel his hardness as he grind to her. "Yuh know yuh want mi, just tell mi dat yuh tink about it," said Zoe as he kisses Sasha neck and then her lips. "There's nothing to think about, we can never be," said Sasha in low whisper when Zoe lifted his head up. Zoe was doing things to her that she never experienced before, and she knew she had to get out and fast. "Ow ole yuh is," asked Zoe as he nibbled on her ear. (How old are you.) "I'm nineteen. Why?" There was a knock on the door before Zoe could say anything. "Mi busy," said Zoe through the door. "Z, we're waiting for you," said a female on the other side of the door "Did yuh hear mi, wait until mi finished," said Zoe through clenched teeth as he pulled Sasha to the side to open the door. "No, were finished," said Sasha as she went around him and bent and went under Zoe arms and walked out the door. "So yuh just gaan ta leave mi like dis," said Zoe smiling and looking down again at his erection. "Maybe she can help you with that," said Sasha as she made her way towards Brittney and a couple more people. "Girl your in trouble," said Brittney as Sasha sat down beside her. "I'm beginning to think so myself," Sasha mumbled to herself. She could feel someone watching her and as soon as she turned Zoe and his whole crew was looking her way. "What the fuck is his problem, he has at less seven girls sitting over there one even sitting on his lap and he's staring a whole in me for what, he kissed me I didn't kiss him," said Sasha getting madder by the minutes. Brittney, spite out her wine cooler at what she just heard. "What did you just say?" "I said he kissed me, he act like I kissed him or something, now he acting like were together," said Sasha looking around the room. "Girl if he kissed you then you're his, it want be long before he have you bag and tag, and than thrown away like yesterday thrash, I've seen it happen." "Well it want be happening to me," said Sasha. "Yeah right, the one sitting in his lap her name is Nancy she been with him for two years, she his main girlfriend or bitch as he calls them. She use to act just like you, kept saying that she wasn't interested in him and then the next thing you know she quit her job and where you saw him you saw her." Sasha was quiet as she looked over to where Zoe was and saw the female looking at her. "The same for all them tricks. You got Meka the short light skin girl on his right. She's his right hand bitch, she sell for him and everything. Mona the dark skin chick wearing the all black she's his ride or die bitch she'll whip anyone ass if he tells her too. Standing next to her is Linda, she's his money maker, she pimps out other females for him, and then you got Lena she's he's brain reliever if you know what I mean. The only one who he's been having problems with lately is Nancy and now Meka, they're jealous ass hell because they want him for themselves, but they know when Z is mad or angry that they stay the hell away from him. They say when he gets angry he blacks out and only when he has gotten whatever anger was in him out is when he stops fighting. I heard he beat a girl so bad that she almost died, if it wasn't for one of his boy who stop by one night to check on him he might of killed her, and the next day she was gone, said her parents came and got her," explained Brittney as she took another sip of her wine cooler. Sasha digested the information. "How do you know so much," asked Sasha not believing what she just heard. "Didn't I tell you I tried to get with him, but when I found out that shit, I thought naw, I'm to beautiful for a nigga to put hands on me, but if he ever do push up on me now that's another story," laughed Brittney. "Your silly, let's dance, it's about time they play something good," said Sasha as she stood up and began to dance to Lady Saw 'I've got your man' and moving and shaking her body to the music. "Hey Sasha, you wonna dance," asked a guy name Steve who Sasha and Janet went to school with. "Sure only if my friend can join us." "Hell yeah, two beautiful female in one night, come on." When they got on the dance floor Sasha was having so much fun dancing and laughing that she didn't see Zoe mean mugging her and Steve. She had taken her hair a loose because it had sweated out and was now hanging down her back. With her eyes closed Sasha was swaying to the next song which was Buju Banton and Beres Hammond song 'My Woman Now'. As she danced to the music her mind clear of the day's problems, she wasn't worried about her grandmother or Zoe all she was feeling and thinking was the music. Than she felt a pair of strong arms circling her waist and thought it was better not to lean in on Steve so she turned and saw no one other then Zoe standing in front of her. As she tried to pull away he pulled her closer to him. "Keep dancing," said Zoe as he held her close to him. Sasha felt his dick get hard against her and swallowed hard. "Wat do yuh want from mi," Sasha asked in a low voice. "Yuh, like di song say, yuh my woman now," said Zoe as he pulled her closer. "You can't be serious, look around you, you have about five females with you, five, and you're here dancing with me not caring of what they think or feel, do you really think." Sasha was silence as Zoe kissed her deeply and as her eyes closed she saw bright lights flashed before her eyes, and the wind caught in her chest, as he was took her on a roller coast ride that she never been on before. When he pulled away she saw that the whole house was now quiet. Stepping back, Sasha slapped Zoe in the face, and ran off the dance floor. When she got to bar on the other side Brittney and Steve was coming towards her. "What the hell was that about, are you crazy why you didn't tell me that you are Z girl," said Steve shaking his head. "I'm not anyone's girl, what the hell am I going to do," asked Sasha fighting back her emotions. "There's nothing you can do, he just claimed you in front of everyone if someone push up on you he's either crazy or have an death wish, and I'm lucky to be still standing here, he usually shot first and ask question later, but it was nice seeing you again Sasha, and tell Jay I said what's up, I haven't seen her in years," said Steve as he turned and went back to where his friends was standing, he wanted to make sure that Zoe saw him without Sasha, he knew in the next minute if he would be dead man or not. When Zoe makes a point it always ended with someone in a body bag or fucked up and Steve wasn't ready to die and he wasn't trying to be in a hospital. Zoe was pissed and he knew he had to find away to get Sasha and quick. Zoe saw Nancy mean mugging him when he went back to the table so he turned the other way from her. "I know damn well you just didn't disrespect me in front of all my friends, you know what, I bet you want like her ass after I fuck that bitch up," said Nancy as she tried to go to where Sasha and Brittney was sitting. "Yuh do and mi will fuck yuh up, now sit the fuck down and shut the hell up mi tired of ya shit, mi will fuck who mi want when mi want, now say someting else and mi will make yuh regret it," said Zoe as he glared down at Nancy. "I hate you," mumble Nancy as she sat back down staring at Sasha. "What do Zoe sees in you and them other bitches I'll never know, hell your playing hard to get when I'll give up the pussy without no hesitation or complaints," said Brittney. "That's where were different at, I just want sleep with just any body, and I've learned two thing and it's that I'll always respect myself and my body," said Sasha pissed at what Brittney just said. "Like I said, what do he sees in y'all?" "Look if you want Zoe then he's all your, but don't start talking down on me, because he didn't choice you but choice me," said Sasha. "Whatever." Said Brittney, as she walked away from Sasha and headed to the door. For the first time in her life Sasha grab a shot of vodka and down it. She wasn't a drinker, but she knew her night was shot-to-hell because Brittney just left her stranded. Three shots later Sasha was finally having some fun and she didn't care if she had a ride home or not, she was tired of not being able to just go out and have fun. She was dancing to the music with her eyes closed when she felt someone watching her, when she opens her eyes Zoe was watching her every move. "Ku at dis." (Look at this) Sasha mouthed to Zoe as she pulled a light skin guy to her and began to freak him on the dance floor. Turning around so her back was against his chest she dropped down and bounced her ass on his dick as he slapped her on the butt a couple times. When Sasha looked up again she saw the expression on Zoe's face and smiled and then to piss him off some more she turned around to face the guy and drop down again and began to work her body upwards like a snake while feeling on his dick at the same time. Zoe friend Gunny came from out of no where, and whispers something in the guy ears and the guy left Sasha on the dance floor. Sasha was mad as hell as she approached Zoe and his whole crew. "Wat di blood clot is ya problem, mi don't want yuh, wat yuh lagga head or someting, now lef mi nuh and galang bout ya bizniz," shouted Sasha with a little slur to her words. (What the fuck is your problem, I don't want you, what are you stupid or something, now leave me alone, and go about your business.) She saw Brittney heading her way and was glad that she didn't leave her stranded after all. "What the hell, I leave you for a few minutes and you get drunk and act a fool," said Brittney. "I thought you left me," said Sasha and bust out laughing. "Girl please leave you for what, my mom said more grimy shit to me then that, now let me take your now drunken ass home before Z beat you in the middle of next week," said Brittney as she helps Sasha away from Zoe and his crew. Zoe looked at the dudes who was dancing with Sasha and was ready to blow both their brains out but thought that if he started killing people he'd end up in jail before he even had a chance to be with Sasha. "Mi ready for yuh ta bounce," said Zoe as he stood and halfway pushed Nancy out his lap. When he got outside he took out his cell phone and pushed a button. "When she gets home yuh galang bout yuh bizniz, do di same ting tamorrow, mi want ta know everything she do," said Zoe in his Caribbean language then closed his cell. "Who was that," asked Nancy. "None of ya bizniz now go get in da car, Gunny take dem home and pick mi up in an hour," said Zoe as he walked back in the party. Making sure his gun was loaded Zoe walked up to Steve and nodded his head towards the back yard. Steve was so scared that he thought his heart was going to come out his chest. "So where do yuh know Sha from," asked Zoe looking out at the night sky. "Um who," asked Steve. "Don't play games, Sasha, where do yuh know her from." "Oh um school, we went to school together." "Ya know who her friends are den." "Well kind of um, well you see I liked her friend Jay, but that was like years ago." "Ya batty bwoy, cool mi don't have to worry about ya, who is dis Jay," asked Zoe still looking at the sky. "Naw man I'm not gay, Jay is a girl, they was friends since kindergarten, I just met Sasha really when I started hanging out with Jay," explain Steve also letting Zoe knows he understood his language. "So dis Jay, where she lives now?" "Last I heard she was in Texas, her mother has a business out there, and they moved five years ago." Zoe was quiet. "So tell mi now have yuh ever touched mi girl," asked Zoe as he turned to look Steve in the face. "Never, like I said I liked her friends Jay, but she moved away, I haven't seen Sasha since we graduated and believe me if I knew she was your girl I'd never have step to her." "Ya can go, mi have a lot on mi mind and right now yuh safe, but if I found out yuh lying ta mi, yuh be dead before yuh know it," said Zoe as he took out a blunt and lit it up and inhaled deeply. When Gunny came to pick up Zoe he headed to Sasha house. Sasha was in her bedroom laying down in her night shirt reading Taught A Lesson by Monica Robinson-Gay, when she heard the doorbell. Knowing that her grandmother wasn't getting up to answer it she went to answer it herself before whoever it was woke everyone in the house. When she opened the door her heart nearly jumped out her chest. "What are you doing here?" Before Sasha could finish speaking Zoe snatched her by the neck and pin her against the side of the house. "If yuh ever, do anyting like wat yuh did tanight ya will pay, yuh mines do yuh understand." Said Zoe as he took her mouth and kissed her deeply not waiting for and respond. As he sucked her tongue softly he heard her moan. Then without breaking contact he took his left hand and squeezed her breast softly and then took his right hand and put them inside of her panties and fuddled her pussy and she came within seconds. When he pulled away, Sasha eyes were still close. "Since mi can't get noting else mi will be satisfied wid dat," smiled Zoe. "I just don't understand you, why me," asked Sasha. "Because yuh untouched, and yuh not battabout," said Zoe as he walked to his car. As the car pulled off Sasha was still thinking of what Zoe said to her. 'Untouched she didn't get, but battabout is a loose woman who sleeps around and she surely wasn't that, so what he meant,' thought Sasha as she locked the door and got back into bed. 'What am I going to do about him,' Sasha asked herself as she touched her lips again and felled asleep with Zoe on her mind and heart. When Zoe and Gunny pulled in his yard he saw Nancy car park in the driveway. "Boss, do yuh want mi ta get rid of her," asked Gunny. "Nuh mi good, mi takes care of her yuh gwan home." When Zoe walked in the door Nancy was sitting on the sofa naked wrapped in a towel. "Mi not in da mood, get dress and gwan home," said Zoe as he passed Nancy and walked over to the bar. "You know what I'm getting real sick of you and your shit Z, who's the bitch you was all over tonight? And then you had the nerves to kiss and claim her in front of everyone, so what she's your new flavor of the month, because if she is then I'm gone, I don't need this shit and I don't need you," said Nancy. "Mi told yuh before mi not in di mood, now get dress or mi call Gunny back and he'll take yuh out of here, yuh choice." Before Nancy could respond Zoe cell phone rung. "Speak," was all Nancy heard before Zoe went the hall to his bedroom. Nancy felled on the sofa and cried. When Zoe came back downstairs four hours later with his suitcases he saw Nancy on the sofa sleep so he went to the closet and grabs a blanket to put on her. As he looks at her he thought she was so beautiful, but she was just like all the other females he was involved with. He remember when he first met her she was working at a bank and he thought she had it going on, but as soon as he got with her she quit her job and expected him to pay her bills, and then to top it off whenever he went out she always showed up, causing a lot of problems. He lost feeling for her ever since then. Now he only wanted one and she seemed to be a challenge, but than again he loved challenges. Zoe walked out his house with only Sasha on his mind as he got in his car and droved off into the night.

Chapter 4

Zoe

Zoe ended up staying two months in California with his mother, sister, and brother. When he got back to Newport News his man Herd who he left in charge had fucked up his money and everyone knew when it came to Zoe money he was a different person. "Wat da blood clot ya mean yuh don't have all mi money, yuh suppose ta be in charge, how ya gaan let dem pussy clot yuh," shouted Zoe as he paced Herd living room. "Boss I'm sorry man, I did everything you said to do, I went to collect on your money every week and everyone said they was short or didn't have it, even shorty grands bucked on me for your cash." "Wat shorty, yuh talking bout," asked Zoe. "You know, you know the girl who works at Mickey D's her grands bucked on your money said she'd pay you when she gets it," said Herd switching the blame on someone else. "She did, did she, yo Gunny let's ride, and Herd yuh got until di end of di week ta get mi money and tell dem ten percent been added, and if dem don't have mi money by the end of di week, tell dem I said ta kiss dem ass good bye," said Zoe as he and Gunny walked out of the house. Herd release this breath and fell on the sofa shaking his head. Soon as Zoe got in the car he pushed a number on his phone. "Where she's at?" Zoe listen for a minutes and then closed his phone. "It's time for mi ta collect mi wife," said Zoe as he smiled wickedly to himself. Sasha was in her bedroom listening to her CD player when her grandmother busted in her room. Sasha never has seen her grandmother look so scared. "What's wrong, are you okay Momma Fill," asked Sasha with concern as she put her things on the bed and stood up. "Mi needs some money, mi knows yuh have it, mi needs it now," said Momma Fills. "All I can give you is two hundred, I was going to put that towards the light bills," said Sasha. "No mi needs five thousand dollars," said Momma Fill with tears in her eyes. Sasha knew at that moment her grandmother had gotten herself in some real deep shit. "Look let me call and see if I can borrow it okay just give me a few minutes, okay," said Sasha as she ran into the living room and called Janet, when she explain everything to her, Janet told her to give her grandmother the money even though she didn't like Sasha grandmother she could tell by Sasha voice that it was serious. Sasha hung up the phone and told her grandmother that she would be back, but as she reached the front room door it flew open missing her by an inch and there stood Zoe and one of his friend. "Where's yuh granni at," said Zoe not looking at Sasha but around the house and her heart stopped beating for what seems like forever as she looked at the man standing before her whom seemed more deadly and dangerous. "Um, um, she's not here what can I help you with." The guy standing beside Zoe tapped him on his shoulder and pointed down the hall. "She's lying, I see movement down the hall want me to check it out," asked Gunny in Spanish. "No you can't go and check it out, I said my grandmother isn't here, now if you'll excuse me I was just leaving," said Sasha shocking them both. Gunny looked at Zoe and then backs at Sasha. "She speaks Spanish ta," said Gunny, surprised now in his Caribbean accent. "It appears she does. Now go check di rest of di house, and see if anyone else is here," said Zoe as he grabs Sasha and pushes her on the sofa. Five minutes later she heard her grandmother yell, and she hopped up, and was push back onto the sofa by Zoe. "What the hell is wrong with you, are you going to let him hurt her," shouted Sasha. Zoe still didn't look at her, when Gunny brought her grandmother in the living room she saw her grandmother was okay, and release a slow breath. "Wat's up B, seems like we have a big situation dat needs ta be cleared like right now, so mi gaan to asked yuh one time where da bumba clot is mi money," said Zoe as he took out his gun and placed it on the table. Sasha looked at her grandmother and then looked back at Zoe. "Look I can get your money if," Sasha stop talking when she heard Zoe laughing. "If ya don't have mi money here den I don't want ta hear shit yuh have ta say, now B from wat mi was told yuh said yuh have mi money for mi when mi get home, mi home now where's mi money," said Zoe. "Mi don't have it Zoe, mi need a little more time," said Momma Fill. Zoe started laughing again. "Ya bummaclot crazy, yuh buck on mi money for two months, now pay mi my money or get a bullet in ya head, now which one," said Zoe picking up his gun and pointing it to Momma Fill head. He wasn't really going to shot her he just wanted Sasha to think so. Bingo. "Please Zoe, can I please talk to you alone," asked Sasha. "Wat we have ta talk about, yuh didn't wat ta talk ta mi two months ago, oh so now yuh need a favor from mi so now mi good enough for ya time," said Zoe as he turned and looks at Sasha for the first time. Sasha didn't say anything but stared into Zoe eyes. "Gunny, take B in di kitchen," said Zoe. When they were gone Zoe just looks at Sasha. "Why are you really doing this," asked Sasha. "Because no bummaclot is gonna steal from mi and live ta talk about it," said Zoe sitting his nine-millimeter back on the table in front of them. "See now shit has changed and here's three option for ya since yuh want ta get involved; one, yuh and yo grands can walk out of here if ya got my ten thousand dollars right here right now." "Ten thousand, she said five." "Because she was ditching mi man for two months I tink dat's a fair amount, mi could raise it ta twenty, after all its mi money," said Zoe. Sasha was quiet, and didn't say anything. Zoe continued. "Or two, yuh can watch mi put a bullet in yuh granni head and then put a bullet in that pretty head of yo's because mi can't let yuh live knowing mi killed ya grands or three yuh can choose ta be mi girl and I'll forget dat she just got mi for ten thousand dollars," said Zoe. "I'll pay you the money, I can go get it right now if you don't hurt us, and I can't be your girl because I'm not going to be here long I'm moving, so see you don't have to do any of this, I can get the money I was about to go get the money when you showed up," said Sasha thinking quick so she can get the hell away from her grandmother and Zoe and all their problems. "Mi don't wat yuh money, mi got plenty money, wat mi want is yuh, and as far as yuh leaving get dat out yuh mind right here right now, like mi told ya before mi always get wat mi want, so wat's it's gaan ta be," asked Zoe. "I can't be your girl you have enough as it is, so why are you so interested in me?" "Yuh untouched and yuh have five second ta give mi yo decision or am gaan ta put a bullet in yuh grands head and make yuh watch." Sasha couldn't believe what was happening. "Yo Gunny bring B in here," shouted Zoe standing up and grabbing his gun. Sasha grandmother and Gunny came in the living room and when she spotted the gun she looked at Sasha and then Zoe. "Times up shorty, wat's yuh answer gaanin' ta be," asked Zoe putting the gun to Betty head.

Chapter 5

Sasha

Sasha was relieved that some of the bruises Zoe put on her was fading away, at one point she didn't recognize her own face and body if she wanted to. She has been avoiding Zoe for the last couple days staying out his way, because lately the littlest thing made him angry. She came home three weeks ago and he took his rage out on her because one of his other bitches as he called them lately made him mad. She knew it was stupid for being with him, but every time she tried to leave he would threaten to kill her grandmother and her and even though she hated her grandmother she wouldn't want any harm done to her and as for herself she was just to scared to see if he would really kill her. Sasha did whatever she could do to keep him happy and avoid everything if she thought it would upset. So in other words she was walking on egg shells trying not to let them crack when he was in a bad mood, so she stayed and put up with Zoe and his many female dramas. On her first week she became a little relax being with him, she was seeing a part of him that she never knew existed, and she was actually enjoying his company. She would clean his house which was an enormous house with four bedrooms, a den, and a huge kitchen where she'd have dinner ready whenever he got home. When he was away and she was alone she'd use her cell phone that he didn't know anything about and call Janet and talk to her and catch on everything with her life. She didn't want him knowing that she had a cell phone because she knew he would ask to see her phone bill to see who she been calling. She was tired of his jealousy and his controlling. Since she been living with him she hadn't put no more then five thousand in her bank account and the only way she could do that was by lying to him telling him that she owed the money to some friends that she borrowed before she moved in with him. Of course he gave her the money to pay them back, but she refused his offer and his money, even thought she was lying, she wouldn't take his money and then be owing him like her grandmother, no way, she already knew how he played his game. Dirty. When Zoe and her was at the house alone he would hold her and for a minute she felt safe and wanted, something she never had in her whole life, he would ask her if she wanted anything or needed anything, but she always said no, not wanting to lead him on to believing that she was feeling him, even though she was. Sasha was confused about her own feeling she didn't know if it was love or lust and since she never been in love or was shown love she figured it was just lust, and she wasn't about to catch feeling for someone who had a dozen of other females calling him and demanding for his attention. Her first couple weeks turned into months, months turned into a year and at first everything with him was pleasant enough, he took her out to fancy restaurant in Hampton, Virginia and Virginia Beach, she forgot the names because she was always nerves when she was with him that she couldn't pay attention on her surroundings. As they talked more then less Zoe talked and she listened, she found out that he was well educated and his streets life started when his father were killed in a drug deal gone badly, so he had to help his mother raise his brother and sister. Sasha heart swelled with emotion as he told her about his life. Sasha also found out that they actually like the same kind of food, music, and movies. He also told her that she was going to be his wifey from that moment on, and the only way she was going to leave him was in a body bag. She didn't understand how he could be so loving and caring and open minded and relaxed on minute and then the next minute he could be mean, dangerous and cold hearted. Sasha was still working but unlike her grandmother Zoe took her check stub to see how much she was earning, and even though he didn't give her any money; not that he didn't offer, but she still had to show him her receipts, on everything she brought. Zoe was against Sasha working and told her that she didn't have to, but Sasha used working as another excuse to escape Zoe and his female drama. Zoe didn't know about Sasha bank account and she was going to keep it that way, when she leaves him she plain on having money to start her new life without Zoe or her grandmother. She just needed the right opportunity to escape. One evening she brought up the subject about going to college, but as far as Zoe was concern college was out the window, he told her that if she wanted to go to college she could sign up for Christopher Newport University which was thirty minutes up the street from where they lived, but other wise she couldn't attend any other college unless it was in area. Sasha later on found out that Zoe had one of his boys following her. She had gone to the postal office to check on her mail and when she got home Zoe choked her out asking her why she needed a postal address when she was living with him, and asked her was she hiding something from him, she lied and said she was checking the mail for a co-worker who was getting off work late. After that she gave her key to Janet and told her to check it for her when ever she was in town. Sasha made sure that Zoe didn't know anything about Janet, when they met they would met in a all women's store knowing who ever was following her wouldn't dare come in there. The only thing Sasha was happy about was that Zoe didn't pressure her with sex, she was real thankful for that. "Yo Sha get in here," yelled Zoe from the living room bring Sasha out of her daydreaming. Sasha was hesitant for a minute she didn't know what kind of mood he was in today since she went straight to their bedroom when she got home from work. Yeah she had to sleep in the same room and bed with him and she had to sleep naked. Sasha was shocked when he told her to take off her night clothes that first night, she never seen a male part but chest and forearm and when he walked in the bedroom butt ass naked she was shocked and surprised when she took in his magnificent body, she still didn't know what he meant when he said she was untouched, and she didn't want to ask him in case it pissed him off. So she hurried in the living room where Zoe was sitting on the floor with his other girlfriend Nancy as she locked his hair that he decided to let grow out. His best friend Jay was sitting in the chair across from them looking at a movie, he was the only one who spoke and as she spoke back she saw about ten more of Zoe's boys, some playing the Wii game and some counting money scattered around the house and some was playing spades at the kitchen table. "Yes Zoe," said Sasha quietly.

"Yuh been avoiding mi and now its gaan ta stop, come here and give mi a kiss and forgive ya man," said Zoe smiling. Sasha obeyed and walked over and kisses him lightly on his lips, but she was surprised when he grabs her head and deepens the kiss using his tongue to open her mouth and she thought her head and heart was floating. When he let her go she ran backs to the room and shut the door. "What the hell was that about, he hasn't kissed me like that in months," said Sasha as she paced the room floor. Taking a deep breath she sat on the bed and cried, before she got in her emotion she wipes her tears away and lay on the bed. She wanted out and she had to plan it safely without Zoe finding out. Sasha couldn't go on living like this, being beaten when she didn't do anything wrong, and for him to bring his other bitches in the house and taking them to the extra bedroom to fuck them and then she had to sleep with him nude. She was thankful that he was screwing them and not her, but she was tired of the disrespect. Oh she heard them talking shit and calling her a bitch this and a slut that, but every time she made her present known they didn't have shit to say, and how come they never had the black eyes or busted lips? After all she was the only one who cleaned the house behind them and cooked his dinner, he claimed it was a wife duty to have the house clean and dinner ready when he gets home or whenever he got there. For the first time in her life Sasha cried herself to sleep. Sasha was in a deep sleep, but when she felt Zoe hands on her thigh rubbing her, she jump and move away from him. "Take off yuh clothes," Zoe said in his thick accent. Sasha looked at the clock and then backs at him. "Yuh areddi ta go ta bed dis early mi haven't cook dinner yet," said Sasha back in her Caribbean accent. When she first moved in Zoe told her he wanted her speaking their native language, so she obeyed not telling him the reason why she hated the language. Every time she spoke it, it reminded her of her grandmother beating her, cursing her, and degrading her, but when Zoe spoke to her, it sent chills down her spine. "Take yuh clothes off," said Zoe again as he began to remove his own clothing. Sasha began to take off her clothes when Zoe stops her. "Den again, let mi." Sasha was confused as she looked into Zoe eyes and could've sworn she saw passion in them but his expression change so fast that she thought she was imagining it. Zoe went slowly as he undresses her taking in her beauty. Hc waited long enough and tonight he was gonna make Sasha his, he was gonna brand her and make her his forever. As he laid Sasha down on the bed he started kissing her on her neck, he felt her tense and told her to relax. "Please stop Zoe, we can't do dis," said Sasha feeling light headed to the sensation Zoe was making her feel. "Look, mi been patient, tanight mi gaan ta make yuh mines, Sasha don't fight mi, just lay back and relax, mi know yuh untouched and I'll go slow," said Zoe as he tried to kiss Sasha on the lips. "Untouched, you said that before, you mean since I'm a virgin you want me," said Sasha shocked and in English. " Wat mi tell yuh, no English and yeah untouched, no one has ever had yuh, now yuh mines forever, I'll make yuh happy Sha." Drawing back Sasha looked into his eyes and smacked him. "How dare you, untouched my ass, I will not give you my virginity. It's bad enough I'm here unwillingly and to have to deal with you and your mood swings, and your females drama, and you taking your anger out on me when theirs the ones who's pissing you off." Sasha said as she took in a deep breath and stared at him. When Zoe didn't say anything, Sasha continued. "I had the only opportunity of leaving this hell hole snatched away from me by you, and if you think for one minute that I'll just lay down and you screw me then you mightiest well shoot me because I'll be damn if I sleep with you or any other man who don't love or respect me," shouted Sasha. Zoe was still quiet as he stood up and walked over to the dresser and opens the middle drawer. Sasha eyes grew big as fifty cent pieces as she saw him take out his gun and pointed it her direction. "Are yuh sure about wat yuh say because if mi can't have yuh no one will, now yuh have five seconds to decide," said Zoe as he took off the safety and cocked the trigger back. "You can't be serious, why are you doing this, what have I done to make you choose me, when you have all these other female who's willing to be your girlfriend," asked Sasha letting her emotion show. "Decide Sha." "I choices death, if I have to give my soul to the devil," said Sasha looking Zoe dead in his eyes. It surprised Sasha when he put his gun on the dresser and crossed the room to her in three strides. "Mi no devil, mi a man who goes after wat mi wats and right now mi wat yuh," said Zoe as he pushed Sasha on the bed and got on top of her. "Please don't do this," cried Sasha. Zoe ignored her cries as he forcefully spread her legs. "Either yuh relax and stop fighting mi and let mi make luv to yuh, or I can go fast and hard and hurt yuh, mi don't want ta hurt yuh but yuh have ta choice and choice now Sha." When he felt her relax in his arms, he began to suck on her breast, and when he heard her moan he worked his way down to her belly button, and licked and kissed there, and then went further. He never given four-play before, but since she was untouched he wanted to enjoy her and both of their experiences. "Oh, my, God," Sasha shouted as Zoe's tongue connected with her clit as he sucked lightly. Lifting his head he smiled up at her. "Oh now mi God, make up yuh mind," teased Zoe as he went back down tasting Sasha sweetness. Zoe sucked, nibbled, and bites on Sasha inner thigh and then he pushed his tongue deep inside of her making her grabs the back of his head to make him go even deeper. Zoe was hard as a rock, and each time he did something she would moan his name with pleasure. When he enter is pointer finger in her, her hips raised up as he finger fucked her nice and slow, when he couldn't take it anymore himself, he raised up and took off the rest of his clothes and for the second time that day he did something he never done, he enter Sasha raw and was shocked when his head became light to the feel of her tightness, and wetness. As he pushed further into her he felt her virginal stretch and cover his length. "Relax Sha, its gaan hurt for a second," said Zoe as he kissed Sasha on the lips to drown out her cries. When he began to go in and out of her he was surprised that she was working her body back to him. "Dat's it baby, damn yuh feel so good Sha," said Zoe as he thrust longer and harder in and out of Sasha. Zoe felt Sasha body tense up and knew she was ready to cum so he stop and went down on her and gave her four-play until she came and he drank every drop of her juices, when her body began to shake from the after shock Zoe reenter her and rocked her world with another orgasm. "Oh Zoe, yes, yes," shouted Sasha as she found Zoe mouth and kissed him deeply. "Dat's it Sasha take dis dick, oh shit I'm fitten ta cum Sha, damn dis pussy is so good," said Zoe as he thrust two more time and filled Sasha up. When he rolled over he pulled Sasha in his arms and kissed her. "If yuh ever try and leave mi I'll kill yuh, yuh mines forever, body, heart, and soul," said Zoe as he got up and went into the bathroom. Sasha was still dazed but she heard him loud and clear. The only way she was leaving him was in a body bag and she wasn't ready to die. Sasha was getting off the bed when Zoe came back in with a warm cloth. "Lie down and let mi clean yuh," said Zoe getting back on the bed. Sasha, did as she was told and laid on the bed. Her nipples harden as Zoe washed them, and her body tingled when he touched her and cleaned her womanhood. "Are yuh sore?" "A likkle." (A little) Sasha said looking away. Zoe lifts her face to face him. "For now on look at mi when yuh talk, were tagether now and forever, I'm yuh man like yo my woman. " Forever, wat is forever ta yuh Zoe, because forever ta mi is wid a man who luvs and respects mi, mi can't live like dis, yuh sleep wid mi den wid di other females, but yet yuh want mi ta be wid yuh forever, again mi ask yuh wat is forever ta yuh?" " Til one of us dead," said Zoe now kissing Sasha neck again. "Yuh can't be serious, yuh want mi ta be wid yuh while yuh have other females are yuh crazy?" "Wat do yuh want mi ta do Sha, mi have other females, dem don't mean anyting ta mi, yuh have noting ta worry about, yuh mi wifey," said Zoe as he began to suck on Sasha breast. "If you want me then leave the other females alone, if they don't mean anyting to you then it shouldn't be a problem, I can't and want be with someone who's sleeping around with other females," said Sasha in English as she pushing Zoe away to look into his eyes. Gosh he was beautiful, if he was a different person in a different place and a different situation she would have no problems dating him, he was that sexy, but she had to focus on what was real and what they had wasn't real. "Why yuh looking at mi like dat for," asked Zoe. "Answer me are you still gonna sleep with them other female?" "Yes dat's money, and noting gets between mi and mi money, no one." Sasha heart crushed in her chest, she was hoping that Zoe would choice her finally, but like always her wishes was unheard. She pushed herself away and Zoe pushed her back down. "Lay down Sha, I wat yuh again," said Zoe as he flip Sasha over on her stomach and enter her from the back. Sasha yelled out from pain first and then pleasure next as she reaches for a pillow to muffle her screams into. Zoe was so deep that Sasha felt him in her stomach, and when she came it was long, strong and hard and she couldn't do anything but work her body to meet with his thrust which was more faster and painful. "Zoe you're hurting me," cried Sasha. "Mi not hurting yuh, mi loving yuh now relax and take dis dick," said Zoe as he kissed the back of Sasha neck and with long steady strokes went in and out of her. When he felt her muscle tighten around him he flip her on her back and enter her fast and hard. "Tell mi yuh never gaan ta leave mi Sha, tell mi yuh mines forever," said Zoe as he worked Sasha over in a five minutes orgasm. "Oh God yes I'm your forever I'll never leave you," shouted Sasha as Zoe and her came together. This time Zoe picked her up and took her to the bathroom and they both took a shower together, which was a first for Sasha. When they finished bathing Zoe carried her to the bed and laid her down, soon as she hit the pillow she was knock out. "Mi will never be able ta show yuh Sha, but mi luv yuh, have for di last two years, now mi gotta try and keep yuh, because I'll kill yuh before mi let yuh go," said Zoe as he watch Sasha sleep. Two months passed since Sasha slept with Zoe, and she was surprised that he didn't bring any of the other females to the house to sleep with. The more they spend time together the more Sasha was falling in love with Zoe. Sasha wasn't going to be stupid and think for a minute that Zoe had stop sleeping with the other females just because they was intimate, plus he still had mood swing when he got home so Sasha avoided being around him giving him some time to get over what was bothering him. He only hit her a couple times since they been intimate, but Sasha was getting tired of his temper whenever he got home and the many phone calls his other females left for him. One evening Sasha was in the bedroom listening to reggae music on the Internet when Zoe came home early. "Take yuh clothes off," said Zoe already taken off his clothing, Sasha already knew what he wanted, so she took off her clothes and lay on the bed. Zoe Obama cologne filled Sasha nostrils as she took a deep breath as he entered her. Their love making this time was different as Zoe stoked her slow and gentle. "Tell mi yuh luv mi," said Zoe as he kissed Sasha on her forehead. "Mi luv yuh," said Sasha meaning it from the bottom of her heart. Zoe deep stroke her took her breath away. "I luv ya Sasha, been luvin yuh for so long." Sasha didn't know what to say so she kissed him and worked her body, making him scream her name. "I'm cumin baby, oh Sha," said Zoe as he thrust a couple more time filling Sasha up with his seeds. "Go in da shower mi be in there in a minute," said Zoe as he sat on the bed and lit a blunt. Sasha went into the bathroom and shut the door turning around she looked at her reflection in the mirror, and then all of a sudden she ran to the toilet and started throwing up. When she was finished she flushed the toilet then went and brushed her teeth after she ran the shower, she sat on the edge for a minute when she started getting dizzy when it passed she got in and began to take a real hot shower, a couple minutes later she felt Zoe hands on her back. "I see yuh like di hot shower now," said Zoe.

Sasha knew he was teasing her because he loves taking a really hot shower to where the water is ready to take your skin off. "If I have to take a shower with you I better get use to it, plus it relaxes me," said Sasha. "Mi better be di only one yuh take a shower wid," said Zoe as he rubs Sasha back. "You'll be the only one for a lot of things," said Sasha getting ready to get out of the shower. "Where yuh gaanin' mi not finished wid yuh yet," said Zoe as he picks Sasha up and lean her against the shower wall. As he enters her Sasha holds on and enjoys the ride Zoe was taking her on. "Yuh know wat mi want ta hear," said Zoe. "Mi luv yuh, mi luv yuh so much, mi never gaanin' leave yuh," said Sasha. "Mi luv yuh ta, mi luv yuh so much," said Zoe. Putting Sasha on the floor Zoe bends her over and enters her doggy style. "Damn yuh pussy is so tight, mi cumin baby," shouted Zoe as he filled Sasha up. Taking a deep breath Sasha leans into him and kisses him on his lips. Holding each other they didn't see the shadow leaving out of the bathroom. Sasha got out of the shower before Zoe and when she walked in the room Nancy was standing at the bedroom door staring her up and down. Sasha quickly grabs the towel that was hanging on the chair, and covered her self up. "Excuse me, but can you leave so I can get dress," said Sasha looking at Nancy. "You will never have him, not as long as I'm in the picture." "You can take that up with Zoe," said Sasha. She was tired of Nancy and Meka and there bullshit, everyday and every night they would leave message calling her a bitch or slut or anything else they thought of calling her, they knew she could hear the message when she didn't answer. "No need I'm going to make Z forget all about you and them other bitches, he's mines and don't forget that," said Nancy as she left the door. Sasha was dressed when Zoe came out of the shower butt ass naked. "Um, you have company in the living room," said Sasha as she went and turned down the volume on the computer. "Wat yuh mean I got company?" "Nancy's here, she was standing at the door when I got out the shower." "Wat di bloodclot, dis girl is asking for it," said Zoe as he went into the dresser and took out a pair of boxers, his black Roca Wear pants, and a Bob Marley shirt out and began to get dress. Sasha knew that when he dressed like that it means he's going out. Zoe went to the other dresser and took out a pair of socks, as he was getting ready to put his shoes on, he looks up at Sasha as she sat at the computer not saying a word. "I'll be back in a few, and mi will handle Nancy," said Zoe as he tied his all black Air Force One up he walked over to Sasha and kissed her on the lips and headed out the bedroom door. Sasha was mad that he just finished making love to her and then leaves to be with someone else, but she wouldn't dare show how she really felt. She got up and went and laid on the bed she was feeling dizzy again so before she knew it she was fast asleep. When she woke up she was feeling much better so she went downstairs to fix her something to eat, she wasn't surprise when she was alone. "What am I going to do, I can't live like this any longer, but I'd be lying to myself if I say I didn't love a man who's not worthy of my love," said Sasha as she grabs some bread and deli meat and fixed a quick sandwich. She took a can of ginger ale to settle her stomach; she knew she shouldn't have eaten all that spicy food earlier now her stomach was upset. When she finished eating Sasha did some work on the internet and when she was finished, she laid down and was knocked-out.

Chapter 6

Zoe

Everywhere Zoe went he thought about Sasha. He knew soon or later Sasha was going to leave him if he didn't get some help, and he wasn't going to lose her for anything so he called and made an appointment with a Therapy in the area, he wanted to start right away in handling his temper. Zoe was feeling real good until he walked into his front door at two in the morning and found Nancy on his sofa. "How di hell yuh get in mi house, mi took ya key from yuh two months ago," shouted Zoe. Nancy didn't say anything just looked at Zoe like he was the one in the wrong. "Yuh can have di key mi locks will be change in di morning, now get di hell out mi house, I don't have time for yuh shit tanight," said Zoe losing his patients. "Why is she still here living with you, hell I been with you for three years and I never stayed the night and then out of the blue you've taken the key you given me back, your not giving me my dick like you use to, and your not answering my calls so what's really good Z, because I can deal with the other bitches you fucking with but I want take you having a live in whore," said Nancy. Zoe started laughing, which pissed Nancy off more. "What the hell you find funny?" "Look I don't have time for dis go home and I'll call ya tamorrow." "I'm not leaving until she's gone, the way I see it if she can live here so can I," said Nancy crossing her legs sitting back on the sofa. Zoe began to speak his native language, which Nancy didn't understand or liked. "Speak English so I can understand you," said Nancy. "I said yuh have no second ta get di hell out mi house before I hurt ya stupid ass, do yuh understand mi now," shouted Zoe. "If I leave it's over, and I want come back," threaten Nancy as she stood up glaring at Zoe. Zoe was in her face so fast that Nancy didn't have time to protect herself from the blow Zoe gave her in her stomach and mouth. "No one threatens ta walk out on mi unless I'm done wid ya, who do yuh tink I am some joke," said Zoe as he slaps Nancy so fast and furious that her face turned red. Sasha jump out of the bed when she heard the commotion in the living room, so she ran out the bedroom to see what was happening, and when she got in the living room she saw Zoe on Nancy and went to pull him off her, and then out of nowhere he haled off and smacked her to the floor. Sasha leaned over to cover Nancy as Zoe went on a rampage and threw blows to Sasha and Nancy as if they were men. Only when he was tired and couldn't threw any more punches did he realized that he was beating on Sasha. When he looked at her she looked as if she was dead. He saw Nancy balled up underneath her and realized that she was protecting her. Zoe lifted Sasha up and carried her to their bedroom and laid her on the bed taking her pulse. Nancy came in behind him a few minutes later and didn't say a word. "She needs ta go ta di hospital, and yuh gaanin' ta take her, if they asked wat happened say some guys tried ta mug her and when yuh got their dem ran off," said Zoe. "Why should I take her, you did this to her, you take her, I'm leaving," said Nancy heading out the door. "Because if anyting happens ta her I'll kill ya ass, and ya whole fucking family. Dis happened ta her because she was protecting yuh, when she gets ta di hospital make sure she's okay, call mi and let me know what's happening and den yuh can go and lose mi number, because if mi see yuh again I'll end up killing yuh, now go in di living room until mi bring her out ta take her ta di car," said Zoe. Before he brought Sasha out he kissed her on her lips and then he took her to the car with Nancy following close behind. Two hours later Zoe was pacing back and forth smoking a blunt when his cell phone rang he flip it over and answered it. "Speak." "She's not waking up, they're running some testes on her, but she's not responding to any of the treatment." "How do yuh know dis." "I told them I was her cousin and we suppose to have met for dinner but she never showed, and then I went to her house and saw her being attack and they ran off when they saw me coming." Zoe was quiet for a long time. "There doing a CAT's scan on her right now to see if she has any swollen on her brains or blood clots, I told them I was going to call our family members to let them know what's happened to her, Z, she didn't look good when I brought her here." "I'll be there shortly, "said Zoe, and hung up the phone. Two hours later Zoe showed up at the hospital and since Nancy told him the room number he went straight to Sasha room, when he got there he couldn't believe he did this to her again, he remember the last time he lost it and blacked out because the bitch Meka tried to run game on him when he went to her house, she was also complaining about Sasha living at his house and threaten to leave him if she didn't move out. The only reason Zoe went over there in the first place was to collect his money, he wasn't planning on sleeping with Meka, but after he slap her around and almost choked her out, he fucked her real good got his money and bounce. When he got home Sasha as usual had the house clean and dinner ready. Then Meka called him thirty minutes later saying if Sasha weren't gone by tomorrow he wouldn't see her anymore and that if he can have a stay in home whore then she can see and fuck whom she wanted to, and just like his pops did his mother he did to Sasha, he blacked out and thinking that Meka was actually there so he beat her and he wouldn't have stop until all the angrier towards her was gone, but something told him to stop and when he did his fist was in the air and Sasha was on the floor bleeding from her mouth and her eye was already bruising. When he reached for her she flinched and wouldn't let him touch her instead she got up and limped to the bathroom and stayed there half of the night crying. And now since everything been going so good between them lately, and Nancy had to start shit, and look at the out come, he hurt Sasha once again over a female he didn't love or want. He saw Nancy in the corner of his eyes so he turned towards her and was shocked to see a police officer talking to her. As he walked closer to them he recognized the police officer as his cousin Drew husband David. "Good evening, I'm a close friend of Sasha Jones, and I came by ta see how she's doing," said Zoe, pretending that he didn't know David; he would call him later and find out what Nancy was talking about. "Oh good evening am Officer Hall, and Ms. Lean was telling me that she went to meet with her cousin when she saw her getting mugged, Mr.," said David playing along. "Ashland, but yuh can call mi Zoe; mi was wondering if yuh can tell mi wat yuh have so far."

"Well Mr. Ashland we was called about an mugging, the victim is unconscious from which appear from multiply blow to the back of her head and face, they also found that she has some fractured ribs, an black eye and some bruises, now would you know anything about any of these things Mr. Ashland," asked David. "No officer mi wouldn't, like mi said I'm just a friend who came ta check on another friends," said Zoe. "Well then Ms. Lean you were about to tell me the name of the victim attacker," said David. "Um, I don't know exactly who would do this, all I know is that she told me that her boyfriend at the time was abusing her, and when she didn't show up for our lunch date, I went by to check on her and that's when I saw a guy running away, but I didn't see his face," said Nancy real quick. "Do you have an address or anything, all we have on Ms. Jones is a P.O. Box and that's about it. " Excuses mi did yuh say she has and P.O. box," asked Zoe looking at David. "Yes, whenever we get a call on a victim of any kind of crime we have to do a back ground check to see if she has a pier history, and she doesn't. She only had paperwork for an P.O. Box in her possessions, so she's was lucky that her cousin Ms. Lean found her when she did, if the police had brought her in it would have taken us days to find out her family and where she lives, she doesn't even have a valid driver license or I.D.," said Officer Hall shaking his head. Zoe didn't say anything else he would call David and get all the information he need about Sasha "If y'all excuse mi, I'm gaan ta sit wid Sasha," said Zoe turning to head back in Sasha room. When he got there a nurse was in there taking her vital signs and written then in the files. When she put the files back at the foot of the bed she spoke to Zoe and left out the room. Zoe walked over and read the information on Sasha chart, and he felt sick to his stomach when he read her pulse when she first got there it was really low, and her blood pressure was also low, when he put her records back he sat in the chair and took her hands. Zoe wasn't stupid as some would think, before he became a drug dealer/ murderer he was a straight A student and would have became a doctor if things went differently, but when his pops died he left over thirty thousand dollars of drugs in their home, and Zoe took it a pond himself to sale it in order for his family to survive. So he called his dad partner and everything else was a wrap. He drop out of school when he was in the eleventh grade and then he became the Man at the age seventeen, and five years later he had bitches riding him literally, and the bitches loved his sex skills and his money so Zoe had in all ten females who he was fucking. It would've been more, but he wasn't greedy, when he got tired of one he replaced her for someone else. But then he met or he should say saw Sasha. She was the most beautiful female he ever seen, working at Mickey D's with the most prettiest smile on her face taking people order, and Zoe knew at that moment he had to have her, and now since he had her he was afraid that he was gonna lose her, and he was to confused to know what to do or think to fix this problem. David stuck his head in and then knocked on the door to get Zoe attention. Zoe closed his eyes and shook his head yes letting David know that he was responsible for Sasha condition. "Call me later I gotta talk to you about ole gurl," said David and then left. Nancy never returned to the room, and Zoe was happy because he would've choked her ass if she came near him. "So Sha yuh did have dat P.O. box all along, I wonder wat's so important that yuh need yuh mail delivered at a post office," said Zoe talking out loud. Sasha was stirring in her sleep and he thought he heard his name but wasn't sure. Two hours later, Zoe had fallen asleep in the chair holding Sasha hands, when he felt her pulling her hands free. Waking up he looked into her eyes. Her expression transformed from frightened to piss. She tried to pull her hand free, but Zoe held on. "Don't, mi sorry I didn't mean ta hurt yuh, mi thought yuh was Nancy I know it's not an excuse, but please forgive mi." Sasha closed her eyes as tears ran down her face. "Nancy told di police dat yuh was getting mugged when she went to your house to meet with you, she said she told dem yuh two are cousin, shorty mi swear I'll never put mi hands on yuh again," said Zoe as he look at Sasha. "I can't do this I want out Zoe," said Sasha. "No, yuh said yuh luv mi, said yuh be mines forever, and mi take yuh word, I can make tings rights, I'll stop seeing dem other females, and be only wid yuh, but I wat let yuh leave mi," said Zoe looking at Sasha. When she was about to say something the nurse came back in and was surprised when she saw Sasha awoke and alert. "Ms. Jones I'm your nurse Gloria and I'll be attending you for the rest of the evening, you gave us a scared there for a moment, how are you feeling." "I'm fine I just want to go home." "Well let me get the doctor so he can look at you, he'll be in here to talk to you in a few minutes, there's some water in the pitcher on the stand and your cup also if you get thirsty." Gloria read Sasha vital signs, and wrote them in her chart, when she left out the room Zoe walked over and opened it and read the last vital records, everything was back to normal, and everything came back negative. "What are you doing with my files? You can't read through my information," said Sasha. "I just want ta check wat she wrote for yuh vital, they're all normal so yuh should be able ta go home, if they say yuh should stay an extra night, tell them yuh be fine and dat yuh going home wid me, since dem only have an P.O. box on yuh," said Zoe as he put the files back at the foot of the bed then turned towards the dresser and poured Sasha some water in her cup. She didn't respond as he handed her the cup and looked into her eyes, he was about to say something else when a tall light skin man walked in followed by the nurse who was in there a few minutes earlier. "Hello Ms. Jones I'm Doctor Howardson," he said as he picked up her files and looked through them. "Everything looks good but, I would like to run another CAT's scan on you to check on the blood clots we saw on the testes earlier, and if everything is normal we would like to keep you over night to monitor you," said Doctor Howardson. "I really do feel fine, if I could I would like to go home and just rest," said Sasha looking at the doctor. "I can only release you if you're going to have someone home with you, who can watch over you," said the doctor. "She'll be going home wid mi, and mi will personally take care of her," said Zoe taking Sasha hands into his. "Alright then, Gloria will take you to the examining room to do another CAT's scan on you and I'll be back in the next hour or so to go over them with you," said Dr. Howardson. "Thank you doctor," said Sasha. "Gloria can you help me fill out some paper work and then you can take Ms. Jones to the back." "Sure, I'll be right back sweetie and relax," said Nurse Gloria as she followed behind the doctor. "Sha I have ta take care of some business, I'll be back in a few, but I hope yuh forgave mi for wat I've done, I'll make it up ta yuh and mi luv yuh and mi sorry," said Zoe as he kissed her softly on the lips and walked out the room. When he got outside he called David. "Wat'd up, can ya talk," asked Zoe. "Yeah I can talk, but I don't think you're going to want to here what I have to say," said David. "Mi all ears man, speak ta mi." "Look you need to cool the fuck down, you're lucky my partner wasn't with me or I'd have to take you down town to question you, she did a total 360 in her police statement man, even though she never said your name, you could guess the attacker was you by her reaction when you showed up, and that's why I asked if you knew anything," said David. "Wat did she say," asked Zoe. "She told me that Sasha and she was dating the same man and that he assaulted her first, and then showed me a huge bruise on her arm, and then she said Sasha tried to stop it, and that's when he started beating on her, when she saw you she changed." Zoe was quiet as he listen to David. "Zoe, I know all about the abuse your mother was going through with your father, and I'm going to tell you like I told your cousin, you need counseling and you need it now, before you end up hurting someone or yourself. Now I love you like you're my own blood but be clear when I tell you this, if anything happens to Nancy or Sasha I will arrest you, the only reason I didn't this time is because I love your cousin with my whole being, but my job comes first and I hate when a man beats on a woman out of anger," said David. Zoe listened to him and was quiet for a long minute. "Yuh right, but mi didn't mean ta hurt her, I thought she was Nancy she was protecting her. I spazed out man, but I promised I'll fix this, mi luv her mon, and mi can't lose her," said Zoe taking in what he just said. "Well if you love her then you better make good of your promises and take care of her, go get counseling man, hell talk to her and see if she'll go with you, I'll talk to you later," said David and hung up the phone. Zoe got in his car and headed home, when he got there he was going to called up his crew to have a meeting, but he decided to call them later he decided to chill for a few and take care of Sasha and prove to her and himself that he wanted only her. So the first thing he did was change his answering machine on his cell phone and home machine, letting everyone know his not available because he's with his wifey and that he wasn't returning any phone calls. Thirty minutes later he had over a hundred messages from his other oomans. He didn't listen to them just deleted them. Then he sat and thought about what he was gonna do about Nancy, he couldn't just let her walk away knowing what he did for living and what he did to Sasha. He thought about what David said and ruled out killing her, he knew David meant everything he said and he didn't want to disrespect his cousin husband, so he did what he knew would keep her mouth close. Zoe called his boy, and best friend Jay, and told him to meet him at the Newport News Park in fifteen minutes. Zoe sat on the bench beside his childhood and best friend Jay and stared ahead. "I want yuh ta take care

Nancy, no dead, but scared," said Zoe as he sat on the bench lighting his blunt. "Aight boss, anyting else," asked Jay. "Naw dat's it don't call mi I'll call yuh," said Zoe handing Jay the blunt and got up and headed towards his candy apple red 2009 Cadillac, which sat on chromes 22's. When he got in he started his car and his CD player blasted I Wayne 'Real' threw his DXM 15's speakers as he pulled out of the parking lot. When he got home he called to the hospital to check on Sasha and when he didn't get an answer he thought she was still getting the CAT's scan done so he went and took a hot shower and when he was finished he got dressed and then headed to the hospital. When he got there Sasha wasn't in the room so he stood by the window to wait for her, when the nurse from earlier walked passed the room, she knocked lightly to get Zoe attention. "Excuse me did Ms. Jones forget anything," asked the nurse. "Excuse mi, I'm waiting for Ms. Jones ta get back from di examining room," said Zoe. "Oh you must be Mr. Ashland, Ms. Jones is already released she told me to give you this envelope before she left, if you'll follow me I have it at my station," said the nurse leaving out the room. When they got to the nurse station Zoe looked around to see who was near, because he knew he couldn't leave from the hospital without knowing who picked Sasha up and where she went to, and if the nurse didn't give it out willingly he had other ways to make her talk. "Here you go," said Nurse Gloria handing Zoe the letter with a big smile. "Excuse mi but do yuh know who picked her up," asked Zoe. "Yes her sister picked her up about thirty minutes ago." "She doesn't have a sister, she's di only child," said Zoe losing his cool. "Well she said her name was Susan Jones, and Ms. Jones went willingly with the young lady, Ms. Jones signed her release paper even when Dr. Howardson told her that her blood clots had increased, but she assures him that her sister would take care of her." "Wat do yuh mean her blood clots have increased," asked Zoe. "It means what the injuries she has occurred we recommend for the patient to stay in the hospital to get the best treatment, that way we can monitor her and see if the medication is working, and since she wouldn't stay Dr. Howardson prescribe some medicine for her to take," said Nurse Gloria as she opened the drawer. "With the blood clots and the fractured ribs she really shouldn't be moving, and I hope when you see her that you remind her to rest and no stress what so ever and any unnecessary movement might damage her ribs so please tell her to stay put," said Gloria as she handed Zoe the envelope. "Mi be sure ta tell her and have a nice day," said Zoe as he turned and walked away. When he got in his car he hit the stirring wheel and curse and banged on the stirring wheel some more. Opening the letter Zoe leaned back and read it.

Zoe,

I'm done, this is my only escape from you, don't try to find me because you want, live your life and forget me.

Sasha

Zoe balled the letter and took his gun from out of the glove box and put it on the seat and started his car and headed to Sasha grandmother house. When he pulled up he saw her sitting on the porch probable smoking his weed with some other people. As he got out his car he saw her mumble something to the lady sitting beside her and the lady turned and looked his way. "Yo B, mi gotta holla at yuh for a minutes," said Zoe looking around to see if push comes to shove how many people he had to shoot if Sasha grandmother wanted to play games. When they got in the house she sat on the sofa while Zoe paced the floor. "Wat can mi do yuh for," asked Betty. "Who's Susan Jones?" "Why yuh wonna know her for ain't Sasha good enough for yuh." Zoe paused and turned to Betty. "Dis is no time ta play games, now answer mi question," said Zoe through clenched teeth. "She's Sasha mother, like I said before why yuh wonna know her for?" "Where does she lives." "Mi don't know, mi haven't talk ta di child in seventeen years, she left her seed and bounced not leaving mi a cent." Zoe pulled out his gun and pointed it to Betty head. "Look, yuh got five second ta tell mi wat yuh know about dis Susan for I blow ya fucking brains out." "Mi don't know noting, she left not telling mi noting, some say she moved ta Florida or LA, and some say she dead, mi really don't know she haven't called mi or anyone since she left," explain Momma Fill as her heart felt it was about to burst out her chest. Zoe put his gun to his side and tapped his leg with it. "Di lady at di hospital said a female name Susan Jones came and picked Sasha up, has she called yuh," ask Zoe looking at Betty. "I haven't seen di child since she moved wid yuh, she's no longer my concern, if yuh having problems wid her den dat's between yuh two, yuh wanted her now ya got her," said Betty standing up. "Since yuh not in it, kick mi my money, I already know yuh lied when we made di arrangement, wat ya take me for a fool, either yuh kick mi money or yuh find her, and if yuh want do either mi can put a bullet in yuh fucking head so choice and choice wisely," said Zoe glaring at Betty. "Wat do ya want from mi, di child is just like her mother, mi don't know where she can be, have yuh checked her job, she be there more den she be anywhere," said Betty. "Naw I'm going over there in a few in the di mean time mi gaanin' have mi boy watch yuh house in case she comes or call, if you try and play mi I'll kill yuh mi own self, dis is not a game and yuh been warned," said Zoe and walked out the door. Betty sat on the chair and took a deep breath. "Wat have I gotten mi self into, dis boy is crazy and mi done put dat child in dis mess, how can I help her when she wat even come ta mi for help, den again why would she I've done noting but be mean and cruel ta her, and why was she at di hospital, had he hurt her." Betty asked herself as she walked outside, when she sat down her friend handed her a blunt and she smoked it without saying another word, she thought of all the horrible things she done to Sasha when she was growing up and came to the conclusion that she wouldn't come to herself for help either. Zoe speed to the McDonald's on Jefferson Avenue not caring if he got a ticket or anything. When he pulled in the parking lot he saw it was empty and he was glad because he wasn't leaving until someone told him something about Sasha. As he walked in he saw Brittney standing behind the cashier and approached her. "Have ya seen or talked ta Sasha?" Zoe got straight to the point why he was there he didn't have time for playing games. "Not in a while, but she called earlier and told our boss that she quit, he just told us about an hour ago." "Where's yuh boss at now," asked Zoe. "He went out to lunch he should be back in thirty minutes." "Do yuh have anyway of contacting Sasha?" "Yeah on her cell phone, she only uses it for emergency, if you can wait a minute I'll go in the back and get it for you," said Brittney smiling. When she came back she handed Zoe a piece of paper and looked into his eyes. "I also wrote my number down if you feel what I'm saying," said Brittney as she winked at Zoe then turn and walked towards the back. Zoe didn't pay her any mind and was concentration on the cell phone number, he been with Sasha for a year and never saw her with a phone. Walking out the building Zoe took out his cell phone and called in for the meeting, everyone agreed to meet at his house at eleven. When he got home it was a little after nine, usually when he got there Sasha would have the house clean and dinner fix, but when he entered it was as he left it, messed up. So he started cleaning and an hour later he was tired and sore so he went and took another shower. When he was finished getting dress his doorbell rang and when he opened it on the other side was a crying Nancy. "Wat di hell yuh wat, I told yuh di last time if mi saw yuh again I would kill ya, wat yuh ready ta die," asked Zoe as he reached in the back of his pants and pulled out his gun. "No I came to say I'm sorry, and I want you to forgive me, I came here also to help you with Sasha, I called to the hospital and they said she was already release so I came here to help, I know what happened to her was because she was protecting me like you said, and I just want to say thanks to her and help anyway I can," said Nancy. "Wat are yuh up ta gurl, mi don't have time ta play ya game, we over and don't come back ta mi house ever again," said Zoe. Nancy grabs his hand, as he was about to close the door. "I'm not playing any games Z, I love you, we been together for three years are you really gonna throw away three years for a female who don't love you?" "She'll learn ta luv mi, but either way she will luv mi." "You'll never understand a woman Z; you can't make someone love you. The only reason you have so many bitches is only because you have money, and without that your nothing, when it comes to real love it doesn't matter who you are or how much money you have, when it comes to love it comes from the heart," said Nancy as she walked away. Zoe just stood at the door and didn't say anything because he knew she was right, in all his twenty-one years he only started being recognized when he became something in his life, he could get all the pussy and dick suck with a show of cash, and to top it off Sasha never asked him for a dime the whole time they was living together, she shopped with her own money and she brought groceries with her own money, hell she was still working when half the other girls he was sleeping with wanted him to pay their mortgage, rent and car notices. "Well all dats about ta change, from here on out my only concern is finding Sasha and letting her know how mi really feel," said Zoe as he walked back into his house. At ten thirty his doorbell ranged again and this time he knew whom it was. "Early as always, come in and get a drink from di bar, I'll be in there in a minute," said Zoe as he let Jay in. When he came back out he had two envelopes in his hands. "Sasha disappeared on mi, and I wat ya people ta find her, I want yuh ta watch dat post office dat ya seen her at, if yuh see her follow her and den call mi, here five thousand for yuh only because I know yuh do di job," said Zoe handing the envelope to Jay. "Dat's okay Z, yuh be easy boss, I got'cha, I see how much she mean ta ya, by di way do yuh still wat mi ta do dat job for ya, I got mi boys lined up and ready," said Jay lighting a blunt. "Naw am gaan ta let it ride, I already talked ta her, Jay man I've been knowing yuh mi whole life and I'm about ta tell ya someting dats gaan ta fuck ya head up but I'm just gaan ta tell yuh," said Zoe. "Wat's up Z, mi never seen ya like dis, talked ta mi," said Jay. "I'm in luv, and di one-woman mi luv don't luv mi back, how's dat," said Zoe as he walked over to the window and stared at the sky. "Mi no noting about luv, mi only Luvs mi mother and sister," said Jay standing by Zoe. "Mi either mon, mi either. I'm gaan ta be leaving again in a few days and I wat yuh ta be head until mi get back, I'll let everyone know when dem get here, I got ta go and clear mi head," said Zoe turning to look at Jay. "Why ya wat mi ta be head, yuh need someone like Gunny or Hell Bent ta be in charge, yuh know half dem nigga don't like mi cause where true boys," said Jay. "I choice ya because I trust yuh, yuh like mi brother, and I already fucked up by leaving Herd di last time, mi money is still short, plus ya have killer heart and a game mind, I watch yuh when ya don't know I'm watching ya." "Mi thought me saw you a couple times," said Jay trying to ease the tension in the room. "Wat ever mon, but mi also choice yuh, because yuh didn't take mi money when dem other nigga would've pocket mi shit, plus I'm gonna put an award out for Sasha ta really let dem look for her." "Well if ya think mi can handle dis for ya den I'll do mi best, but just be ready for mi call ta tell ya ta bring ya ass back, mi not patient when it comes ta nigga's, mi shoot first and den ask question," said Jay laughing. "Dat's wat yuh suppose ta do, when I'm gone don't take no shit from no one, yuh know mi schedule, pick up mi money and I'm gaan ta tell dem dat if dem late or short it's a ten percent fee on mi money," said Zoe as he walked back in the living room and poured him a glass of Gray Goose on ice. As him and Jay sat on the sofa they talked for a few minutes and then Zoe doorbell rang again, when all fourteen members of his crew enter his house he wasted no time beginning the meeting about Jay taking over and handling business until he returned, and the ten percent fee if anyone was late or short with his money, and he also reminded the ones who still owed him to give the money to Jay and if Jay called him for any reason at all and he had to return there would be blood shed, last he told them that he had a ten thousand dollars reward for whoever finds Sasha. When everyone was gone Zoe went in the back room and laid on the bed, when he closed his eyes Sasha batter and bruised face pop in his mind and the only thing he could do was think of all the things he done in his life and when did he fall in love. He knew without a doubt that he loved Sasha and he knew the only way he could get her back was to change. He just wished he wasn't too late. He reached in his pocket and pulled out the number Brittney gave him. Sitting on the bed he dialed the number and when he heard Sasha voice he took a deep breath. "Mi sorry, and I wat yuh ta come back home ta mi," said Zoe. In her native language Sasha held control over her emotions. "Ya no see it, mi luv yuh wid all mi heart, but mi gaan, all mi feel is hot when mi wid yuh, and now the hot is ova, yuh cyaan cold up mi anymore yuh cyan ave di odda ooman mi finished. Now lef mi nuh, and galang wid yuh life," said Sasha. (You know I love you with my whole heart, but I'm gone, all I feel is pain when I'm with you, and now the pain is over, you can't humiliate me anymore you can have the other woman I'm finished. Now leave me alone and go along with your life.) "Yuh are mi life, mi want yuh, yuh said ya would never leave mi, mi took yuh word, yuh said yuh luv mi, did yuh lie," asked Zoe. Sasha was quiet for a minute as tears ran down her face. "Mi didn't lie, mi luv ya, but mi cyaan be wid yuh, don't call mi again or mi will change mi number." "Look don't vex mi know, or yuh gaan ta regret it, either yuh come home or mi kill yuh granni just ta prove ta yuh dat mi not playing," said Zoe using his only trap card. "Zoe mi don't care anymore, it's not like she cares about mi, after all she pimp mi ta ya. Believe mi she'll be di last person mi will ever call. Now please don't call mi again Zoe, galang wid yuh life and forget about mi." " Yuh is mi life, and mi will find yuh Sha, mi luv yuh forever," said Zoe as he hung up the phone.

Chapter 7

Janet and Jason (Jay)

As Janet listened to her friend she couldn't have been more sad and hurt and then relieved and then proud. Sasha had finally gotten away from her evil ass grandmother and that psychopath Zoe. She was calling Janet to see what time she was coming home because she just got her license and brought her first car and wanted Janet to see it. A year had passed, but Janet was still worried that Zoe would find Sasha, and when he did the out come would not be pretty. Janet was getting out of her car, when the wind blew opened her door, making it hit the car beside hers. "Oh my god, SaSa gurl I gotta call you back I done hit this man car," said Janet as she hung up before Sasha could respond. "I am so sorry, the wind just flew it open, I can give you my insurance information, and they can pay for the damage," speed talked Janet. "Dis okay shorty, madda nature was just doing her ting," said Jay, as he looked Janet up and down. "Yuh not from round here," asked Jay. "Um not anymore I use to live around here years ago." "Yeah mon, mi name is Jason, but everyone call me Jay wat is yuh name?" "Janet, but everyone calls me Jay to." "J J, mi like dat, where ya headed ta," asked Jay. "Aren't you a little concern about your car, it has a big dent in it," said Janet. "Naw mi handle dat later, mi more interested in yuh." Janet taken aback she stared at the handsome man. "Wat don't tell mi yuh don't date, ya ta beautiful not ta," smiled Jay. "No it's not that, it's that your car, I feel really bad about it, here's my insurance information so you can get it fixed," said Janet as she handed him her insurance card information. "Like mi said before I'll take care of dat later, who knows mi might leave it ta remind mi of di most beautaful lady mi met." "Wow your good, but I really need to be going before the post office close." "Dat's wat's up before yuh leave can I get ya number, I would luv ta take yuh out one day, get ta know yuh." Janet looked Jason up and down this time and she couldn't lie the brother was sexy as hell. He was about 5'11 and weight about 200 evenly, he was light skin with a dread locks and a nice trimmed beard, the only problem was that she just gotten out of an relationship and promised herself she wasn't going to rush into another one. "Um, I'm kind of in a relationship right now, and I wouldn't want to lead you on or anything," laid Janet. She wanted to lead him straight to her bed, hell it's been over a year since she broken up with her ex. "I feel ya, but wat yuh can't have a guy friend, or do all ya friends have ta be gurls," teased Jay. "Now since you put it like that, why don't you give me your number, when I see how my schedule looks I'll give you a call," said Janet as she took out her cell phone and put in his name and number as he gave them to her. "Mi hope ta hear from yuh soon," said Jason as he got in his car and left. Janet couldn't believe what just happened. She went into the postal office and did a change of address for Sasha as she was signing the paper work her cell phone started ringing and startled her. "Hello." "Girl you had me worried when you hung up the phone after you told me you hit someone's car, is you okay, what's happening now," asked Sasha. "Girl I'm okay the wind blew open my door and it hit this guys car, everything is fine, what's up?" "Nothing, just wanted to make sure you was alright," said Sasha "Did you call your grandmother yet and talk to her," asked Janet. "I'm not calling her J, if she's sick then let her call her kids or other grand kids, she never loved me, all I ever was to her was a burden, my own mother didn't want me." "SaSa, you have to forgive your grandmother for her evil ass ways, because you don't want anything to happen to her and you never have the chance to make amends, you owe yourself to have closer and you know the reason why I'm pressuring you," said Janet as she handed the paper work to the clerk. "Yeah, I'll call her later on to see how she's doing, are you sure they said she had a heart attack," asked Sasha. "Yes, now don't wait to long, I don't like the way she treated you all these years but she's still your blood and from what I hear none of her kids been by to see her since she been back home," said Janet. "Okay I'll call her, but what if she starts asking me question?" "Well it has been a year SaSa, of course she's going to ask you some question, just don't tell her where you are, I'll be home in two days, and I picked up your mail and change the address, now kiss my babies for me and tell them I'll be home tomorrow, and I want you to get some rest," said Janet as she hung up the phone. When Janet got to her rented townhouse she headed straight for the bathroom, she took a hot steamy shower and when she was finished she went in the kitchen and heated up her Chinese food she order early and went and sat on the sofa. The house was to quiet and she wish she was at home, but she had to come to Newport News on business for her mother. She like the city but she knew Sasha hated it. So after she picked Sasha up from the hospital they stayed with her mom in Texas for five months and than her mom opened her business in Richmond, Virginia so her and Sasha decided to move down there to run the business and to start over. Janet still couldn't believe what Sasha was going through while she was living with Zoe, and she always knew Sasha grandmother was nothing but trouble, but when she found out that she was sick and how her own kids was treating her she had to let Sasha know. She thought it was time for Sasha to heal and the only way she could do that was to forgive her grandmother. At ten o'clock Janet was bored so she decided to call Jay and see what he was up to, he answer on the third ring. "Who's dis?" "It's Janet, um Jay, I met you at the postal office earlier today, are you busy." "Mi surprised yuh called, mi little busy, wat's up." "I just wanted to know if you wanted to go out and have a drink or something to eat, I know we just met and it's late, but you're the only one I know here, I mean I know other people," Janet feeling like a fool. "Tell mi where yuh want ta met," laughed Jay, as he keep his eyes on Sasha grandmother's house. "There's a nice Caribbean restaurant on Jefferson Avenue next to Speedo's called Caribbean Soul I could meet you there in thirty minutes," said Janet getting excited. "Mi see yuh there," said Jay as he hung up. Janet quickly ran to the room and changes she put on some lip-gloss and light make-up, pulled her hair in a tight ponytail. She chooses a red and white Baby Phat dress outfit with her four inch red heels. When she looked into the floor to ceiling mirror she like what she saw and left out. When she pulled up the restaurant was pack. Quickly checking her make-up she got out her car and walked inside. The aroma from the food made Janet hungry all over again, she took a sit at the bar and waited for Jay to arrive. A man sitting down from her order her drink and Janet didn't want to be rude so she accepted it and nodded her thanks. Ten minutes later someone tap her on the shoulders and she almost spilt her drink. "Mi sorry mi scared yuh, yuh look real nice Ms. Jay, are ya ready ta eat, dis place made mi hungry," smiled Jay. "Yes, I was thinking the same thing when I walked in, come on we can sit in the corner if you like," said Janet pointing to the booth in the back. "Dats fine," said Jay as he took her hand and lead her to the table. When they took their seat, a waitress came to take their order. "Hi, I would like your curry chicken with white rice, some goat meat also in curry, and a large Mountain Dew," said Janet. "And wat would ya like?" "Mi have da same, but mi wat a large green tea," said Jay. When the waitress was gone Jay stared at Janet. "So tell mi, are yuh happy wid yo man," asked Jay. "Hmm, oh um, I wasn't quite honest with you earlier, you see I'm not in a relationship, actually I just got out of one and I wasn't trying to rush back into another one," said Janet in one breath. "Mi see, he hurt ya and now yuh don't trust anymore." "I trust, not just whole hearted, so what about you do you have a girlfriend?" "Mi has lots of girlfriends, but noting serious." "You have a lot of girlfriends, wow." "No wow, like mi said it's noting, when mi met Mrs. Right mi will leave dem alone, but right now mi single, mi happy." "Okay, so what do you do for a living," asked Janet changing the subject. "Mi not gonna lie ta yuh, but mi hired help." "Hired help, what's that," asked Janet. "Mi take care of tings make problems go away, wat do yuh do for a living?" "I work with my mom in her computer business, she just started her second business in Richmond, and I came down here to help a couple clients." "So yuh live here or in Richmond," asked Jay. "Actually my friend SaSa and I just moved to Richmond, but I have a townhouse in this area for when I come down for business, it's a lot cheaper then staying in hotels." "Mi know di feeling mi travel a lot, and di hotels are noting ta joke about." "I like your accent," said Janet out of the blue. "Mi thanks yuh, mi like yuh voice, smooth like honey." Janet blushed so hard that she was about to turn red in the face. When their food arrived they ate and talked some more when they were finished the restaurant was getting ready to close. "I had a wonderful time with you," said Janet as she looked into

Jay's eyes. "Mi ta, maybe we can do it again." "I'd like that, I'm only here for one more day then I'm going home, but if I finish early tomorrow would you like to go out, I heard it's a nice ocean front restaurant in Virginia Beach that has a wonderful Caribbean food by the water. I wanted to try it out before I go home, SaSa said she ate there once and the food was mouth watering." " Mi have someting ta do, but call mi and let mi know when yuh finished, mi should be free round ten or eleven," said Jay as he took her hand and walked her out of the restaurant. "Okay thanks again for coming out with me." Without thinking Janet leaned in and kissed Jay on the mouth, when he deepened it she felt as she was floating. When they pulled apart Janet held eye contact with him. "See yuh tomorrow Janet," said Jay as he walked off and got in his car. Janet stood where she was in daze. When she got in her car and was about to start it until Jay tapped on her window. Janet turned the switch back and let the window down. "Mi had ta give yuh dis before yuh left," said Jay and leaned in and kissed her once again on the mouth. When he lifted his head he had a big smile on his face. "Mi definitely will see yuh tomorrow." And with that he left leaving Janet breathless and with a big smile on her face as well. When Janet got home it was two o'clock, she jump back in the shower and when she was finished she got in bed. The whole night she thought about Jay and the kiss, she been kissed plenty of times but she never had the sensation of the after affect, her mouth tingled and her heart had beat faster and she honestly thought she was floating. "Wow if a kiss make me feel like this no telling what else he can make me feel," said Janet as she lay on the bed. When she was finally comfortable her cell phone rang making her jump. "Hello." "Mi call ta see if yuh make it home safe," said Jay. "That's so sweet, and yes I'm home, I was going to call you but I didn't know if you was busy or not." 'Now why did I have to say that, now I'm sounding jealous,' thought Janet. "Yuh don't have ta worry about anyting like dat, yeah mi have girlfriends but mi sleep alone at home, mi bring no one where mi rest mi head." "Oh." "But mi just wanted ta let yuh know dat mi had a wonderful time wid yuh tanight." "I had a wonderful time too; actually I haven't been on a date in so long I forgot how it felt." "Why yuh not date, yuh ta beautaful ta be sitting at home looking at di for wall," laughed Jay. "I go out with my friend SaSa, but going out with you tonight it was much, better," Janet admitted. "Well mi glad yuh had fun, now get some sleep and mi see ya tamorrow beautaful lady," said Jay as he hung up the phone. Janet smiled to herself as she remembers the kiss and fell asleep with a big smile on her face.

Chapter 8

Janet and Ed

When she woke up the next morning, it was nine o'clock, and she was, well-rested even if she did toss and turn all night. When she went into the bathroom to take a shower her cell phone rang and she rushed to answer it. "Hello." "Hey baby, I'm just calling to remind you of Miss. Heather hearing, her daughter Jessica called me last night and she said you might have to speak up in order for her to hear you, and they just want you to fix the web for the internet, Jessica thinks her mother deleted it off the computer by accident, but any ways what did you do last night," asked Marcy. "Well if you must know I went out to dinner." "Stop playing, who did you have dinner with?" Janet loved her mother; they act as if they were sister beside mother and daughter. "Well when I went to the postal office yesterday the wind blew open my car door and it hit this man's car, when I say hit I mean hit he had a huge dent on the side, but he didn't seem to mind, actually he said 'dat's okay madda nature doing her ting.' Janet said using an accent as she talked to her mother. "So he's Caribbean I take." "Yep and mom you should hear him, his voice is so, I don't know what to call it, but it's nice." "Well as long as you had fun that's all that matter, oh Sasha called last night she's going to start work in another week, I've already talked to Lisa and Mecca and you are doing the training of course, but any ways I'll call you later and see how everything went and Jay don't be stubborn, if you need to call me to get some input then call." "Okay mom, love you and

I'll talk to you later," said Janet as she hung up the phone. Two hours later with her hair in a French braid and wearing a gray and black Lisa Lo business suit Janet was at Miss. Heather desk finishing her computer. When she stood up Jessica walked into the room. "So do you know what the problem was," asked Jessica. "You were right she deleted it off the computer, but I restored it and if you come closer I can show you where you can locate it just in case if she deletes it again or if you want to add the updates and different profiles to your page." When Janet was done it was going on one o'clock. She went to Subway and orders a ham, turkey and roast beef cold club and a bottle Mountain Dew for her late lunch. When turned to find a seat, she saw a black couple sitting in the back with there backs towards her and two white couple sitting down eating, so she took the table to the front. She only had an hour before she went to her next client and decided to call Jay and see if he was busy. When she pressed the send button on the phone the man who's back was to her phone rang, and Janet didn't pay it any mind until she heard his voice a few feet from her. She quickly closed her phone, and was gathering her food when her cell rung. Cursing herself again for not turning it off, she made a dash to the door, but fall on her butt, when she slipped on something. Standing Janet brushed her pants off and froze when she felt a hand on her arm. Turning Janet saw Jay and a beautiful female standing behind him. Now Janet knew she look good also she was 5'7 and weight 145, she was light skin with long straight shoulder length hair, which she could say was hers, but the female standing before her was model type fine. "Um, excuse me," said Janet. "Jay." "Oh, um, hey Jay," stutter Janet. "Lynn dis here is Jay di one mi was telling yuh about, Jay dis mi sister Lynn," said Jay, as he looked Janet up and down. "Your sister, boy don't I feel stupid." "Nice ta meet yuh," said Lynn shaking Janet hand. "Mi sorry ta run off but I have ta get back ta work, call mi later Jay," said Lynn as she walked out of the restaurant. "I must look like a fool," said Janet as she bent down to pick up her food and purse. "Yuh look beautaful, come let mi order ya someting else ta eat," said Jay as he took Janet food from her hand and threw it in the trash. When she reorders they sat at the table Jay and his sister just left from. "So ya thought mi was wid another girl after our date last night?" "Yeah." "Look Jay, mi like yuh, and wants ta get ta know ya better, yuh already know mi have girlfriends but dem don't matter, mi don't play games and don't like dem, mi have mi own money, house and cars, wat I want is ta enjoy ya company wat do yuh say," asked Jay looking at Janet. "I'd like that very much," said Janet. "Good, now eat, mi has ta leave soon, but I'll be free round ten." "Okay, you can go I have two more clients, and than I'll call you when I'm finished," said Janet. Jay leaned in and kissed her on the lips, it was nothing like the night before, but Janet felt her heart skip a beat when he backed away. When Jay was gone Janet blew a long breath. 'Man if he keeps kissing me like that my mind want be any good with the clients," thought Janet as she finished her sandwich. An hour later she was pulling into her second client driveway, she was amazed at the surrounding the view was breath taking. As she made her way to the door she saw a middle age woman come from the side of the house dressed in a pair of overall and garden tools in her hand. "Hey you must be Ms. Day, I'm Joyce." "Hello, how are you today, and you can call me Jay, so where's the patient," asked Janet referring to the computer. "If you follow me you can get started," said Joyce walking into the house. Joyce left Janet left alone, and as she began working, her cell phone started to vibrate so she ignores it and continued working. Two hours and about twenty missed calls later she was finished, and was heading towards her car when her cell phone rung again. As she scanned the phone it was a block caller so she sent it to voice mail. When she pulled out of the driveway her phone ranged again displaying the same thing. "Hello," said Janet as she made a left on Warwick Boulevard and headed to her next client home. "I see your dating again, don't forget what I told you, and make no mistakes I know your every moves so don't try me." Janet heart stopped as she slammed on breaks. "Ed, how the hell did you get my number?" "Don't worry about that, I saw you last night hug up on that nigga, don't let me see you with him or anyone else or your going to pay." "Fuck you and stop fucking calling me, nigga you choice who you wanted now be happy with that stank," said Janet as she looked into her rearview mirror to see if he was following her. Ed Gray was Janet ex-fiancé she caught him in bed with a girl name Pamela and broke it off with him, and a couple months she heard they was married and that Pamela was pregnant. "Fuck her I should've never fucked with her to begin with, let alone marry the bitch, but she said she was pregnant, and you know I've always wanted kids, but you know what the bitch did she went and had an abortion after I married her," said Ed yelling. "Look that's on you, I'm not your counselor and I really couldn't care less, you reap what you sow," said Janet. "Oh I'll reap with I sow alright, I'll see you when I see you," said Ed as he hung up the phone. She sat in her car as tears felled down her face. Ed was three years older then her, he was about 6'1 and weight about 270 the most, dark skin with a low hair cut with light brown eyes, he was a goddess and Janet was in love, he was the first and only person she slept with. She was with Ed for three years and they were suppose to have gotten married on her eighth birthday, but she went by his house early one day to surprise him and got the surprise instead. Not saying a word she watch as Ed fucked the girl in the ass without no protection and when he was cumin she walked in the room and just started swinging, they was lucky that she didn't own a gun or she would've caught two cases. Leaving everything she had there she left got in her car and never looked back, that was a year ago. Then five months ago he started calling her on her cell phone telling her that he wanted her back and that he was going to leave Pamela. She blew him off and stop answering his calls, then he started leaving threaten message on her phone telling her if he saw her with any other guys he was going to beat her ass and beat the nigga she's with, so she changed her number all together so he couldn't call. For two months Janet was scared, not leaving out to go anywhere, and then she was like fuck him, he was the one who cheated and even though she didn't date it wasn't because of him and his threats she realized that when she met the right person she'd date than. Wiping her tears from her eyes Janet pulled back to the main highway and went to her last client house. She thought Jason was the right person and couldn't wait to go out with him tonight it's been a long time since she been on a date and thought it was time for a change. When she pulled in the driveway it was a long dirt road off the main road it was going on five o'clock. She looked at the paper work again and saw the client name was Raymond Allen, he was a new customer and called in saying his website wasn't showing on his computer and he needed his feedback from his project as soon as possible. Janet didn't talk to him, but her mother did over the phone trying to resolve the problem, but with no luck. Janet continued to drive until she saw a big bight yellow house, and it also had all yellow flowers in front. The view was beautiful and as she got out she locked her door and walked up to ring the doorbell. A couple minutes later her breath caught in her chest as Ed grabs her hands and pulls her into the house making her fall on the floor as he locked the door behind him. Bending down he picks her up. "Get the fuck off me," yelled Janet as she fought to get away from him. "What's the matter baby, you're not happy to see me," said Ed as he started kissing Janet on the neck while squeezing her breast through her shirt. "I mean it Ed, let me go," said Janet feeling sick to her stomach. Looking around to find any kind of weapon she saw nothing. Ed picked her up and tossed her over his shoulders and walked up the flight of stairs as if she weight no more then a bag of potatoes even though she was fighting and kicking. Kicking the master bedroom door open he throws her on the bed and just looked down at her. "Your still sexy as hell," said Ed as he licks his lips. "I want you to move so I can leave Ed, it's over between us, and I don't want to be here with you," said Janet sitting up on the bed. "But you're here and you know what I want," said Ed as he walked over to the bed and grabs Janet by the neck and squeezed real hard. When he felt that she couldn't move he took her mouth and kissed her lips hard and rough as he laid her on the bed. Taking his other hand he pushes it up her shirt to feels her breast and squeezes it so hard that Janet screams out in pain. "Oh yeah I'm gonna love this," said Ed as he rips off Janet shirt popping the buttons in the process and then lifted up her dress and rips off her thongs with one hand. Still holding Janet by the neck he pulls down his pants and with on quick thrust he enters her hard and fast. "Uhhhhh." Janet screamed as Ed squeezed harder on her neck and pumped into her. "Damn I miss this pussy, Pam don't have shit on your pussy," said Ed as he moves his hand from around Janet neck and grabs both Janet hands in his to pin her hands over her head. Janet couldn't believe this was happening to her, she couldn't believe that she was being rap by a man she once loved. "Please stop Ed, please stop." Ignoring her, Ed kissed her on the mouth. "Ouch." Shouted Ed as he lifted his hand to touch his lip where Janet bit him and saw blood. "Do that again and you'll regret it," said Ed as he held tight of her both her hands with one of his, and reached for a tissue that was on the dresser, and wipes his lip. Looking down at her he smiled as he got his paced back and thrust in and out of Janet. "I know you missed this dick, now work my pussy for me Janet," said Ed as sweat pour from his forehead as he pushes deeper inside of Janet. "I hate you, I hate you so much," said Janet as tears ran down her face. Ed stops and looks down at her. "I want you to have my baby Jay and I know one thing about you is that if you ever get pregnant you want get an abortion, because you don't believe in that shit you love kids always have." For the first time Janet realized Ed was fucking her raw without any protection. "Get the fuck off me right now Ed, are you crazy I'm not going to have your child," shouted Janet as she tried to push Ed off her with no luck. "Oh yes you are, I know for a fact that you don't believe in birth control so I'm not going to stop until I fill you up and get you pregnant, then were going to get married and your going to be with me like we planned," said Ed as he pushes deeper and deeper inside Janet making her feel him in her stomach. "Oh Janet, I'm cumin baby," shouted Ed as he filled Janet with his sperm. Collapsing on top of her he took in a deep breath and held her to him. "I fucked up Janet, please forgive me," said Ed as he sat up on the bed. Janet whole body was numb, and when she got her barring she tried to sit up, only to be push back onto the bed. "Where do you think your going, were not done," said Ed. At that moment Janet cell phone began to ring and she tried her best to answer it but Ed snatched her purse from her reach. "What that's your nigga on the phone calling you, well guess what he can't help you, you see I'm going to keep you here with me until I know your pregnant," said Ed as he hit the end button sending the call to voicemail. "Why are you doing this to me Ed, for god sake you cheated on me, you left me, and you're the one who got married, just let me go, I want tell anyone what you did, I swear to God, if you just let me leave right now I want press charges against you," said Janet pulling down her shirt and dress. "Do you really think I give a fuck about you pressing charges against me, have you forgot my father is the best damn lawyer there is in this city, or have you forgotten that my Uncle Frank is Mayor of the city of Newport News," laughed Ed. "Everyone knows we was together and that you was hurt when I married that bitch, believe me I still have all the letters you wrote saying how you was going to make me pay for cheating on you, do you take me for a fool," said Ed looking at Janet. She did forget that she wrote him that letter out of hurt and anger. Her cell phone ranged again and Ed answers it. "Hello." "Sorry mon mi must have di wrong number," said Jay. "Naw nigga you got the right number Janet is taken and stop fucking calling her she's on my dick," said Ed looking at Janet. "Help," was all Janet got out before Ed hung up the phone. "So ya fucking a rude boy now," said Ed in a fake Caribbean accent. "Look you can't keep me here, he knows where I'm at and so does my mother and SsSa," lied Janet. "How about this you give me what I want and I'll let you go," said Ed. "And what do you want Ed," asked Janet. "You, I want you to make love to me like you mean it, I want you to work that pussy like I taught you, and I want to be able to touch you the way you like me to touch you, I didn't want to fuck you just now, but I had to have you, and damn your pussy is still the bomb," said Ed licking his lips. "If I have the sex the way you want, you promise you'll let me go." "Yeah I promise, but you're gonna have to do it the ways I taught you," said Ed. "Okay," said Janet. Ed had a devilish smile on his face as he leaned over and kissed Janet on the lips, when she opened her mouth and received his tongue and sucked on it just the way he like his dick harden insistently. Taking her free hand she rubs his head and deepens the kiss. When Ed pulled back he looked into her eyes and she saw the love that was still there for her, but she wasn't a fool, she knew the only way to get the hell away from Ed was to give him what he wanted and if that mean sleeping with him then that's one thing she was willing to do. After Ed lifted her dress up she felt him going down on her she took in a deep breath and moaned real loud when his tongue played with her clit. She grabs his head the way he like and pushes his face deeper inside her pussy rotating her hips as he gave her head. When she came in his mouth he sucked up every ounce of her juices, lifting his head up he pulls her down and kiss her letting her taste herself, when he got on top of her this time he enter her slow and easy. Janet body betrayed her and so did her heart, she was lost when Ed touched her gently and kissed her on her neck softly and she was dazed when he told her that he loved her, but at lease her mind was still sane and she kept telling herself to be numb, but once again her body betrayed her and the next thing she knew she was making love to Ed. "That's it Jay work my pussy, work it baby, damn Jay I love you baby, tell me you love me Jay," said Ed as he circled his hip and thrust deeper in her making her cry out his name. "Tell me you love and forgive me," said Ed kissing her forehead and neck and hitting her g-spot. "I love and forgive you E," moaned Janet as she wished he'd hurry up and finish. When she called him his nickname he pulled out, and turned her over on her stomach and enter her from behind. Stroking her long and deep he fucked her slow and then fast pounding into her, making her scream his name and when he felt her muscle tighten around his dick was when he came hard and long filling her up a second time with his sperm. Weak and tired Ed rolled over bring Janet with him, she laid there not saying a word and when she heard his soft snore she eased herself out his arms. When she was off the bed she quickly pulled her ruined shirt together and pulled down her dress and grabs her phone and purse and ran like hell out the house, when she got to her car she didn't look back. An hour later Janet was packing her suitcase when her cell phone ranged scaring her, she scanned the number and when it showed unavailable she hit end sending it to voicemail a few minutes later it chimed letting her know she had a message. Grabbing her things as fast as she could she hurry to her car, when she was putting her things in the car her cell phone ranged again and it showed the same number, hesitant she answer knowing already who was on the other end. "I'm sorry if I hurt you, I don't know what came over me, I did this so I could talk to you, and I know I fucked up, but I love you," said Ed. Janet couldn't believe her ears. Ed has never said sorry to anyone, he always said when someone said they was sorry really meant they're really a sorry ass person. "Look save your sorry ass excuses you rape me, I should have your ass arrested for what you did to me," shouted Janet. "Whatever you do then just do it, I don't regret what I did, what we did, not when I was so deep inside my pussy, and not when I can still taste you in my mouth and that I could hear and feel your heart beat the same beat as mines, and I can't regret when you told me that you love and forgave me, and you can't tell me that you didn't feel it to Jay." "I didn't mean any of that shit, I only said it so you'd think it so you'd let me go," said Janet. "What if you're carrying my child, do you really think I'm just going to let you leave me when you could be pregnant." "Fuck you Ed, and I swear if I'm pregnant I'll get an abortion," said Janet. "Yeah right, you don't believe in abortion and you despise female who kills innocent baby, I know you and I know you want hurt our baby if you're pregnant." "Whatever I may or may not be it's no concern to you, and I mean it Ed leave me the hell alone," said Janet as she hung up the phone

Chapter 9

Janet and Jason (Jay)

Janet was a ball of nerves as she paced her bedroom floor. "How the fuck did this happen," Janet, asked herself the hundredth time since she been there. She took three hot scorching hot showers, scrubbed her body until she thought she was going to bleed and when she still felt dirty she poured a whole bottle of lavender bleach and took a tub bath. Now three hours later she still could feel Ed hands and mouth on her. "How the fuck did this." Janet cell phone went off stopping her from finishing her sentences. Walking over to the bed she saw it was Jason calling. Not knowing what to say she sent the call to voicemail. Janet began to pace the floor again as her cell phone went off again. Knowing who it was already she answered it. "Hello." "Wat di bloodclot is gwan'in on, mi told yuh before dat mi don't play games," said Jay in a calm voice. "Um, I'm sorry about earlier, um, that was my ex-boyfriend and." "Mi don't care who di bumbo clot is, yuh should've said yuh was involved, mi already told yuh dat mi have other ooman, mi just don't understand why yuh had ta lie, and tell mi dat ya single when yuh not, but don't worry dis be mi last time calling yuh, ya lucky because mi don't take no disrespect lightly get yuh shit tagether," said Jay as he hung up the phone. Janet couldn't do anything but cry, because she didn't know how to tell him or anyone what Ed did to her. Thirty minutes of dwelling in her self pity Janet got up and put on her tan and brown K.C. Spencer outfit, she looked at her neck and saw that it was still red with Ed handprint and decided to wear a tan scarf. She let her hair hang down and added a little make-up and perfume and grab her car keys. She wasn't going to sit in the house and let Ed win she was going out, so she decided to go to the restaurant that she had told Jay about. An hour later she was sitting at a table by a window, and view that was breathtaking. She order some curry chicken and white rice with a glass of sparkling water. When her food arrived she was about to put the fork to her mouth when she saw Jason sitting across the room with a female who looked to be in her mid twenties. Janet heart crashed in her chest, as she saw the female kiss Jay on the mouth as she rubbed his thigh. Turning her head she didn't miss the evil look Jason gave her. Trying to stay focus on her food she was only able to eat half when she gave up. Picking up her purse she headed for the register to pay for her food, when she was walking out she bump into Jason. "Sorry I wasn't looking where I was going," said Janet glancing up at Jay. He was so sexy she thought, he was wearing a black and sliver tuxedo and he had a fresh hair cut and she wanted to taste his lips so she could erase the memory of her kissing Ed, and she wanted to feel his hands on her to erase where Ed had his hands. "Na yuh good," said Jason walking away. Janet knew she had to tell him because she didn't want him thinking she was playing any games. So taking a deep breath she walked behind him as he headed towards the bathroom, and when he was about to open the door she called his name. "Wat do ya want, mi have noting ta say ta yuh," said Jay as he turned to look at Janet. Without another word Janet kissed him hard and hungry on his lips, sucking his tongue softly as she ran her hands from his head down to his dick that was big and hard and she massage it through his pants, finally erasing all memory of Ed from her mind she steps back only to bump into Jay's date. "What the hell is going on Jay and who the hell is this bitch kissing you and shit," yelled the female. In a daze of his own Jay only looked at Janet as she tried to leave. Grabbing her hands to stop her only to have his date slaps him in the face. Fully focus now Jay looks at Janet and then at his date. "Go home Sara mi call yuh tamorrow," said Jay not reacting to the slap. "Go home, nigga you asked me out and now your trying to play games with me," said Sara. "Now mi telling yuh ta go home, yuh know mi don't play games either, so yuh either go home and mi call ya tamorrow or yuh stay here and get played." "No I'm sorry I shouldn't have kissed you, it was a mistake," said Janet as she ran out of the restaurant. When she got to her car she just sat there and cried. "What's wrong with me, I was just rape by her ex-boyfriend and now I'm acting like a whore by kissing Jay when I know he's with another female," Janet said to herself as she sat in her car. When she was about to start it, her car door flew open, and was snatched out the car, and pressed against it by Jay. "Wat di hell is going on Janet, mi don't like playing fucking games, wat's di deal wit yuh," asked Jay as he looks into Janet eyes. Holding her head down tears began to fall more freely. "I'm so sorry, I had no right to do that," said Janet. Lifting her face up to him Jay leaned in and kissed Janet. Pulling her out of the car he lifts up her dress and fuddled with her clit through her panties. Inhaling deep Janet was shocked and scared of the feeling she was feeling. "Please stop, I can't do this," said Janet as she pushed against Jay's chest. Letting her down Jay takes a step back. "Wat di hell is yo problem, first ya kissing on mi and den di next ya pushing mi away." "It's not that, my ex," said Janet as she started to cry and shake all over from the memory. "Ya ex wat Janet," asked Jason as stood in front of her. "Oh God Jay, he rape me," said Janet as she slide into her car seat shaking and crying. "Wat did yuh say." "Before you called he," Janet couldn't finish as she broke down and cried harder. Jay picked her up and held her against him. "Come on yuh go home wid mi, I'll get mi boy ta pick up yuh car in di morning." "No I'm fine." "No ya not look at yuh, yuh shaking and ya can't drive like dis, come get ya things and lock up yuh car, yuh stay wid mi," said Jay not taking no for an answer. When Janet locked her door Jay was on his phone talking real fast in his language, so Janet step back to give him space, than he held up his pointer finger telling her to stay where she was. "Wat is ya ex name," asked Jay as he held the phone to his ear. "Ed Gray. Why?" " Ya mon, Ed Gray," said Jay and then continued in his language, a couple more question later he hung up his phone and they walked to his car. Thirty minutes later they pulled into Jay's driveway and Janet was taken-aback again. "Wow, your house is beautiful." "Thank yuh," said Jay, as he went around and open Janet's door. A man came out of nowhere and scared Janet half to death. "Sorry mon, mi didn't mean ta frighten yuh." "Oh, that's okay," said Janet. Jay began speaking his language and then asked Janet for her car keys. When Jason handed her keys to the man he said nothing else and the man left as Jay and Janet went inside the house. “Oh this is real nice,” said Janet as she looked around the house. “Thank yuh, do ya want anyting ta drink.” “No really I’m fine, I can go home now, I don’t want to invade your privacy, and you told me before that you don’t bring anyone to your home.” “Yuh fine just relax have a seat and I’ll bring ya someting ta drink.” Taking a seat on the sofa Janet closed her eyes. She didn’t want to go home and was happy that Jay brought her to his house. “Look, tell mi wat happen?” said Jay handing her a drink. Swallowing the unknown drink down with on gulp it instantly burned Janet stomach. So she told Jay what happened, when she was finished Jay had a look of murder on his face. “Di bummaclod, when mi find him he dead,” said Jay. “No, please, you don’t understand his father is a well known Lawyer and his Uncle is Mayor of this city, just.” “Just wat Jay, ya want mi ta let a man like dat breath after wat he did ta yuh, fuck dat he dead.” Janet leaned over and took Jay hands. “Jason I need for you to understand, he doesn’t matter I’m here and for now on I’ll take someone with me, he’s not worth it,” said Janet looking into his eyes. Removing his hands Jay stood up and paced the floor, the way she said his real name made him hard and he didn’t want to think about sex when she was just rape. Taking in a deep breath Jay sat back down beside Janet. “Look where mi from we treat our woman like Queens, dis I can’t let go, wat he did need just and wat if yuh pregnant.” “I’m not pregnant I take birth control pills, have been on them since I was with him that’s why I couldn’t get pregnant by him when we was together, he doesn’t know this because I told him that I didn’t believe in them,” explain Janet. “So ya sure dat yuh can’t get pregnant?” “Yes.” Leaning back Jay closed his eyes and thought about the hit he just made on Ed. He opened his eyes when he felt Janet kiss his lips. “I want you to erase him from my mind,” said Janet as she looks into his eyes. “Naw mi want take advantages of ya like dis, yuh not tinking straight and I don’t want yuh ta have second thoughts later on.” Taking her hands she ran her hands down his pants and squeezed his dick lightly. Leaning further over Janet began kissing his neck, going down to his chest. “Make love to me Jason and erase him from my mind,” said Janet as she unbuttons his pants and taking his dick in her hands. Jay just sat and looks at her as she flicks her tongue on his dick and began to suck softly. “Mi trying ta be a gentleman, ya not tinking right, when mi in yuh I want yuh ta know its mi and not him.” Janet deep throated him making his hips lift off the sofa and moan deep in his throat. Lifting her head she pulls off her shirt and stands before him. "I know where I am and I know that I want you Jason, I want you right here and right now," said Janet as she took off her dress and stood before him in her matching red thong and bra set. Standing up Jay lifts her in his arms and carry her up stairs to his bedroom cutting on the lights as he carried her inside. Laying her on the bed he kisses her on her stomach and when he got to her belly button he flicks his tongue in her naval teasing and making her shake. Janet felt his dick harden as he made his way lower. Lifting her hips in the air he removed her thongs and then her bra leaving her completely naked. "Yuh so beautaful." "And your so damn sexy," said Janet. Jay began to take his clothes off when Janet took over; with each button she open she kissed its place. When she was at his pants she used her teeth to open the buttons then using her hands she pulled down his pants freeing his dick. "Wow," was all she could say when she saw the full length of him. "Yuh changed yuh mind already," teased Jay as he lean back on the bed. "Oh no, I want you even more," said Janet as she climbs on top of Jay. "Do you have a condom?" Reaching over to the nightstand Jay took out a pack of brand new condoms. Laying Janet down Jay put on the condom and then began to kiss her neck, and when he got to her breast he paused and took in her beauty. Jay sucked and nibbled on her breast and when he looked at her neck more clearer he paused and sat up. "What's wrong did I do something," asked Janet when she realized that he was looking at her neck she took her hand and covered it up. Pulling her hands from her neck Jay began to kiss the bruises licking and sucking on it lightly. When Janet felt his dick ready to enter her she tensed up, but soon relaxed. Jay was way bigger then Ed so he worked his dick in and out of Janet until he filled her. "Let mi know if mi hurt yuh," said Jay as he kissed Janet on the forehead and pushed a little further in her. "Oh Jason you feel so good," said Janet as she worked her body meeting Jay's thrust. Jason lifted Janet's ass in the air, as he squeezed and rotated his hips as he worked her over. "Damn yuh pussy is so tight." "No your dick is just big, now fuck this pussy Jason," said Janet as she took his full length in her. Flipping over Jay sat Janet on his dick. "Ride mi dick Janet." Without any question asked Janet rode Jay fast and hard, when she was about to nut Jay lifts up and walked over to the wall and fucked her standing up. "Oh my, gosh, that's it Jay, that's it I'm cumin," shouted Janet as an orgasms so big made her head dizzy. "Take dis dick baby, say mi name." "Jason, oh Jason, Jason," shouted Janet. "Mi cumin baby hold on tight," said Jay as he pumps a couple more time filling the condom with his sperm or so he thought. "Oh shit da condom broke," said Jay as he looks at Janet. "What?" "Mi said da condom broke." Yep, Janet look down, she saw that the condom had bust. "Yuh said ya on di pill right." "Yeah, but still Ed had sex with me without any protection." "Mi know, look it's okay mi wanted ta have di sex so it's my fault ta, we can get checked out in a week and see wat a doctor say," said Jay as he pulled Janet into his arms. "Okay, you're not mad." "Na mi good, now lie down and get some sleep we worry when we need ta worry," said Jay. They both felled asleep in each other arms. The next morning when Janet woke up she was confused where she was at until she remembers that she was at Jason house. When she was about to get out of bed Jay walked in the room fully clothed smiling at her. "How did yuh sleep," asked Jason as he sat on the edge of the bed. "Wonderful, thanks again for letting me stay the night, I don't know what I've would've done if I went back to my house, shit I don't know if he knows where I stay," said Janet getting scared all over again. "Do yuh have someone ta stay wid yuh when ya get home," asked Jay. "Oh me and my best friend lives together, I'll tell her when I get home what happened I can't tell her over the phone then she'll be worried, and then she'll come all the way down here, and believe me she hates Newport News," said Janet. "How about if mi follows yuh home," said Jay. "No really I'm fine, your probable busy and I've held enough of your time, can I take a quick shower before I leave." "Look yuh good, mi just want ta make sure yuh get home safe, and yes yuh can take a shower everyting is already out for yuh, mi be downstairs when ya finished." Janet got out of bed and headed towards the bathroom, when she got in she put the water on fully blast and stayed there and let the water beat against her skin, she jump when she felt hands on her back. "Sorry mi startled yuh but ya were just ta tempting mi had ta join yuh in di shower," said Jay as he began to rub Janet back and then breast. Lifting her up he enter her slow, but he felt her tense up. "Protection," said Janet. "Ta late for protection now, plus mi only been raw wid yuh no one else," said Jay. "But still." "Just relax Janet, mi want yuh raw." And with that Jay fucked Janet to the point where she thought she was going to faint, she never experience orgasms after orgasms before but she did with Jason. When they was finished he cooked her breakfast and then Janet went to her townhouse and packed the rest of her things and headed home, she never knew she was being followed by Jay friend to make sure she got home safe, but what they didn't know was that they were also being followed.

Chapter 10

Zoe and Brittney

Zoe was walking towards his house when his cell phone rang. "Speak." "Hey baby, I was wondering what you want for dinner," asked Brittney. "Wat ever yuh cook is fine I'll be there later," said Zoe. "Okay see you later baby," said Brittney as she hung up the phone. Zoe shook his head as he open the door and saw Jay sitting on the sofa talking on his cell to his new girlfriend Janet. As he made his way to the bar he smiled because he was happy that his best friend and now partner had found his soul mate. In a couple months they were to go to Richmond to Janet girlfriend SaSa birthday party. Zoe told Jay that he couldn't make it because Brittney family was having a dinner and they wanted Zoe to attend. Even thought he wasn't feeling Brittney that way he told her he'd let her know if he could make it or not. He was only dating Brittney because she were friends with Sasha, and he knew if Sasha called or contacted Brittney he would know because he had one of his boys break her password and checked her phone records without he knowing. He wasn't born yesterday he knew if Sasha called Brittney she would erase it off her phone, that's why he was always a step ahead of her. Sasha didn't lie when she told him if he continued to call she would change her number. He called her and begged her to come back and when he called her the last time he got the recording saying the number was change, and he still didn't know where she was he even tried the tracking device but she didn't have one on her phone. Zoe went over and poured him self a glass of Jamaica rum and went to his study. Twenty minutes later Jay walked in with a big smile on his face. "Wat's up mon ya ready ta go ta dis party or wat," said Jay as he poured a glass of Vodka. "Yeah mon, I need ta get away from Brittney, she's a pain in di ass, don't yuh know she quit her job, den she want mi ta pay her rent, yo she's trippin hard mon," said Zoe sitting down on the chair behind the desk. "Man, yuh need ta let her go, ya making a mistake being wid her, if Sasha comes home and your wid Brittney wat yuh gaan ta say or do?" "I know yuh looking out for me and everyting but mi know Sasha is going ta call her, they're friends," said Zoe. "If she hasn't called her in a year then I don't tink she's going ta call." "She will." "If Sasha does call Brittney, y'all know either ya wid her or not." "Mi know wat ya saying, but mi want ta do it dis way, so enough about mi problems how's business in Norfolk." "Mon it's crazy, but good, when ya said yuh was going legit mi didn't know ya was planning dis, three restaurant and two night clubs, work is really good," smiled Jay. "Yeah mon, di night club in Hampton is doing good also, last night we had a full house, couldn't let anyone else in and we still had a line outside, we had ta give dem a free pass ta di other club ta get in for free," said Zoe as he lit a blunt. "I know wat yuh mean, wat do ya have plan for tanight." "Nothing mon, Brittney cooking mi dinner again, she's good peps but she's not mi type, she's too clinging want ta be where mi be everyday and night, and I'm gaan ta do wat yuh said, and leave her alone, because when Sha gets home I don't want no shit poppin and di way Brittney is clinging she's just gaan ta be more trouble and mi don't want dat," said Zoe standing up walking towards the window. "Good mon, she's bad news mon, bad news." "Mi know, mi gaan head over B house and check on her, she didn't look ta good di last time mi saw her." "Mi know mi saw her sorry ass kids at di club last night probable spending her money, it's a shame dat dem treat her like dat, mi madda would've kicked mi ass if I didn't help her out," said Jay shaking his head. "Well I'll call yuh later," said Zoe as he walked out the door. Forty minutes later he was pulling in Betty house and saw a lot of cars parked in front. When he got out he heard loud music coming from out the house. As he walked up the steps he saw Betty's daughters sitting on the steps smoking a blunt and bobbing their heads to the music. "Wat do ya want, mi madda not feeling well and she don't want no company," said Helen the oldest daughter. Ignoring her Zoe went into the house and he's eyes almost pop out his head as he saw Betty house, it was fucked up. Zoe walked over to the stereo and turned it off. "Wat di bloodclot is going on here," shouted Zoe. He been paying for a maid to come and clean up the house because he knew Betty was still to weak to do it herself. Looking around Zoe saw beer cans, liquor bottles, and food, weed stems, everything everywhere in the house. "Ya mon keep ya voice down mi madda is resting," said Hue looking Zoe up and down. "Wat ya say boy," said Zoe to Hue who was at lease ten years older then him. "Ya heard mi, wat ya here for, yuh done ran off mi niece, ya made mi madda sick from stressing her and shit, wat yuh coming here for now." "Mi want all ya out of here in the next five seconds or ya gaan ta find out wat mi want," said Zoe as he took out his gun and pulled back the trigger. "Mi go no where, I want ya out of mi madda house, because yuh do noting but cause problems." "Mi cause problems, nigga yuh have di nerves ta talk, ya madda had a mild heart attack and none of ya came here ta check on her in over two months, now ya here and her house is fucked up just like y'awl ass, now yuh have two seconds ta get di hell out of here before mi put a bullet in ya ass," said Zoe pointing the gun towards Hue head. Betty came out at that time and put her hands to her chest. "Oh Jah no, please don't shot mi boy Z," said Betty as she watched with horror at what was going on. Lowering his gun Zoe looks at Betty. "Mi didn't mean to scar yuh, mi only came ta check on ya, when mi see dem and di house it vex mi," said Zoe. "It's mi fault mi let dem come here because mi was lonely Z, mi only see yuh and Gunny and he not been here in a long time, when mi kids called and asked could they have a get tagether mi said yes." Zoe help Betty seat down on the sofa. "Where is di maid mi paying ta come clean ya house?" "She came by and saw di house and she quit, Hue and Helen is gonna clean up." "Well they need ta get ta work, yuh can't live like dis is bad for ya health, look go grab a couple outfits mi get yuh a suite so yuh can relax for a couple days," said Zoe standing up. Surprised Betty looks into Zoe eyes. "Why ya doing dis for mi, mi don't know where Sasha is, if mi did mi would really tell yuh, yuh help me a lot dis pass months," said Betty. "Na mi good, when mi time ta finds Sha mi will find her and bring her home, right now mi worried about yuh." Betty was speechless. Going to her room Zoe turned to look at Hue. "Ya right mi was di cause for ya mom ta get sick, but now mi making it up ta her, but when she gets home in a week dis house better be spick and span, or yuh gaan ta regret it, if it wasn't for the luv for Sha and B yuh be dead," said Zoe. "Yeah right, yuh luv mi niece but fucking her friend, if dat's luv den mi niece needs ta stay where di hell she's at, yuh want ta play games wid her, she ta good for yuh and ya wicked luv ya wicked mind, mi know yo type, mi is ya type," said Hue. Zoe was quiet as he looks at Hue still standing in front of him. Then Zoe cell phone rung, easing the tension in the air. "Wat dat saying, yeah, saved by di bell, but in yuh case ya phone," smiled Hue as he walked out the house. "Speak." "When are you coming, I've been waiting for you all evening," said Brittney. "Mi not coming someting came up," said Zoe. "But I need for you to come I have something to tell you," said Brittney. "Wat ya got ta tell mi," said Zoe getting irritated with Brittney. "I want to tell you face to face, I'll be waiting," said Brittney and hung up the phone. "Yo B are yuh almost ready," asked Zoe as he walked in the back of the house. He was glad that this area was clean. He knocked on Betty bedroom door and when she didn't answer he opens it only to find her sitting on her bed crying. "Wat's di matter B," said Zoe as he sat beside her on her bed. "Mi so sorry Z, I haven't been honest wid yuh," said Betty as she looked into his eyes. "Wat yuh talking bout?" "If ya only helping mi ta find out where Sasha is, will mi sorry ta tell yuh dat she'll never call mi, hell she probable hates mi," cried Betty. "Wat yuh talking bout B?" "Mi treated her bad, all her life mi treated her bad, not showing her di luv she deserved, mi took mi anger out on her when her madda left, mi beat and punished her for noting, now she's gone like her madda." "We'll find her, just don't get upset, mi wasn't right by wid mi did either, but mi luv her we just have a different way of showing our luv," said Zoe. "Yuh a good man, but mi didn't know dat at first mi only saw ya as a weed man who had plenty money, now I see yuh a good man wid a good heart, but if yuh just being nice just ta find Sasha ya wasting yuh time, she want call mi, I'll be di last person she calls," said Betty wiping away her tears. "She'll call yuh, but when she calls yuh need ta talk and put di past behind ya, if she calls yuh can tell mi only if ya wants ta, right now mi gonna stop trying ta find her, when she or if she comes den it be on her and not because mi found her, and now since we got dat out di way are yuh ready ta go, mi have ta go somewhere," said Zoe standing up. "Yeah mon mi ready mi just hopes dat she's okay, mi miss her so much," said Betty. "Yeah, mi ta B." After Zoe drops Betty off at the In House Suites he headed to Brittney house. As soon as he walked to her door it flew open and there stood Brittney in a see through teddy. Ignoring her Zoe walked passed her as she closed the door. "So I guess you were with one of your other bitches that you didn't have time for me," said Brittney. "Look Brittany, mi have no time for ya bullshit, wat do yuh have ta tell mi?" "I'm pregnant." "Okay wat dat have ta do wid mi," said Zoe. "I'm pregnant by you motherfucker," spat Brittney. "Nuh, mi don't tink so, mi never hit dat raw, wat ya take mi for a fool." "Oh it's yours I made sure I got pregnant by you, I put wholes in all the condoms we used, why do you think it always leaked when we was finished," said Brittney. "Wat di bloodclot yuh say," said Zoe as he walked up to Brittney. Backing away she took a deep breath. "I put holes in your condoms so I could get pregnant, I knew if I got pregnant you'd forget about Sasha and then we can be together and be a family." Zoe laughed so hard that he had tears in his eyes then he began to talk in his accent and Brittney looked at him confused. "What the hell you're laughing at, and speak fucking English," shouted Brittney. Just as quick he laughed was as quick as his whole face expression changed. "If ya pregnant den yuh better get rid of it, mi don't want ya ass or ya baby, wat yuh tink ya di first one ta claim ta get pregnant by mi, ask ya self dis, do yuh really tink mi would let yuh have mi baby when mi in love wid Sasha, and den ask yuh self dis, once ya told mi dat yuh pregnant do ya tink mi would let yuh have it, tamorrow mawning yuh be un-pregnant," said Zoe as he flip open his cell phone and called someone. "I'm not having no abortion, I'll leave town first before I kill my baby," said Brittney as she walked to the bedroom and slammed the door. When Brittney heard the doorbell she came out of the bedroom to see who it was. When she walked into the living room she saw Zoe opening the door and letting a tall dark skin man and four other guys behind him in. Brittney noticed in their hands looked like a folded table in a big long case. Zoe began to speak his language to the four men. When he was finished three of the men grabbed Brittney, and carried her to the back bedroom, while the other two took back the equipment. Zoe walked over to the stereo and turned it on and up a little, and then he went to the back room where the men had Brittney in a position of having a pep smear on the recliner chair. "Ya really didn't tink mi would wait until tamorrow do ya, mi can't have no baby by yuh, ya noting ta mi but a wet ass, den yuh had ta go and do dis, if ya claim yuh pregnant den after dis ya want be anymore, and after dis is over don't fucking call mi or I'll kill yuh," said Zoe and then he started laughed really hard. "Yo mon, she put holes in mi condoms ta get pregnant," Zoe told the men still laughing. "Mon, how many is dis, thirty, forty," said Zoe as he lit a blunt and puffed on it. "Brittney, Brittney yuh not di first ta lie and say ya pregnant by mi, but after dis procedure, if yuh pregnant or not it want make it, this here is wat mi call getting down ta the truth and when its over mi don't want ta see or hear ya voice or ya name and if yuh see mi go the other way, mi have a bullet wid yuh name on it, hurry up and get dis over wid mi want ta blow dis bitch head off just by looking at her," said Zoe. Brittney finally found her voice spoke for the first time since the men came into her home. "Please don't do dis Zoe, please don't kill our baby I'm, really pregnant by you, and I have a doctor notes you can even call her," cried Brittney. Zoe paused where he was standing and turned to look at Brittney. "I'm not lying I went to the doctor a week ago, I was going to tell you but you been busy, I'm almost three months," said Brittney. Zoe spoke his language again and the men untied Brittney and let her down and gather there things and walked out the room. "I should kill yuh, but if yuh really carrying mi seed mi let ya live, but if I find out yuh lying ya gonna wish ya was dead," said Zoe as he walked out the room. Brittney walked over to the bed and cried, she was so happy to be pregnant, but she wanted Zoe to be happy to. How was she going to get him to forget Sasha when she had a hold on him that she didn't know she had? 'Well at lease I'm pregnant, with our baby he'll forget about Sasha.' thought Brittney as she got off the bed and went to take a shower. She had one more surprise for Zoe. When Zoe got home Jay was once again on the phone talking to Janet. When he saw Zoe he ended his call and approached him. "Wat's up Z, I thought yuh was going ta Brittney house." "Yeah I did, but I stopped at B's house first and you want believe wat mi saw." "Don't tell mi she let her kids back in right." "Yeah mon, house was tore di hell up dem do noting. I guess because mi not in di game anymore nigga's tink mi soft or someting. Sasha Uncle Hue tried mi taday, if it wasn't for B he be sleep right now, and ta top dat off Brittney trap mi by getting pregnant, ya know mi so when she told mi I called Head and he showed up and handle dat only ta found out dat it's true she has doctor papers and I talked ta her doctor before I left out," said Zoe as he walked over to the bar and poured him a Gray Goose straight. Taking a big gulp Zoe emptied the glass and poured another shot. "Hey mon take it easy, ya know yuh can't handle ya liquor," joked Jay trying to calm his friend. "Jay mon dis shit is driving mi crazy, so as of taday mi no longer gives a fuck about Sasha, mi moving on wid Brittney and dat's dat." "Wow, but mi don't understand, just because she's pregnant ya gaan ta stay wid her," asked Jay "Yeah mon, I can't abandon mi seed, plus if mi told ya di truth yuh wouldn't believe mi." "Try mi," said Jay. "Sasha uncle Hue, he said someting about wicked luv wicked minds and he's right, mi wicked, dat's why mi going ta work tings out wid Brittney, I'm going ta take her ta Florida wid mi so she can met mi madda, everyting in Norfolk is already taken care of and I'll get everyting in order in Hampton for di reggae club down there before mi leave." "So how long yuh gaan ta be gaan dis time?" "Mi family reunion is next week, I forgot until mi sister Rhonda called ta remind mi so I should be gaan for two weeks tops." "Dat's wat's up, mi got dis end yuh go and take it easy have some fun," said Jay. "Yeah mi just hopes dis bitch ain't playing no games because mi will catch a murder charges," said Zoe as he went down the hall to pack his things. Brittney was so happy to be going to Florida with Zoe that she began to pack the same day he told her he was taking her. She remembers when he first called her and how they talked on the phone for three hours straight they mostly talked about Sasha and if she knew anything, which at that time she didn't. Then when he came and picked her up to take her out to dinner. Oh boy she was so happy to be in his present that she didn't care what he talked about, she been dreaming of dating Zoe for so long that she actually pinched herself to see if she wasn't dreaming. And then exactly five months later she finally had sex with him, he never kissed her to claim her, but when he sexed her the way he did it had to mean something to him, it felt, as he was making love to her soul telling her that he was her soul mate. Yeah she knew she was wrong for trapping him, but she was losing him each and everyday and she didn't want that so desperate people do desperate things. One day while he was in the shower she went inside his nightstand and took out his condoms and put holes in them, she knew he wasn't sleeping with anyone else, after Sasha left he broke up with all his other girlfriends, so what was she to think when he approached her. Brittney cell phone rang and she answered it without looking at the number. "Hello." "Hey stranger." "Who's this," asked Brittney already knowing it was Sasha. "Don't be like that how are you, sorry I haven't called you in a while, how's things going," asked Sasha. "It's going, when you're coming back to this side of town." Brittney asked because she was worried that if she came back would Zoe leave her and the baby to be with her again. "Be for real, I'm never coming back to Newport News, I like where am at." "Where's that again," asked Brittney already knowing. "Richmond, girl you should come visit me, you know I miss you right." "Look Sasha I gotta tell you something and I don't know how you're going to take it but I can't keep this from you any longer." "What's wrong, are you okay," asked Sasha concern. "Zoe and I are together and I'm pregnant by him," said Brittney wanting to hurt Sasha and make her jealous. "Wow congratulation and I mean that, you deserve all the happiness you're receiving." "So you're not even a little mad that were together," asked Brittney shocked. "Girl please I've moved on and dating this guy who just moved down here, he respects me and loves me so to answer your question hell no I'm not mad," said Sasha. "Okay I just wanted to make sure," said Brittney angry that her news didn't upset Sasha. "Well I got to go, but I'll call you later to check on you, when your due dates." "Girl on Valentines Day can you believe that, I'm so excited and Zoe taking me to meet his family next week, girl he's everything I've dreamt of," brag Brittney. "Well congratulation again and if I came down there I'll stop by to see you," said Sasha as she hung up the phone. Brittney flip closed her phone and was looking through her mail when she came across a late notice for her rent, since she quit her job Zoe been giving her checks to pay her bills down to her car payments and she realized she needed to called him so he could give her a check to take care of both of them for her right now, she couldn't wait until she had her baby and then her and the baby would live with Zoe and be a family. Smiling she dialed Zoe cell phone. "Speak." "Hey Jay this Brittney is Zoe around I need to speak to him." "Zoe not here, he says if yuh calls ta tell ya he'll call yuh later." "What do you mean he's not there, your answering his cell so where the fuck is he," said Brittney pissed off. "Look mi not his secretary mi just telling ya wat he said," said Jay as he hung up the phone. Brittney looked at the phone and then flips it closed. Pissed off because of the disrespect Jay gave her Brittney walked into her bedroom and got dressed. 'If he wants to play games then let's play.' said Brittney as she put on the most reviling dress in her closet, she knew about the party and was going, why should she sit in a house when her man will be there, and she was going to keep the other bitches away, Brittney knew she was playing with fire, but what the hell, if she can get an reaction out of him then that meant that he cared. Looking at herself in the mirror once again Brittney left her house on a mission. Thirty minutes later she pulled in the parking lot of club Rude Style and got out, she knew she was the bomb and with the extra weight she gain, her curves was dangerous. Walking pass all the other female Brittney looked them up and down and rolled her eyes at them and walked right in the club not even caring about the loud out burst the other females were saying to her. When she walked in she spotted Zoe up stairs with a light skin female sitting on his lap. Making her way upstairs she bust in the VIP room where Zoe was. "Well I guess I see why you was to busy to return my calls," said Brittney as she glared at Zoe and the girl. "Wat do ya want, mi busy go home mi will call ya tamorrow," said Zoe ignoring her. Well that told her a lot, he still wasn't feeling her, next plan, thought Brittney as she walked back down stairs and started to dance to the music, a few minutes later a tall dark skin guy came behind her and started grinding against her. She looked over her shoulder and Bingo Zoe was coming towards them. "Yo mon, ya can have her for di whole night for di right price," said Zoe looking at the guy. "Oh shit for real, how much." "Ten dollars," said Zoe. "You son of a bitch," said Brittney as she tried to slap Zoe. He caught her hands in mid air. "If yuh ever raise ya hand at mi again mi gaan ta forget ya pregnant and put mi foot in ya ass, now dis is mi last time telling yuh ta go home, mi not feeling yuh like dat, and di only reason mi here talking ta ya is because yuh carrying mi seed, don't get it twisted," said Zoe walking off. "Fuck you then I just want have your seed as you call it then, how about that, I'll go and get that abortion tomorrow you was so willing to give me," shouted Brittney over the music. Soon as the words came out her mouth she regretted because Zoe was grabbing her by the neck pulling her out of the club, when she got to the door she slip on something so not stopping Zoe dragged her with her neck around his arm in a choke hold and kept walking. The same females she walked pass looking up and down and rolling her eyes as she came in, was passing her laughing at her as she was being drag back out. "Let me go," gurgled Brittney as Zoe continued to drag her to the car. She lost her shoes on the way and the road was scratching her foot and leg as she tried to find a footing to walk on her own, but the way Zoe was choking and pulling her she was lucky she would live through this. When Zoe finally got to Brittney car he shoves her against it real hard taking her breath away. Pacing the road Zoe walked over and slap Brittney so hard in the face she saw stars. "If yuh ever in ya life talk ta mi like dat again mi will kill ya, now go home and don't fucking call mi at all, if yuh do yuh gaan ta regret it," said Zoe as he turned and walked away, pausing he turned and looks at Brittney. "And ta tink mi was gaan ta give yuh a chance, ya not worth it," said Zoe as he continued to walk away. Brittney was shocked when she heard Zoe say that, once again she done fucked up. Getting in her car she went home and cried, she didn't call Zoe at all instead she was going to change her ways and let Zoe do whatever he wanted to do, after all he was with her and she was having his baby, no one could give him what she was giving him and that's a baby. Getting her nightclothes she went into the bathroom and took a shower when she was finished she got in the bed with a big smile on her face. He was going to give her a chance and she wasn't going to fuck it up, one chance was all she wanted and needed. Now she just needed to find away to get rid of Sasha and than her relationship with Zoe would be perfect. 'I'm going to make sure that Sasha and all those other bitches will never be on your mind, I've been and did to much to get you Zoe Ashland and I'll be damn if I let you go without an fight.' Brittney said as she put on her nightclothes. When she laid her head on the pillow she smiled to herself. 'Momma if only you could see me know, oh but you best believe that I'll be calling you and letting you know for a fact that I'm pregnant and I'm with the man that I love,' said Brittney as she felled asleep with a smile on her face.

Chapter 11

Sasha and Roy

Sasha was sitting on the bed rocking her four month old son Zoe Jr. when her daughter Zara woke up crying. She still couldn't believe that she was a mother of twins, but she was happy to have a part of Zoe that was lovable. When she found out she was pregnant she was going to get an abortion until she remember that Janet didn't respect females who would kill an innocent baby, so she kept her baby only to find out when she was five months that she was having twins. She promised herself that she would never degrade her children and shower them with her love something she never had when she was growing up. She was still hesitant about calling her grandmother, she was afraid to call her at first because she thought Zoe was still looking for her but when Brittney told her the news she wanted to jump up and down because he had finally moved on with his life. "Knock, knock yuh need some help," asked Roy Sasha boyfriend. "Yes, if you can take Z.J. I can feed Z, she's been fussy lately," said Sasha handing the baby to Roy. "Hey there man, ya full now ha, just like a man eat and den fall asleep," said Roy as he places the sleeping baby on his shoulder to burp him. "Hey there what's wrong with momma princess, oh my, she's hot," said Sasha. "Take her temperature ta see how high it tis." Sasha laid the baby in the basket net and took her temperature. "Oh my 102, I need to take her to the hospital, what kind of mother am I, I let her get this sick," said Sasha rushing to put the baby clothes on her. "Hold on SaSa, ya a wonderful madda and mi don't want ta hear yuh talking like dat, now calm down, mi here ta help ya and don't forget dat," said Roy as he kisses Sasha on the lips. "Okay, it's that I don't want to mess up, I want to be the best mom I can." "Ya already da best mom, yuh taking care of two babies by ya self, dat takes love and patients of a wonderful caring mother." Sasha was use to the words of endearment from Roy; he always said the sweetest things to her. "Now let's go and see wat's wrong wid princess," said Roy as they walked out the house. Five hours later Sasha was pacing the hospital floor. "What the hell is taking the doctor so long to get test results back," said Sasha as she opened the hospital room door and looks down the hall for the tenth time. "Patient SaSa, they'll tell yuh wat's wrong, she looks better since dem given her di Tylenol." Sasha closed the door and sat in the chair. "Yeah your right, gosh I'm just so scared." At that moment the door open and a young female doctor came into the room. "Hello Ms. Jones, I'm Dr. Lane, and sorry for the wait, we're short on staff tonight, but I've looked over all the testes and it seems that Ms. Zara has an ear infection, it's common for babies, so I prescribe some drops that you'll use for one week, drop two drops in each ear and she should be all better in a few days," said the doctor. "Oh thank you so much," said Sasha. "And you're free to go all you have to do is follow up with her doctor." "Thanks again and have a good night," said Sasha as she and Roy gathering the babies things. When Sasha got home it was ten o'clock on the dot, putting the babies in their crib Roy and her crashed on the sofa. "Here give mi yuh feet so mi can massage dem for ya." Obeying Sasha put her feet on Roy lap as he rubs them. "Now that feels good, and thanks for going with me, but I know you're tired you been here since you got off work, are you hungry I can cook something for us to eat," said Sasha as she began to move her legs. "Na mi good, mi want yuh ta relax," said Roy. Sasha closed her eyes and thought about the first day she met or she should say bumped into Roy. Sasha was shopping and didn't know where anything was, and when she turned the corner she bumped into another chart knocking over the shelf behind her as she jumps back and felled. Helping her up he introduced himself as Roy Towards and they been talking ever since. Two weeks later Sasha told him that she was pregnant and he was cool with it, he didn't have a girlfriend or kids so he welcome Sasha friendship and her pregnancy that was nine months ago. Sasha opened her eyes when she felt Roy mouth on her now bare toes. Taking a deep breath she let him continue, he already told her that he was a toes person the first time he saw her wearing sandals, and warned her that she better hide them from him, now it was too late because the feeling was something Sasha never felt before unless she wanted to compare it to the sex she had with Zoe. Shaking her head she didn't want any thoughts of Zoe tonight he was with Brittney and she had to live with the decision she made. Moaning softly Sasha felt herself get moist between her legs as she creamed her panties. Kissing his way up Sasha legs Roy began to rub and massage her legs and thighs until his head was buried between Sasha dress pushing her thongs to the side he tasted her for the first time. "Oh, my, gosh Roy," shouted Sasha as Roy pushed his tongue deep inside her. As Roy sucked and licked sucked and licked some more Sasha came fast and hard. Sasha was shaking as she looked down into Roy gray eyes and was lost. Roy stood 6'2 and weight 300 evenly, his hair was in dread locks and he had a mustache and goatee that connected, he was seven years older then she and he could eat some pussy, but Sasha wanted to know what else he could do. Taking a chance Sasha worked her pussy in Roy mouth and then she sat up and removed her clothes. "Do you have protection," asked Sasha hoping that he did. Roy pull three condoms out his pocket and Sasha took and rip it and sat it on the table. As she unbuckled his pants, and when his pants and then boxer hit the floor Sasha thought she was going to hit it behind it, Roy was big. Since she was single she wanted to try everything so she got on her knees and began to suck Roy big dick. Sasha got half of him in her mouth and began to bob her head to a slow pace. "Oh SaSa, dat's it suck dis big dick," said Roy as he thrust his hips making his dick go further in Sasha mouth. "Oh baby, now dis feels good," said Roy teasing Sasha. When he couldn't take it any longer Roy picked Sasha up and laid her on the floor. Reaching over he grab the condom and shield himself. Taking his time he enters her slow, when he got half of his dick inside of her he began to pump long study strokes in and out of her making her cum on the condom. "Oh Roy your so big," said Sasha as she grind her hips taking more and more of his length. Lifting both Sasha legs in the air, Roy spread her legs eagle style, and deepens his deep stroke. "Damn ya pussy is so tight." Moaning and sweating Roy made love to Sasha slow at one minute and then fast and hard the next making her body shakes with each thrust. "SaSa mi cumin baby," said Roy as he filled the condom with his sperm. Still thrusting in and out of Sasha she screamed out her own orgasm. Both panting and breathing hard they both started laughing. "If mi known ya pussy was so deadly mi would have married yuh first," said Roy. "If I've known you were packing like that I would've been more prepared," said Sasha. "Wat yuh mean more prepared if ya were anymore prepared mi would've had a heart attack," laughed Roy. "Your silly, let me go check on the babies, do you want something to eat, I can fix you something after I take a shower," said Sasha as she straighten her clothes. "Na mi good, but can I wash up," said Roy wiggling his eyebrows. "Yeah come with me," said Sasha as she walked into the bedroom. The babies were asleep, so Sasha and Roy headed to the bathroom when Sasha cell phone ranged. "I'll be in there you can find everything in the cabinet in the bathroom," said Sasha as she went to answer the phone, she didn't recognized the number and was going to send it to voicemail but answered it thinking it might be a client since they was calling on her business line. "Hello Your Dream Design, Ms. Jones speaking how I may assist you," asked Sasha in a cheerful voice. Click the phone hung up in her ear. "Well you could've said wrong number or something," said Sasha as she closed the phone. When she went back to the bathroom she admire Roy body, but still, she thought Zoe had the perfect body. As soon as the thought came to her mind was as quicker she erased it, she just finished having the most wonderful sex, and she wasn't going to think about Zoe. Sasha got in the shower behind Roy and wrapped her arms around his waist. "I hope this doesn't change our friendship," said Sasha. Turning around Roy held her against him. "Na mi good, yuh good," said Roy as he looked down at her. "Is that all you say 'mi good, don't you say anything else." "Mi love ya and wat us ta get married," said Roy looking into Sasha eyes. "Wow, I ask for a little and get a lot," said Sasha. "SaSa, mi be in love wit yuh di first day I meet yuh, mi fell more in love wid yuh when yuh had yuh babies." "Wow." "Come now say someting anyting," said Roy. "I don't know what to say." "Will yuh tink about it." "Yeah, I'll think about it." "Den mi good, now take ya bath, mi be in di bedroom waiting for yuh," said Roy as he got out. While Sasha took her bath she couldn't think. She felted it and knew that she was still in love with Zoe, but she also knew she would never act to those feeling. Thinking of her future she decided to do the safest thing and marry Roy. Sasha knew that if she married him he could protect her and love her and her kids. When she went back to the bedroom Roy was sleep on the bed, so she just put the sheet over him and got dressed, she only put on a T-shirt and shorts and headed to the kitchen. She saw Janet talking on the phone and waved to her. She was furious when Janet told her what Ed did to her, but she thanked Jah for letting her escape and un-pregnant. As she walked closer she saw her friend since childhood wearing a big smile and was indeed happy for her. Twenty minutes later Janet got off the phone. "So I guess you finally stop being afraid and let him hit dat," said Janet teasing Sasha. "You're so silly, but on the real I need to talk to you," said Sasha sitting down at the table. "What's on your mind, are you and the babies okay," asked Janet concerned. "Yeah, we took Zara to the hospital she had a temperature 102, they said she had and ear infection, but I wanted to talk to you about Roy." "What about him, he didn't please you in bed, if that's the case try and try again until y'all get it right," smiled Janet. "Get your head out of the gutter, he asked me to marry him and I'm going to say yes, and before you talked me out of it let me tell you that I talked to Brittney and she's with Zoe and she's pregnant so you see I can marry Roy and be free of Zoe and don't have to worry about him finding out about the babies." "Are you serious, SaSa your thinking with your mind what does your heart says?" "No, it doesn't matter what my heart says damnmit, I want to move forwards not backwards." "Do you love Roy the same way you love Zoe, because if you don't love him then I advise you not to marry him, he seems like good peps and everything, but what do you know about him besides the sex, you don't know where he's from or if he has any sisters or brothers." "Come on Janet, you slept with Jason not knowing any of the things you just mention, I can learn to love him, he's a good man, who owns his own construction business, but most he's good with my babies, hell he stayed after I told him I was pregnant. How many men do you know would stay with a female who's already pregnant?" " A man who wants something more," said Janet as she walked up behind Sasha, and hugs her from behind. "I love you, you're the sister I've always wanted, and I just don't want you to rush into anything that will backfire later on down the road." "I'm not going to regret marrying Roy we can make each other happy," said Sasha holding on Janet arms. "Okay if your sure about this then I'm with you one hundred percent." Turning around Sasha hugs her. "Thanks Jay, knowing your behind me means a lot to me, and now I think it's time to call Momma Fill and see how she's doing and tell her the news," said Sasha as she went into her bedroom to get her cell phone. Going back into the living room Sasha dialed her grandmother number. "Hello." "Hey Momma Fill this Sasha." "Praise Jah, Sasha where are ya child are yuh okay, where have yuh been," asked Betty as tears ran down her face. "Momma Fill you okay? I'm sorry I'm just calling, but I didn't know if you wanted to hear from me." " "Sasha mi sorry, mi sorry for all di mean tings mi did ta yuh when yuh was growing up, mi was mad at ya madda for leaving and took it out on yuh and dat wasn't right, will yuh forgive mi." "You're already forgiven Momma Fill." "Call mi grandma, mi was wrong for telling yuh not ta." "Grandma," said Sasha real slow. "You're already forgiven, how are you feeling I heard you had a mild heart attack are you really okay, do you need me to come and help you with anything, or do you need any money or anything," asked Sasha with real concern for her grandmother. "No mi good, Zoe been helping mi, even hired a maid ta clean mi house," Betty said laughing. "Why is Zoe coming over there, he's not bothering you is he." "No child he's a good man Sasha, and mi not just saying day because he has money or anyting he's been helping mi a long time now, even got mi a room in one of those fancy hotel, motel ya know wat mi mean, and got ya uncle ta straighten out and everyting." "Wow, well I'm happy he's change, maybe him and Brittney can make their relationship work," said Sasha slipping out that she talked to Brittney. "So yuh do call dat gurl?" "Yeah sometimes, she told me that she's with Zoe and that she's pregnant, I'm really happy for them, Momma." "Grandma," said Betty cutting Sasha off. "Yes that's right well grandma the reason I called is to let you know that I have twin babies and I'm getting married," said Sasha. Betty was quiet on the other end of the phone. "Hello." "Yeah mi here, so mi a great grandma, wow so when is the big day." "Um I don't know for sure, but I'll let you know I want you to be there," said Sasha. "Mi wouldn't miss it for di world, Sasha thank yuh for calling mi, it means di world ta mi ta know yuh alright and ta let mi know mi have great grandbabies." "I love you grandma always have always will and I can't wait for you to meet your grandbabies and my friend, his name is Roy." "Well just let mi know when yuh want mi ta met dem, ya know Zoe was right." "Zoe, what was he right about," asked Sasha. "He told mi ta talk ta ya and forget about di past and move towards di future, it means a lot ta mi ta know yuh forgave mi." Sasha began to cry on the other end of the phone. "It means a lot to me to, I'll call you later on to let you know the date." "Okay baby call mi, no matter when or what time I'm gaan ta be here for yuh," said Betty. "I know and I'll be here for you whenever you need me bye grandma," said Sasha as she closed her phone. In her bedroom Roy listen to her whole conversation. Laying back on the bed he punched his fist into the bed wishing it were Zoe. He didn't know who he was but he had a feeling that if he ever came back in the picture he'd get Sasha back. Roy knew right than that he had to marry Sasha quick fast and a hurry. He been waiting nine months and Sasha was going to finally be his until death do them part. Any means necessary. A month later Sasha and Roy was married and Momma Fill and Janet were the only ones there to celebrate her happiest.

Chapter 12

Sasha and Roy

Sasha was sitting in the bedroom trying to put the fussy Zara to sleep when she heard the front door slam shut waking Z.J. up. Laying Zara down she went to pick Zoe up when Roy busted through the door startling her. "Where di hell ya been, mi been calling yuh for di last four hours, ya didn't answer ya cell or di house phone," shouted Roy. Dumfounded Sasha looked at Roy as he had two heads instead of one. "Lower your voice you just woke Zoe up, and I've just got Zara to sleep," said Sasha in a low voice. Walking up to Sasha Roy slaps her across the face. "Don't yuh ever talk back ta mi, now answer mi question," demanded Roy. Grabbing Sasha by the arms he didn't wait for her to give him an answer he picked her up and throw her on the bed ripping her shirt and skirt from her body. "Yuh been fucking dat nigga behind mi back, is dat why ya didn't answer yuh phone," said Roy as he pushes two fingers inside of Sasha checking to see if she was wet. "Your hurting me Roy, stop your hurting me," shouted Sasha. Taking his fingers out of Sasha wetness he sniffs his fingers and then tasted them. Pushing Sasha back he stands up and takes off his pants and boxers. "Mi gaan ta make sure yuh ta sore ta fuck anyone, yuh hear mi," said Roy as he climbs on top of Sasha and enters her with one powerful quick thrust. "Ahhhh, Roy, please stop," cried Sasha as Roy pumps harder and faster inside of her. Taking her hands she slaps him in the face and it seems as if it didn't faze him as he fucks her harder and harder, when he came Roy got up and walked over to the crying baby. Roy picked Z.J. up and he quiet insistently. "Wat's wrong wid daddy man, yeah daddy got ya, now go back ta sleep," said Roy as he laid Zoe back in the crib. When he walked over to the bed Sasha flinched when he rub her cheeks. "Next time when mi call, yuh better answer di fucking phone," said Roy putting his boxers and pants back on. "If you ever hit me again I'll leave you," said Sasha. Pausing Roy turned towards her. "Do as yuh told, and ya want have ta worry about mi hitting yuh, now answer mi question why di fuck didn't yuh answer di phone." "Because I turned the ringers off, every time the phone rung it woke the babies and I was working and didn't want to be disturb, you act like you don't know my routine I've worked the same way every since I started dating you and after I had the babies," cried Sasha. Roy was quiet as he looks at Sasha. "Mi sorry, mi just don't want ta lose yuh." "Lose me, what are you talking about Roy I'm with you, were married for God sakes how can you lose me," asked Sasha confused. "Do yuh luv mi or Zoe?" "What kind of question is that," asked Sasha looking away. "Yuh luv dat nigga more den yuh luv mi, mi know mi can tell by di way ya look at ya babies or when yuh call prince Zoe or hold him close ta ya heart," said Roy getting madder from the thoughts. "He's my son of course I'm going to show him my love I hold Zara the same way, but that doesn't mean that I'm in love with their father." "Mi dem father, mi takes care of dem and love dem, and I want ya ta change his name, mi want yuh ta name him after mi." "No, I told you before we was married that I wasn't going to change his name and I meant it." "Mi not asking mi telling yuh, mi wants his name changed." Sasha couldn't believe Roy, she knew something wasn't right because he never called her son Zoe he called him Prince and Zara Princess never calling them by their names. Taking a deep breath Sasha got off the bed and stood up. "I'll think about it," said Sasha as she walked into the bathroom shutting the door softly behind her. A few minutes later Roy joined her and started kissing her on her neck and fuddling her pussy. Sasha didn't want him to touch her, but she didn't want to argue or upset him so she gave him what he wanted. Dropping on her knees Sasha took Roy dick in her mouth and sucked on it long and hard. After they were married Roy taught her how to give him head the way he liked which was long and slow. Taking most of him in her mouth Sasha imagines she was giving head to Zoe, she imagined she was pleasing him instead of her husband and then she started feeling guilty. When Roy was ready to cum Sasha stood up and let Roy enter her from the back. Pumping a couple times Roy filled Sasha up with his seed. For once Sasha was happy that she got the Depo shot after she had her babies. Roy been hinting that he wanted his own kids and Sasha just didn't want to have any with him just yet, now she was happy that she never told him. When he left out the shower Sasha cried the whole time she was in there. 'Please help me Jah in my marriage, I can't go through this again,' said Sasha as she went to the bedroom to face her husband. Four months into their marriage and she was already his punching bag, she thought Zoe was controlling, but Roy was way worst. "How do I find men who treat me so bad," Sasha asked herself as she looked at Roy sleeping on the bed. Sasha went back in the living room and called Janet and they talked for a while and when they got off she did some work and when she thought Roy was deep in his sleep she went to the other side and got in the bed, she didn't want him touching her so she made sure that she wasn't close to him. 'Jah please let my marriage work,' said Sasha as she felled asleep.

Chapter 13

Betty and Zoe

Betty was sitting on the porch when Zoe pulled up. She was so excited that she couldn't keep still, so she got up to met him. "I got here as fast as mi could, are yuh okay," asked Zoe. "Ya mon mi fine, mi got some good news and bad news dat mi thought ya want ta hear." "Okay, wats up." "Sasha called me when yuh was away, we made up, and she forgave mi," said Betty with a big smile on her face. "Dat's good B, but wats so bad about dat, mi happy for yuh, um, how is she?" "Um, dats di part mi really don't want ta tell ya, but ya gaan ta find out anyway." "Come now yuh know mi don't like playing games B, wat's wrong wid Sasha?" "Um she got married a couple months ago, and she done had twin babies," said Betty looking at the ground. Zoe heart broke in a million pieces. "But dats not all Zoe mi have someting else ta tell ya." "Mi listening." "Mi tink he beating on her, when she calls mi, mi can feel someting not right, she's not happy like she was at first." "Wat do yuh mean?" "When she first told mi she was happy, cheerful, talkative, but now she's always quiet and she calls mi when he's not there so dat says a lot." "B, mi luv Sasha very much, but wat do ya want mi ta do, she's married." "Noting mi just want ta let yuh know in case someting happens ta her ya would already know wat's going on." "Well mi gotta go, Brittney has an appointment in an hour, but mi be back later ta take ya out ta eat so be ready, and thanks B for telling mi about Sha, when ya talk ta her tell her she'll always have mi heart, and even though she got married on mi that mi still Luvs and wants her," said Zoe as he walked off the porch getting into his car. When he pulled off Betty house phone rung so she got up and went to answer it, on the other line was her daughter Susan and she thought her heart was going to burst out her chest. "Mom you still there," asked Susan. "Yeah mi still here, mi just, mi just, where ya have been, mi been so worried, mi thought yuh was dead," said Betty as tears of real happiness ran down her face. "Mom mi wanted ta call ya but it was complicated, can mi come home we needs ta talk," said Susan. "Yeah come home baby, mi missed ya so much, when are ya coming." "Mi be there in da morning and mom where mi daughter is?" "She lives in Richmond; she's married now wid twins babies." "Oh my mi a grandma, I'll see ya in di morning mom, and mom." "Yeah," asked Betty. "Mi luv yuh mom, and mi sorry for leaving," said Susan holding back her tears. "Mi luv yuh ta," said Betty as she hung up her phone. Betty called only one person and told him the news, ten minutes later Zoe pulled back in Betty's yard in his hand he was carrying Misty a Jamaica restaurant bags in both hands. "Mi thought yuh might be hungry, so mi picked up sometìng for yuh ta eat," said Zoe as he places the bags on the table. "Ya ta good Z, ta good, so how's Brittney and di baby." "Mi didn't go, when yuh called mi, mi came here instead, mi go ta di next one, plus all Brittney does is complain so mi needed ta get away from her for a while," said Zoe as he went into the kitchen and took out two plates. "So do ya know where ya daughter been all dis time," asked Zoe when he came to the living room and sat beside Betty. "Nuh mon, she just said she'd be here in da mawning so we can talk." "Dats good, so why ya looking sad for," asked Zoe. "Mi just worried about Sasha, she usually calls mi by now, but she hasn't called mi in weeks, mi got a bad feeling dats all." "She'll call, I been calling her business phone every week and she been answering it, she doesn't know its mi because mi hang up or describe mi voice and say wrong number, but she always answers, ta make ya feel better mi gonna call her right now and yuh can talk ta her ya self," said Zoe as he pushed the number one on the phone to speed dial Sasha number. "Hello you've reached Your Dream Design and this is Sasha Towards, sorry to have missed your call, please leave a full description of the problem you're having and I'll personally get back in contact with you ASAP. Have a good day." Zoe closed the phone and looks over at Betty. "Ya mon, she didn't answer, mi try later, but don't worry if she needs yuh she'll call." "Don't take mi for a fool Z, mi know about yuh hitting her, but ask ya self dis, if she never told mi about yuh putting hands on her den wat makes yuh tink she gonna tell mi dat her husband is," said Betty. Zoe was quiet for a long minute. "Okay mi get mi boy ta go and check on her." "No, no guys if you can get a female ta go and make it seems that she's at di wrong address dat would be fine, Sasha did tell mi dat he's real jealous, no men." "Okay, now eat and stop worrying. Mi have ta get her address, and den mi get someone ta go over there and check on her mi promise." " Dats easy for yuh ta do, mi just getting ta know mi granddaughter and mi don't want noting ta happen ta her Z, her mom is back in mi life and for once mi feel whole knowing dem both are giving mi another chance." Taking Betty hands in his Zoe held her hand firm but tight. "Thanks Z, thanks a lot." Zoe stayed until Betty ate a plate of food then he left to go home. Betty went in her bedroom and took out her night clothes. When she was on her way to take her bath she stopped dead in her tracks and did something she hadn't done since she was a little girl. She fell on her knees and prayed to Jah to watch over Susan and Sasha and to let them return home safely. When she was finished praying she went and took her shower then got in bed and fell a sleep. Zoe wasn't taking the news about Sasha getting married at all. 'She was suppose ta marry mi, not no other nigga, but hell wat can mi do now especially when Brittney carrying mi seed.' When Zoe got home he went and took a shower and got in bed with Sasha on his mind.

Chapter 14

Janet and Jay

Janet was pacing her house floor when she called Sasha for the hundredth time, she haven't talked to Sasha in a month and that was something that never happen, she called Sasha at home and on her cell only to get her voicemail for both. She wouldn't be back in Richmond for another two days she'd to come to Hampton for a client whose website had been hi-jacked to spread porn. The customer didn't know how to stop it, even after Janet's mother explained it to them repeatedly over the phone. Things turned into an emergency when the business began getting e-mail from customers blaming them for sending them porn. Soon as Janet flips her phone closed it rang startling her. "Sasha, where are you," asked Janet not scanning the number. "Nuh is mi, who's Sasha," asked Jay. "SaSa, I've been calling her but she's not answering her phone and it's not like her she always answer her phone when I call, and I'm so worried that she might be hurt or what if the babies hurt," said Janet as she started crying uncontrollable. "Sasha, mi knows dat name where she's from, maybe mi can go check on her for ya." "You know my best friend SaSa, she used to live in Newport News but she left because she was in an abusive relationship, so she moved to Texas with me until we got a house together in Richmond, Virginia remember I went to her wedding a couple months ago." Jay was quiet for along time, he couldn't believe that all this time SaSa was Sasha, she been under his nose all this time. "Jay, are you still there?" "Yeah mi still here, give mi her address and mi get someone ta go check on her for yuh." "I don't think that's a good idea, Roy is a fucking control freak, she didn't tell me herself but she cut back on her work and that's something SaSa never does so it had to be Roy who didn't approve of her working that many hours. I haven't seen her in a month, something not right, when I'm finished here I'm going over there to check on her myself." " Nuh mi go wid yuh, mi met yuh at mi house when ya finished just call mi when ya done." " Okay, Jay I love you so much, I don't know what I'd do without you," said Janet. "Mi luv yuh ta now hurry so we can check on ya friend," said Jay as he hung up the phone. Jay leaned back in his chair still shock and glad for the information he just got, he opens his phone and pushed the number two and speed dialed Zoe phone. "Speak." "Wats good mon, mi know yuh already told mi dat yuh not looking for Sasha but mi found her," said Jay. "Wat da ya mean yuh found her?" "Ya not gaan ta believe dis but SaSa is Sasha, she's Janet best friends." "Yo man dis is crazy, mi and B was just trying ta find her, B is worried dat sometings wrong, Sasha not answering her phones," said Zoe. "Mi knows Jay is worried also, we leaving when she finishes work den were going over there ta check on her." "Thanks mon, call mi when ya find out someting mi gaan ta let B know wats up," said Zoe relived that Jay come through when he needed him the most. Five hours later Janet and Jay pulls into Sasha driveway and got out. They saw that the lights were on, as they made there way to the door they could hear the babies crying. Knocking on the door Janet and Jay waited and when the door opens they couldn't believe what they saw. Sasha face was bruise badly, and the long beautiful hair that she once had, were cut off to a short in a style Janet didn't know, and she looked as if she lost weight. The sight undid Janet as she walked to her best friend and hugged her for dear life. "What the hell is going on, did Roy do this to you," asked Janet. Shaking her head Sasha started to cry when her body was about to give way Jay picked her up and carried her to the sofa. "Fuck that lets get their shit and get the hell out of here," said Janet as she walked over and picked up the crying Zara and began to rub her back to keep her quiet. Sasha noticed Jason for the first time and pulled away from him. "Jay what are you doing here," asked Sasha. Confused Janet looks to the shock Sasha and the all too quiet Jason. "How do you know Jay Sasha?" "He works with Zoe, his one of Zoe's boy," said Sasha sitting up. "No, SaSa his name is

Jay but he doesn't work for Zoe, don't you think I'd know if he was working with that psychopath." "Mi only came ta see if yuh was alright, ya grandmadda was worried about yuh, Zoe mean no harm Sha, yuh wasn't answering ya phone, den Jay said ya name and mi so happy ta find yuh, we gotta get yuh out of here," said Jay standing up. "What a fucking minute, you work for Zoe," asked Janet surprise. "Yes mi did work for him but now we partners, mi was his hired help, we went legit a year ago, mi didn't know yuh know Sha until taday when yuh said her name, mi only knew her as SaSa," explain Jay. "Look were going to talk about that later, right now we need to get her and my godbabies the hell out of this house," said Janet. "I can't leave, he threaten to kill me if I do, and the only reason I didn't call you is because he knows where you lives, he threaten to kill anyone who tries to help me even you, Janet I'm so scared. Every time he leaves he takes my cell phone, house phone and car keys with him saying I'm talking to Zoe, and that Zoe's this and Zoe that." " When did this happened SaSa," asked Janet getting pissed. "A couple months after we got married, one day I cut the phone off because it kept waking the babies and then he came home and slap me, accusing me of sleeping with Zoe." "How the hell does he know about Zoe, do you think he listen to our conversation when we were living together?" "I don't know but that's not all, he wants me to change Z.J. name and name him after him." "Z.J." asked Jay. Sasha cursed herself as she forgot Jay was there. "Um yes Zoe Jr.," said Sasha lowering her head. "Wat do ya mean Zoe Jr. yuh telling mi dat dem babies is Zoe," asked Jay. "Yes, and you can't tell him, I know your close friends, but Zoe can never know about my babies, he's with Brittney and they're starting their own family, I have to make this work between Roy, I know he loves me, he's just." "He's just what Sasha, the nigga is crazy have you seen your face, he's beating you like a fucking man and your standing here making excuses for him," shouted Janet. Just then they all heard a car pull up and Sasha knew Roy was home. "Please just go along with me okay, don't do anything or say anything to make him upset, his temper is worse then Zoe if you make him angry, just think about me and my babies, I can't let anything happen to them," said Sasha pleading to Janet and Jay. "We are tinking about ya babies and yuh, mi going ta give yuh one week, one week ta get di hell out of here or mi gaan ta tell Zoe about his babies mi want let anyting happen ta his seeds," said Jay. Before Sasha could say anything Roy walked into the house with a frown on his face. "Hey baby Janet stop by to visit, and this is her friend Jay, Jay this is my husband Roy," said Sasha. Jay looked into the man eyes and almost died. "Wat di hell is yuh joking mi," said Jay looking at Sasha and then back at Roy. "You know him," asked Janet. "Yeah mi know him, he's mi cousin," said Jay as he looks at Roy with hatred. "What" said Sasha and Janet in unison? "Mi know yuh not di fussy boy who did dis ta her," asked Jay. "Look dis is mi wife, and yuh have noting ta do wid mi and mi wife business," said Roy as he went and stood by Sasha. Taking out his gun that Janet didn't know he had, he pointed it to Roy head and cocked the trigger. "Let mi say dis one time and one time only, for now on dis is mi bizniz, mi know all about yuh past and di trouble yuh caused mi aunt, if mi come back and she hurt again mi will kill yuh wid out blinking," said Jay. For the first time Sasha saw fear in Roy's eyes. "Sha like mi said before yuh got one week," said Jay. "One week for wat," asked Roy looking down at Sasha with panic in his voice. "Um, before you came he gave me one week to let him know if I could do his web site for him, but since I'm not in the position to go any where, I was wondering if Janet could do it, I can do all the designs and all she has to do is add the events and pictures on his website," lied Sasha. "Na mi wats yuh ta design it, it's yuh project now, be ready in one week mi have ta take ya ta mi restaurant so ya can get di feeling of di place," said Jay. Pulling Sasha to the side Janet pulled her in her arms for a hug and then kissed her bruised face. "You know I love you right, and no matter what happen I'm always going to love you, but Jay's right it's not good for you and your babies to be here, he's dangerous, and I hate to do this to you but I'm also going to give you one week." Shaking her head Sasha agreed. "I'll leave if he hits me again, if he can change then I'm staying, I really want our marriage to work, he deserves that much, it wasn't right for me to marry him when I was still in love with Zoe, and I have to give him a chance Jay." "I don't care one week." "Okay, I'll call you in one week and let you know my decision," said Sasha as she hugs Janet back. When they left Roy looks at Sasha and walks into the bedroom without saying a word to her, and for the first time in months Sasha was relieved. When Jay and Janet arrived at her house the whole way there Janet was quiet. As they made there way to the door Jay pulled her in his arms and kissed her hard. Pulling away Jay looks into Janet eyes. "Mi don't want dis ta come between us, mi luv yuh and I hope ya understand dat mi can't keep any of dis from Zoe, yuh don't know mi cousin, he's not screwed ta tight in di head, di only way mi gonna keep Sasha and her babies safe is for mi ta tell Zoe," said Jay. Opening her house Janet went to sit on the sofa. "What makes you think Zoe is any better, have you forgotten that he beat my friend the same way your cousin is doing, all I'm asking is that you give her a week to leave, you can tell Zoe everything else but not the babies, I know Sasha will leave Roy, but we gotta be by her side when she does," said Janet. "Yuh di first person ta ever make mi lie ta mi best friend, mi only going ta give her one week, if she don't call, mi gaan ta tell Zoe," said Jay as he kissed Janet on the lips. "Okay, that's all I ask," said Janet taking off Jay's shirt and then pants and shoes. Only in his boxer with a hard on and she fully clothes she eyes him up and down licking her lips. "Ya know yuh got mi heart any time mi standing in di middle of yuh floor hard and ya teasing mi, but someting missing," said Jay as he strokes himself. "What's missing?" "Yuh not naked," said Jay as he traces her to the bedroom. When he finally caught her they felled on the bed and started kissing and caressing each other. "I want you to promise that you'll never change or disrespect me or put your hands on me if were going out or if we ever get married," said Janet as she looks into his eyes. "Yuh don't have ta worry about dat, and ta prove it ta ya if mi ever hit ya, yuh can call mi sister, and she will personally beat mi ass," laughed Jason. "Mi not like mi cousin Jay, we were brought up differently, but he knows it's not right ta hit on female, I didn't want ta tell ya dis but mi have ta, Roy was in jail for five years for assault, he beat his ex-girlfriend until she was in a coma, she survived but he's dangerous when he's angry," said Jay. "I just don't get it, all her life she was abused, and now she has to go through it as and young adult and with her husband." "She'll be okay mi cousin might be crazy but he knows who's di craziest when it comes between us, now enough talking about dem, get naked for mi bust in mi boxers," said Jay as he pulls Janet on top of him. The next morning as Janet was getting dressed her cell phone rang so she rushed to answer it. "Hello." "I see you're still fucking hard headed, so you're giving my pussy to another nigga," said Ed. Janet pushed some buttons on her phone for the recorder on her phone and recorded their conversation. "Look Ed, if you keep calling me I'm going to file harassment charges against you, please leave me alone your married and I'm in a relationship, if you continue to harass me I'll call your father and tell him that you rape me and held me against my will two months ago." "I don't give a fuck who you tell who do you think is going to believe you, you're lucky that's all I did to you, your mines I can still taste your pussy in my mouth and my dick can still feel your wetness, and I have to have you again, I'm tired of imagine Pamela ass you, I be fucking the bitch in the mouth and all the while I'm thinking it's your mouth that's wrapped around my dick, then to get a good laugh at the bitch, I fuck her in the ass thinking it's you, oh I can feel you right now Janet, everything I do reminds me of your pussy and I can't and want wait any longer, this time when I get you am going to make sure I tie your ass up so you want escape this time," said Ed. "You know what Ed Jerome Gray?" "You're playing games now, you know I get hard when only you say my full name, so does that mean I can come and fuck the shit out of you." "Are you really that stupid leave me that hell alone or I'm going to make copies of this recording I'm doing right now and send them to your wife, your father and uncle then I'm going to the police station and have your ass arrested for raping me," shouted Janet. "Yeah right, your not recording me; are you really recording me," asked Ed all of a sudden getting scared. "You damn right I'm recording you, and for the last time stop fucking calling me, go bother your wife and leave me alone," shouted Janet as she hung up the phone. Janet hurried and got dressed then she called her mother to let her know what just happened since she finally gave up and told her about the incident, and went to Kinko and made copies of the recorder, she mailed one to her mother and one to herself and one to her job, next she called Jay and told him what happened of course he was pissed because if he had his way Ed be dead right about now, so he told Janet he was coming to her house to listen to the recording and make a copy himself.

Chapter 15

Brittney

Brittney was sitting on the sofa when her cell phone ranged. She recognized the number and smiled a devilish smile. "Hello." "Wats up, mi wonna see ya, can mi meet yuh some where in ya area." "Are you crazy, Zoe is watching my every move?" Brittney lied. Zoe could care less about what she did or who she did it to. "So mi want ta see yuh, mi close ta ya area, meet mi at our spot." The phone line went dead in Brittney ear as she hurried to get ready; when she was putting her make-up on she heard Zoe in the living room talking on the phone. Easing her way to the door she put her ear against it and listen to his conversation, as usual he was speaking his language but she knew he was talking about Sasha because he said her name. Walking back to the bed Brittney sat down fuming. 'When will dis bitch learn her lesson, I went through a lot to keep her out of the picture and she still popping the fuck up.' Said Brittney as she put her three-inch heels on and walked out the bedroom. When she walked in the living room Zoe was sitting on the sofa and turned when he heard her approach. "Mi call ya back," said Zoe as he closed the phone. "Wat ya doing here, mi thought yuh was gaanin' shopping wid yuh friends," said Zoe as he walks over to the bar and pour him a glass of Vodka on ice. "Well if you wasn't always busy you'd know what I'm doing, but anyway I got other plans," said Brittney. "Cool mi see ya tamorrow," said Zoe. "Tomorrow where the hell are you going now?" "None of ya business, where are ya gaanin'," asked Zoe losing his patients. "Why, if you can't tell me where you're going then don't worry about where I'm going," said Brittney picking up her purse. "Wat ever mon be gaan mi busy," said Zoe as he pushed a button on his phone. Walking out the door Brittney knew who he was trying to call, she went through his phone one night when he was sleep and saw Sasha number programmed in his phone. He had the nerves to have Sasha as number one, and she was under Mistake. The next morning she called Sasha to see if she was actually talking to Zoe behind her back, when a better idea pops in her head when Sasha husband answered the phone. It was easy planting a seed in Roy head, everything she told him he believed. 'Sucker,' thought Brittney. Shit she wished Zoe was that gullible. Then she wouldn't be going through the shit she been going through. Than all of a sudden Zoe started fucking different bitches again staying out all night, and not returning none of her calls, she was tired of being last so that's why when Roy asked if he could met her face to face she agreed with no hesitation only to be pissed at Sasha all over again. Roy was fine as wine, hell she'd leave Zoe and be with Roy if she was given a chance and the sex was wicked, she never thought she's have as many orgasms as she did the first time her and Roy had sex. She was whip and wasn't afraid to admit it, but she knew she had to spice up the sex in order to keep Roy nose wide the fuck open and she had the perfect plan. "That bitch Sasha has all the luck in men, shit every nigga who tried to holla at her was fine as hell including that dude Steve, hell I was only the bitch friend because she always held the guys attention. Hell if I admit it I couldn't get a man on my own if I tried, not that I haven't tried." Brittney said to herself as he droved down 143 heading to Williamsburg. "I tried everything to get a man only to be fucked over and then dumped, hell the only reason I'm with Zoe is because Sasha left town, and even though I'm fucking Roy on the side he's still that bitch husband, why does this bitch has all the luck." Brittney said as she bang on the stirring wheel. When she pulled into King William Inn in Williamsburg she saw Roy leaning against his dark blue Bentley and all the hatred for Sasha resurface. Getting out of the car her bulging stomach stuck out as she walked up to Roy and kissed him on the lips, as they made there way to the room Brittney miss the shocking eyes of Jay as he was leaving out of the parking lot across the street. Soon as they got in the room all their clothing was remove, as

Roy hungrily sucked and kissed Brittney. "Mi so glad ya made it, mi couldn't tink of anyting but ya sweet pussy," said Roy as he picked Brittney up and ate her pussy while she was press against the wall. "Oh shit daddy, that's it eat this pussy," said Brittney as she worked her pussy in his mouth. Sliding her down Roy bent Brittney over and reaches in his coat pocket and took out the KY gel and lubricates his dick then he put some on his finger and stuck it in Brittney ass and with one quick thrust he enters her and starts pumping in and out of her asshole. "Mi luv yuh ass, mi hook on ya ass," said Roy. "Oh shit baby slow down your hurting me," said Brittney as sharp pain hit her in the stomach and back. "Mi can't, ya feel so good, mi been waiting for a whole week ta fuck dis ass," said Roy as he slaps her on the ass. Not able to take the pain anymore Brittney pushes Roy back off her. "You're gonna hurt my baby, now go slower or you're gonna have to stop," said Brittney wiping sweat off her face. "Okay, mi go slower," said Roy as he pumped slow at first and without a word he shoved his dick so far in Brittney that she saw stars in front of her eyes. Pulling out he flips Brittney around and kisses her softly on the lips, when the pain was gone Brittney relaxed as Roy enter her with powerful thrust that had her cumin in a matter of seconds. "Oh shit baby, you feel so good," said Brittney as she pumped her pussy harder towards Roy dick. "Tell me my pussy is better then Sasha," said Brittney. "Ya pussy is way better den Sasha, mi luv yuh pussy," said Roy as he pumped in and out of Brittney. "Talk to me daddy, tell me what I want to hear," said Brittney. "Mi want yuh, and only yuh, mi want us tagether, mi luv yuh and yuh pussy." "Whose dick is that," said Brittney as she thrust her hips up in the air the way she knew Roy liked. "Mi dick is yuh baby," said Roy. When they both came they fell on the bed breathing hard. Sitting up Brittney looks at Roy big dick and started sucking on it, lifting up she looked at Roy. "I have to ask you something," said Brittney. "Wat's up?" "Did you give Sasha her phone back," asked Brittney guessing that he did since she didn't see the other cell on the table? "Yeah, why yuh ask?" "Um, I think she was talking to Zoe earlier today," said Brittney. "Wat di fuck ya mean yuh tink, either she was or she wasn't," said Roy pulling his dick from Brittney hands and getting up off the bed. Thinking fast Brittney made up a lie. "Well I heard him say her name when he was on the phone, and when he saw me he told her that he would call her back." "Mi will handle her when mi gets' home." "I thought you said you had her under control, she's still calling Zoe behind your back, and they making us look like fool," said Brittney planting more seed in Roy head. "Look mi will handle mi wife, but wat about yuh, ya man is still calling mi wife, mi thought yuh had him in control," said Roy as he started putting on his clothes. "I got Zoe, once I have our baby he'll forget all about Sasha. Thank God he doesn't know about Sasha babies, and then we would've done all of this for nothing," said Brittney as she sat up on the bed. Soon as she stood up a sharp pain shot through her stomach making her lost her breath. Bending over she saw a big glob of blood roll down her thigh. "Oh Roy my baby, I need to go to the hospital," cried Brittney. "Hold on, mi gaan ta take ya, yuh gaanin' be alright," said Roy as he help Brittney get dress, when she was fully cloth they walked out the door not seeing Jay and Zoe sitting in the car parked across the street. On there way to the hospital Brittney tried to reach Zoe to let him know what was going on but only got his voicemail. When they got to the hospital they checked Brittney and then rushed her to have a surgery. Six hours later Brittney still haven't heard or seen a doctor. An hour later a doctor walked into Brittney room followed by a nurse. "Ms. Will I'm Doctor White." "How's my baby, is my baby okay," asked Brittney cutting the doctor off. "I'm sorry Ms. Will but you had a miscarriage," said the doctor. "I had a what," shouted Brittney as tears ran down her face. "I'm sorry, but I have some more news Ms. Will, I'm also sorry to have to inform you that in the process of the miscarriage that one of your fallopian tube burst." "Fallopian tube, what's that," asked Brittney crying and confused. "Fallopian tubes is what produce your eggs, you have one on the right and left of your oval." "Okay, so what is it you're saying." Looking at the nurse the doctor continued. "Ms. Will your right fallopian tube burst and if you ever get pregnant again it's a high risk that you may miscarry again," said the doctor. "But I can have another baby right," asked Brittney. "Situation like this is hard; during your miscarriage your left fallopian tube was also damage, and I'd say it's a fifty-fifty chance that if you ever get pregnant again that you wouldn't be able to carry to full term." "But I have to get pregnant, I went through to much to get pregnant, I have to have another baby," cried Brittney. The doctor nods his head towards the nurse. "Ms. Will nurse Angle is going to give you a sedative something to relax you," said the doctor. Rubbing an alcohol swab on Brittney arm the nurse gave her a shot, ten minutes later Brittney was out cold. As Brittney slept vision of Zoe, Sasha and Roy flashed in her mind eyes, and what she saw hurt and angered her at the same time. As she dreamt, she was seeing Zoe, Sasha, and Roy in a room, and she saw how all attention was on Sasha, how they ran their hands on her curvy body, and how they caressed her breast and sucked everywhere they touched. "You had both of them, but you had to be greedy and now look at you, you lost your baby because you wouldn't leave will enough alone, and know your suffering just like you made me suffer," Brittney heard Sasha say. "Now you'll have none of them, they're mines forever," Brittney heard Sasha say. "I hate you, I hate you so much Sasha, and I'm going to make sure you suffer like you never suffer before," shouted Brittney, as she fought in her sleep. Zoe stood at the foot of the bed with Brittney files in hand and paused when he heard her say Sasha name. "We'll see whose gaan ta suffer," said Zoe as he put the file back on the bed and walked out the room. Brittney woke up the next morning alone, no flowers, balloons nothing. Brittney reached for her purse on the chair for her phone. She checked her message, but only had one from Roy just checking on her and telling her that he would call her later. Brittney closed the phone not wanting to see Roy or hear his voice, as far as she was concern Roy was dead like her baby was. She called Zoe but once again she got his answering machine so she left him a message telling him that she was in the hospital, leaving out that she lost the baby and hung up. An hour later Doctor White came into her room, carrying her chart. "Good morning Ms. Will, how are you feeling today," asked Doctor White. Brittney didn't say anything so the doctor continued to talk. "I'd like for you to stay another day to check on things, but everything looks fine, when you go home I'd like for you to follow up with your doctor." "Everything is fine, motherfucker I just lost my baby how the hell is everything's fine," shouted Brittney. "It'll get better in time, maybe the baby father and you can try again, like I said it's a fifty-fifty chance, but at less you can try." Brittney turned and looked at the doctor for the first time. "Try again, do you know what I went through to get pregnant, look just sign me the hell out of here I'm tired of looking at you and hearing you," Brittney spat at the doctor. He quickly handed over the paper work that he usually gives to the nurse to go over it with the patient, to Brittney and walked out the room closing the door behind him. Brittney got dressed fast and when she was standing in front of the hospital she remember that her car was at the motel, so she called a taxi and waiting another forty minutes for it to pick her up, Brittney was so mad she could spit bullets. When she finally got to the King William Inn, Brittney was confused when she didn't see her car parked where she left it. "Now I know damn well I'm not going crazy, where the hell is my car," said Brittney looking around the parking lot. "Ma'am is you getting out or not I have another run," said taxicab lady. Brittney gave the lady her address and sat back and closed her eyes. Another hour the taxicab pulled in front of Brittney building and Brittney almost had a heart attack. Jumping out of the taxicab Brittney rushed over to the people taking her personal belonging that was scattered everywhere. "What the hell is going on, get the hell away from my things," cried Brittney. Her eighteen hundred dollar bed set was missing the dressers, and her fifteen hundred dollars flat screen television was missing and a couple of people were walking off with her brand new sofa set. Reaching into her purse she called 911 and ten minutes later the pulled up and Brittney rushed over to them. "Look at this they're stealing all my things," cried Brittney. "Calm down ma'am, can you tell me what's going on," asked the officer who name tag read Ross. "I just came home from the hospital and all my things was out here and all of those people was taking my things," explain Brittney. At that moment the rental office manager pulled up and got out of her car. Brittney looks her up and down. "I'm glad you're here Ms. James, can you tell me why the hell my things are put outside, and just to let you know I'll be taking you to court to replace all my things that is missing," shouted Brittney. "Excuse me," said Ms. James. "You heard me, I'll have your job do you know who my boyfriend is," asked Brittney carrying on. "Look Ms. Will as you called him, your boyfriend Mr. Ashland came to the office yesterday evening and demanded all his money that he's been paying, or should I say that you been stealing, he said he checked his bank statement and without him knowing you been forging his signature on his checks to pay for you rent, and he did show me receipts of everything that's sitting outside, he told me to have the maintenance men to take everything he had an receipt for and put it outside or throw it away," said Ms. James. Brittney couldn't believe her ears. "This can't be happening I don't care what Zoe says these are my things, mines and you can't just put it out here and let these people take my things," shouted Brittney. "Oh I can, and I did, as of right now your evicted and I want you off the primes and since you already have a police officer here with you he can escort you to the apartment to get your belonging," said Ms. James. "What the hell do you mean I'm evicted, I just paid my rent," said Brittney not believing what she was hearing. "No Mr. Ashland was paying your rent without knowing it, and the only way you can get your apartment back is if you can pay the remaining balance." "Okay and how much is that," Brittney asked trying to remember how much money she has in the bank. "Three thousand, seven hundred and fifty dollars," said Ms. James looking at the folder Brittney just noticing. "What?" "Yes, you're now five months behind in rent, and you have two weeks to pay this months rent which is an additional seven fifty." "I don't have that kind of money, I'm not even working, how can Zoe do this to me, I'm having his baby," Brittney stops talking and rubs her stomach. "He knows," Brittney said out loud. "Excuse me," said Ms. James. "Ma'am I've been quiet long enough, now I know you said you just came from the hospital, but I can't help you here, now either you pay the money and keep your apartment or I'm going to have to escort you to get your things and then off the property," said officer Ross. "Um excuse me, but you still owe me for your fair," said the taxicab driver. Brittney asked if she could wait a little while longer as she went into her apartment to retrieve her belonging. The only thing that was still there was everything she bought with her own money which wasn't a lot, the officer stood by the door as Brittney threw all her clothing in the suitcase, she noticed that every pair of shoes Zoe brought was gone including all the outfits, purse, perfume everything he brought was gone just like him.

Chapter 16

Betty & Susan

Betty Fills couldn't believe her eyes when her daughter whom she hasn't seen in eighteen years walked into her house. She was just as beautiful as the last time saw her. "Oh mi Jah," said Betty as she took Susan in her arms and held her tight. "Mi sorry mom, I'm so sorry dat mi left di way mi did and mi hope yuh can forgive mi." "Yuh forgiven Su, mi forgave yuh when yuh called and mi found out dat yuh alive," said Betty as tears rolls down her face. "Mi know its mi own fault dat yuh ran away, mi never showed ya any luv, mi was hard on ya and mi sorry Su." They both went and sat on the sofa and held each other hands "Mi can't lie, ya were one of di reason for me leaving, but mi has ta be honest wid yuh, after mi had Sasha mi was on drugs real bad." Susan paused a minute and the tears rolls down her face. "Mi was tinking crazy and mi didn't want ta hurt Sasha so mi left, everything went downhill after that, I started prostitution and doing drugs even worse." "Why didn't yuh tell mi, mi would've help yuh, mi never meant ta hurt ya," cried Betty. "Mi know, mi seen how ya madda treated ya when mi was young, and even though it took mi a long time mi understand dat yuh luv mi no matter wat." "Yeah, mi luv yuh so much, so wat have ya been doing since, yuh look as beautiful as di last day mi seen ya." Susan smile. "I was living in New York and mi was beaten real bad by mi boyfriend, beaten so badly dat mi didn't remember who mi was, I was place in a shelter and den mi meet Allen, he's a good man madda, and he doesn't beat mi or disrespect mi, mi wanted ta tell yuh first because mi want ya ta meet him, we got married five years ago," said Susan. "Mi so happy for yuh, and mi would luv ta meet him, but mi have ta tell yuh someting about Sasha." "Is she okay?" "Mi hope so, but mi want ta be honest wid ya, mi treated her badly after yuh left, even though she forgave mi, mi can't forgive mi self mi want ta fix wat mi done ta her. Mi pimped her off to Zoe not caring wat happens ta her, den she disappear like ya did, and mi haven't seen or talked ta her in almost two years, and den she calls mi ta tell mi she's getting married, she was so happy Su, but now she's not calling mi, and mi tink her husband is beaten her." " Oh Jah no, do ya know where she lives," asked Susan. "Nuh mi only have her number, mi can try and see if she answers it, Zoe tried yesterday, but she no answer." "Well lets hope she answer dis time," said Susan as she took out her cell phone and handed it to Betty. "She doesn't know yuh number, she might not answer." "Well try and if she doesn't then we can call from di house phone." Betty dialed Sasha number and on the third ring she was about to hang up when she heard Sasha voice. "Your Dreams Design Sasha Towards speaking how I can help you," said Sasha cheerful voice. "Sasha dis yuh grandma, mi was calling ta see if yuh was alright, yuh haven't called mi in a while, and mi was worried," said Betty. "Momma Fills," asked Sasha surprised. "Yeah, are yuh okay Sasha?" "Um, yes um how are you feeling, I'm sorry I haven't been calling you, um I been a little busy are you okay do you need anything," asked Sasha. "Well since ya mentioned it, mi do need yuh ta stay wid mi, mi heart been bothering mi again, di doctor tinks mi stressing again, so mi wanted ta asked if ya and mi great grandbabies will come stay wid mi for a while," lied Betty. She prayed that the Lord forgive her for lying. Sasha had to admit she was happy to hear her grandmother voice the only reason she hadn't called her was because Roy took her cell phone and house phone with him when he left for work telling her that they can leave a message and then she could call them back. Plus she only had a day to leave Roy or Jay would tell Zoe about her babies, so she did what she knew she must do, leave Roy, and protect her babies from their father. "Okay, I'll call Janet and see if she can help me get packed," said Sasha already knowing Janet and Jay would be at her house early in the morning. "Okay, and Sasha mi have a surprise for yuh, now go get packed and call mi if ya need anyting," said Betty. "I will, now go get some rest, I'll see you tomorrow," said Sasha as she hung up the phone. "Why didn't you tell her dat mi home," asked Susan. "Yuh di surprise, now let mi go clean up," said Betty, as she was about to stand up. Susan stops her. "Wat'd yuh mean dat ya heart been bothering yuh again, are ya okay madda." Betty looks into her daughter eyes. "Mi had a mild heart attack, but mi fine, mi just said dat so Sasha will come home, mi know she would come if mi mention mi heart, but mi fine really not worrying so much, ya daughter and grandbabies and mi granddaughter and great grand babies are coming home in di morning," said Betty truly happy. Susan looks towards her mother and saw the happiness in her mother eyes and wondered if Sasha would welcome her back in her life with open arms or a closed door. Either way she wasn't going to back out and let her daughter down any more because she needed this chance to prove to her daughter and to herself that everything she done was a mistake and she was there to fix what she messed up.

Chapter 17

Sasha and Roy

Sasha was putting Z.J. in the crib when she heard the living room door slams. She hasn't seen Roy in a couple days because he said he had to go out of town for some business, but he was back early then usual. "Give mi yuh phone," said Roy as soon as he walks into the room. "My phone for what, not this again Roy I really want our marriage to work, but if you keep accusing me of things I'm not doing then." "Den wat Sasha, ya gaan ta leave mi," said Roy looking at Sasha. "Yes, if you keep hitting me, and accusing me of things I'm not doing then yes, I'm going to leave you. Roy I love you, maybe not at first when we got married but I do love you now, I married you because you was the first person to show me love and I want that back," said Sasha holding back her emotions. Roy was quiet as he went and sat on the bed. "Mi been told dat yuh been talking ta Zoe behind mi back, yuh know how mi feel about him, so tell mi Sasha have yuh been talking ta him," asked Roy. "Roy I swear on my baby's life that I haven't talked to or seen Zoe, and I don't know who's telling you these things but they're lying to you trying to break us up. Roy, Jay gave me until tomorrow to leave you, and if I don't then he's going to tell Zoe about my babies, I told him that I want to make my marriage work, but he thinks your going to hurt me, and I need to know right here and right now that if I stay are you willing to change, because I can't and want go through anymore of your abuse," said Sasha. "Mi shouldn't have listen ta her, but she said yuh was talking ta Zoe, and mi got so angry, mi do luv yuh." "She, she who," asked Sasha sitting on the bed and taking Roy hands into hers. "Brittney, she tells mi dat ya trying ta be wid Zoe again and dat yuh talk ta him behind mi back." "Brittney, how do you know Brittney?" Roy was quiet for a minute and then stood up and began to pace the floor. "She called ya phone after we got married, she tell mi dat yuh was calling her boyfriend and dat yuh was trying ta ruin their relationship, after she hang up mi call ya but yuh not answer." The memory of that day came to Sasha as if it happened yesterday. "Let me get this right, your telling me that, that day when you came home and slapped me and then force yourself on me was because Brittney told you that I was talking to Zoe." Roy only shook his head yes. "Why would Brittney tell you lies about me, she's suppose to be my friend, and now you're telling me that she was the cause of all the pain and suffering I endure for the last couple of months, there have to be more to this then what you're telling me," said Sasha as she walked up to face Roy. "Dats all, if mi had known she was lying mi wouldn't have talked ta her, but she say she wasn't lying and mi believed her." "You believed a complete stranger that I was cheating on you and since you never asked me you beat me, made me cut off all my hair and took my cell and house phone, and car keys because you thought I was calling and seeing a man whom not only I didn't want to be with but ran away from because Brittney told you that I was talking to him behind your back," shouted Sasha. "Ran away from, wat are yuh talking about," asked Roy. "You don't get it do you, the same hell your putting me through Zoe was doing the exact same thing, why do you think I don't want him to know about my babies, he didn't know I was pregnant when I left, I left him after he almost beat me to death and I'm telling you if you ever put your hands on me again I'll leave you, am sick and tired of all the abuse you caused me only to find out you took a bitch word over me, I'm suppose to be your wife," said Sasha as she walked into the bathroom and slammed the door shut waking Zara and Zoe at the same time. Roy walked over to the cribs and picked each baby up and held them in his arms. "Wat have mi done, mi gaan ta fix dis, okay mi gaan ta fix dis and make ya madda happy," said Roy as he kissed both babies on their forehead. A few minutes later both babies was asleep again. Roy put them both in their cribs when his cell phone vibrated in his pocket, he looked at the number and saw Brittney number, he hit end sending it to voicemail he put it on the nightstand and laid on the bed. When Sasha came out the bathroom Roy was knocked out on the bed snoring lightly, she saw his cell phone on the nightstand vibrating so she went and picked it up, looking at the number her heart sank as she saw Brittney number. "Some friend you are, I want be surprised if your fucking my husband like your fucking Zoe," said Sasha as she put the phone back and went and got in the bed. She made sure that she wasn't touching Roy. They haven't had sex in months and now she knew why. Sasha closed her eyes and before she knew it she was sound asleep. The next morning when she woke up Roy was gone as usual and soon as she went into the kitchen her doorbell rung. Opening the door she saw Janet and Jay standing there with a demanding face, stepping aside she let them in. "Why aren't you dress, and where are your things," asked Janet as she came in the house and scanned the area. "I'm not leaving, I'm giving Roy another chance to make our marriage work, we talked last night and he told me why he's been acting the way he has," said Sasha as she walked into the kitchen. Sasha fixed herself a cup of coffee as she looked at Janet and Jay. "Do you guys want any?" "Don't change the subject SaSa, you're leaving and that's final, I want stand by and watch him beat you and treat you the way he's been doing." "Mi can't let Zoe babies be around him either, he may make yuh tink him change but he evil Sasha, mi know him better den yuh, he has a temper dats not good especially around ya babies," said Jay. "Look he told me that Brittney has been telling him that I've been talking to Zoe and trying to get him back, apparently she called my cell phone after we got married and told him a bunch of lies and he believed them, but we cleared it all up last night, and I also let him know if he ever hit me or anything that I'd leave him and I mean it you guys, I want my marriage to work, and I want you to trust my judgement, if he do anything to harm me or my babies I'll leave, I'll call the both of you everyday and let you know how's everything is going, but I can't walk out of this marriage until I know it's not worth saving," said Sasha. Janet looks at Jay and Jay looks at Janet. When Jay was about to say something they heard Roy car pull up. "Please trust me that's all I'm asking, just give us time to fix all the damage Brittney cause because she's the real reason why our marriage went wrong," said Sasha as she heard the front door open. Jason didn't say anything as he watched his cousin walked into the house. "Damn mi can't go and get mi wife a surprise unless mi comes home ta mi cousin and his girl," teased Roy. "Wats up mon, we came ta check on Sasha and ta see if she can fix mi computer," said Jay mean mugging Roy. "Yeah she told mi about ya computer, but mi just want ta say dat mi sorry and dat ya going ta have ta find someone else ta fix it for ya, mi have a lot of making up ta do," said Roy as he handed Sasha a dozen of red roses and a shopping bag. "Thanks but what's all these for," asked Sasha. "Mi wanted ta do it alone, but since we have company mi just want ta tell yuh dat mi sorry for everyting and mi hope ya can forgive mi, mi luv yuh," said Roy. Tears felled freely down Sasha face as she went and hug Roy. "I love you to, and I mean it from the bottom of my heart," said Sasha as she kissed Roy softly on the lips. "Okay enough with all that mushy stuff," laughed Janet. "But let me make myself clear if you hurt her you want only have to worry about Jay you'll have to worry about me also, now she told me what's been going on and since she's my sister and best friend, I'm going to give you another chance to prove to me that she'd made the right decision of giving you an second chance," said Janet. "Mi want let ya down, and Jay if mi lay a hand on her mi give ya permission ta bodily harm mi, ya know how mi grew up, mi never had any luv, and if Sasha can forgive mi, mi hope yuh can ta," said Roy. Jay was quiet as all the backstabbing he was doing to Zoe at that moment hit him hard. "How would Zoe feel if he ever finds out that he has babies and that mi didn't tell him," said Jay as he stared at Sasha and Roy and than Janet. "Zoe is mi best friend, and for mi ta keep someting like this is wrong of mi, mi have an honor wid him dat mi want break, and mi can't and want hide dis from him," said Jason as he stared only at Janet on that comment. "He has a right ta know about his babies, as far as ya concern Roy, mi never liked ya ways but yuh as a man and as mi blood mi luv yuh, yuh can take wid mi say lightly or serious but mi want betray Zoe dis way, when mi get home mi will tell him about his babies," said Jay "If yuh had said dat yesterday mi would have fought yuh and lost, but after last night mi know Sasha luvs mi and not Zoe, and ya right he needs ta know," said Roy. Sasha was shocked and surprise. "No, no, no it's not any of your business to let Zoe know about my babies, he's with Brittney and they're starting a family together, I don't care what she did or all the lies she told, all I want right now is to move on, and I want to put the past in the past and concentrate on our future," said Sasha looking at Roy. She saw the way Roy and Jay was looking at each other and paid no mind to it. "Yuh right, but we do have ta talk about it, mi want ta do everyting di right way, mi want yuh ta know mi trust and believe in yuh," said Roy. "Thanks Roy, but I don't want to tell Zoe about the babies, not right now," said Sasha. "Whenever ya ready mi be ready," said Roy. "Oh I forgot to tell you that Momma Fill called last night, she needs me to stay with her for a few days, she said her heart has been bothering her and she said the doctor said she was stressing again, so I told her that the we'll come down and stay for a few days if its okay with you," asked Sasha. "Nuh, yuh good, mi go another time, plus mi gotta go out of town for a few days," said Roy. "Are you sure, we can go another time when your off, its that I know she's been worrying about me, I haven't been calling her like I use to and I just don't want her getting sick again," said Sasha. "Look mi want yuh ta go and spend sometime wid yuh granni, mi was wrong ta take ya phone ta begin wid, mi never should've listen ta another female when mi married di one mi heart loves," said Roy as he kissed Sasha again on the lips. "Okay, well I'm going to go get pack, how long will you be gone," asked Sasha turning around to look at Roy. "Three or four days, mi want know until mi see di area." "Well call me and let me know we'll stay at Momma Fill until you come back," said Sasha as she hurried into their bedroom to pack. Janet and Jay sat on the sofa and talked to Roy. Deep down Roy was feeling guilty about what happened to Brittney, and he had to see her to make sure she was okay. Even though Roy promised himself that he wouldn't tell her that he knew she was lying to him, he would let her know that after tomorrow he wouldn't be involved with her and that he was going to work on his marriage. He just hopes that he wasn't too late. When Sasha and her babies pulled in front of her grandmother house she was surprised to see no one standing or sitting on the porch. As she took Z.J. and Zara out of the car and stood them by her leg as she bent down for her now baby bag bookbag off the floor. Taking their hands Sasha kicked the car door shut and headed to the house. When she was ready to open the house door she got the feeling she was being watch, so she turned and saw a baby blue Bentley with dark tinted window drive slowly by. She only looked at the car for a quick second before Z.J. started crying. When Sasha opened her grandmother door she was surprised to see all different shapes and colors balloons floating everywhere. "What in the world is going on," said Sasha as she sat her bookbag purse on the floor and letting Zara and Z.J. crawl on the floor. When she was ready to call her grandmother she saw movements behind her in the den, and when she turned she thought she was looking at an older version of herself. "I'm sorry I didn't know my grandma had any company, I'm Sasha." "Mi knows." "So who are you, I've never seen you before, are you one of her sisters that I haven't met," asked Sasha as she watched Zoe and Zara play on the floor. "Um no, actually mi ya madda," said Susan as she looks into Sasha eyes when she turned back to look at her. "My what," asked Sasha confused? "Sit so ya want faint on mi," said Susan as she helps Sasha on the sofa. "You can't be my mom, Momma Fill said." "Mi know wat mi madda said, and she didn't have any right ta tell ya dat, but mi ya madda." "Momma Fill, Momma Fill," called out Sasha as she looks around the house for her grandmother, when she rushed into the living room she stops and look at Susan and then Sasha. "Wats wrong, are yuh all right, yuh bout ta give mi another heart attack," said Betty as she went and sat on the sofa beside Sasha catching her breath. "Oh I'm sorry, but who is this lady, because what she just told me can't be true, you always told me that my mom." "Mi know wat mi told yuh, but mi lied and mi sorry, dis is ya madda, dis is Susan." Sasha eyes flooded with tears as she looks at the lady standing before her. "Wow after all these years I always imagine what I'd say to you, but at this very moment I'm happy, mad, and confused," said Sasha. "Mi understand and mi also understand if yuh never forgive mi for leaving ya di way mi did, but mi was young and on drugs real bad, so mi thought mi was doing di right ting by leaving yuh," said Susan as her own tears rolled down her face. "Did you ever love me, or was I a mistake," asked Sasha. Shaking her head Susan kneed down in front of Sasha and took her hands into her owns. "Mi swear ta Jah, mi luv yuh so much, it was di hardest ting for mi ta do, but di drugs was stronger den mi and mi didn't want ta hurt yuh so mi left, mi know it's gaan ta take a long time for ya ta forgive mi, but mi wanted another chance wid yuh, and mi will be here when ya ready," said Susan. Sasha was speechless. When Z.J. and Zara started to cry Sasha went and picked them both up one at a time. "Hey, I want you two met your grandma, her name is Susan, um mom these are your grandkids, Z.J. and Zara," said Sasha as she handed Zara to her letting her know that she was forgiven.

Chapter 18

Sasha, Zoe, Roy

Sasha had enjoyed the last two days with her mom and grandma, her mom told her about her husband and they planned to set up a date so Betty and Sasha could meet him. Susan sister and brothers came to see her and they had a big dinner to celebrate. Sasha found herself telling them about Brittney and the lies she told Roy. "Mi knew dat gurl was Red Eye," said Betty. "What does Brittney have to be envy of me about, I don't have no more than what she has," said Sasha. "Ya got a good heart, and mi know for a fact dat yuh will do anyting ta help someone out even when dem don't deserve it," said Betty. "That's behind us now, and Roy and I are going to work on our marriage she may have tried to ruin it but she didn't, and I really hope you'll give him another chance Momma Fill." "Mi gaan ta tell yuh for di last time, mi want ya ta call mi grandma better yet NaNa is even better," smiled Betty. "Okay NaNa," said Sasha. The doorbell ranged and woke up Z.J. while Susan picked him up Sasha went to answer the door. When she opened it her heart fell to her stomach. "What are you doing here," Sasha asked Zoe. Damn he looked even sexier then she remembers him being. She began to fell self-conscious about her looks remembering that all her hair was now gone she had it cut into a short bob which help hide some of the bruises that was fading, and she lost so much weight that she wanted to just disappear. "Is dat a way ta answer someone else's door, mi come ta check on B, she haven't called mi in a couple days and mi wanted ta make sure she was okay," said Zoe as he walked into the house. "Ya still look beautaful Sha, and mi like ya hair cut, mi liked it long, but mi like di new yuh," said Zoe. "Um, thank you," said Sasha feeling pretty all of a sudden. When Zoe walked into the living room his heart stop beating and his face froze when he saw Susan lifting a baby in the air and started kissing his stomach making him laugh. Turning around he looks into Sasha eyes as she started backing up. Sasha starts biting on her bottom lips, something she found a habit of doing when she was nerves or scared but at that moment she was petrified. Zoe turned around and walked further into the room, when Betty spotted him she smiled and stood up giving him a big hug, Sasha was confused. "Wat brings ya by Z," asked Betty as she sat back down. "Mi came ta check on yuh, yuh haven't called mi in a couple days and mi was worried, so how do ya feel," asked Zoe as he turned back to look at the babies more clearly. "Oh am Boonoonoonous now dat mi daughter and granddaughter and great grandbabies are here, wid more could mi ask for," said Betty. Walking over Zoe picked up the now crying Zara and she quiet instantly. "So wats ya name little princess," said Zoe as he turned again to look at Sasha. "Um, her name is um Zara," said Sasha as she walked over and took the baby out of Zoe hands. "Zara, dats pretty, and wat is little man name," asked Zoe as he leaned over and looked at the baby boy who Susan was holding. "Um, um, look why don't you come by later on we where just getting ready to eat," lied Sasha. "Good mi luvs ya grands cooking, so wat's ya son name, do ya mind if mi hold him," Zoe asked Susan. Susan hands Zoe the baby and moved so he could sit down, then she went and sat in the chair giving Zoe more moving room. "Um, his name is Z.J.," said Sasha. "Z.J. wat's his real name," said Zoe looking into Sasha eyes. He already knew what she wasn't trying to tell him, he saw that both babies looked just like him. "Um, his name is Zoe Jr. okay is that what you wanted to hear," said Sasha as she shocked everyone in the room as she ran out. Sasha locked herself in the childhood bedroom and paced the floor. She didn't know what Zoe would do to her for not telling him about the babies, but she wasn't going to let him beat her for hiding the fact that she had his kids. A few minutes went by and Sasha heard some mumbling down the hall, to her surprise Zoe didn't kick in the door. A soft knock made her jump, but she didn't say a word. "Sasha baby it's mi ya madda, open di door." "Is he gone," asked Sasha as she cracked the door? "No, he's sitting in di living room playing wid di babies, he said he wat's ta talk ta ya." Sasha opened the door wider and they went and sat on the small bed. Sasha looked into her mother eyes. "You knew he was my kid's father didn't you?' " Yeah," said Susan as she took Sasha hands into hers. "Why you didn't say anything?" "I was waiting for you ta tell mi, plus madda told mi about Zoe, and when yuh called him Z.J. mi put two and two tagether." "Do you think he'll forgive me for deceiving him this way?" "Di only way yuh gwan ta find out is for yuh ta go out there and find out, and don't worry, mi and madda is right here if yuh need us," said Susan. "I love you mom, I never stopped," said Sasha. "Mi love yuh ta, we'll get through dis, mi never gwan ta leave yuh again," said Susan as she hugs her daughter tight. "We'll I better get this over with," said Sasha as she stood up and walked out the door. When she walked into the living room Zoe was holding both babies in his arms. Rising his head he looks into her eyes and she saw the anger and than saw the pain. "Why yuh not tell mi," asked Zoe now looking at the babies. "How old is mi babies," asked Zoe not waiting on a responds. "They're seven months; they'll be eight months on the twenty-first." Just then the doorbell ranged so Sasha excused herself and went to answer it, on the other side was her worst nightmare. "Surprise," said Roy as he walked into the house. "Um, Roy what are you doing here I thought you had to be in D.C.," said Sasha, "Mi left early, mi wanted ta take yuh and ya grandmother out ta eat, where is she," asked Roy and then froze when he saw a man holding the babies and knew he had to be Zoe. "It's not what it seem," said Sasha as she clarified his thoughts. "Den wat di bloodclot is dis, and why is he holding mi kids," asked Roy as he studied the man. Zoe stood up and put the babies in the floor. Standing straight with his hands placed in front of him he looks Roy up and down and then sat back down. "Yuh say ya kids, but mi just found out dem mi kids," said Zoe looking at only Sasha. "Look, Roy I swear I didn't know Zoe was going to be here, he came to check on my grandmother, when he saw the babies he started asking question and I didn't mean to tell him I know we said we'd tell him together, but it slip out," explained Sasha. Roy took a deep breath and released it slowly; pulling Sasha in his arms he kissed her hard on the mouth. "Mi good, we was going ta tell him any ways dis better because now we can start our MARRIAGE wid no more secrets," said

Roy using the word marriage as a point to Zoe. "You really mean it, your not upset that I told him without you," asked Sasha. "Mi mean it, mi luv yuh and want ta make yuh happy and di babies needs ta know him, he is dem father, and mi want stand in di way." "I love you to Roy, very much," said Sasha as she kissed Roy on the mouth. Zoe was pissed and wanted to kill Roy for putting his mouth and hands on Sasha. He didn't care if she was his wife, but he stayed cool, because what Roy didn't know Zoe was going to have Sasha for once and for all, he just had to find a way for Sasha to know about Roy and Brittney without him being involved. Sasha caught Zoe evil stare and pulled away from Roy. "Um, Roy I want you to meet Zoe, Zoe this is my husband Roy," said Sasha. Nodding his head Roy sat down and pulled Sasha in his lap. When Zoe was ready to say something Susan and Betty walked into the room. "Hello Roy, mi didn't know ya was coming, Sasha said ya was out of town," said Betty. "Hey Momma Fill, mi came early ta surprise her, so how do yuh feel," asked Roy. "Boonoonoonous, now dat mi daughter and granddaughter are back in mi life." "Roy I want you to meet my mom Susan, mom this is my husband Roy," introduced Sasha. "It's nice ta met yuh, ya daughter is a luving woman and mi will take good care of her," said Roy. "Well mi hope yuh keep ya word, and it's nice ta meet yuh ta, so are yuh gaan ta stay for dinner, mi make mi special curry chicken and rice, mi even made some bulla," said Susan as she tried to ease up the tension in the living room. "Mi would luv ta." "Sha can mi talk ta ya for a minute alone," said Zoe not caring how Roy felt. "Go, mi gaan ta help ya madda and grandma in di kitchen," said Roy as he kissed Sasha on the lips and left out behind them. Just then both babies started crying so Sasha picked up Zara while Zoe picked up Z.J. "Mi want ta know why yuh didn't tell mi dat yuh had mi babies," asked Zoe as he looks into Sasha eyes. "Are you serious, you know why I didn't tell you about our babies? I didn't run away from you just to come back because I was pregnant." "So ya keep mi seeds from mi, mi should kill yuh for dat, but ya still breathing." "That's why I didn't tell you, all you do is threaten me, and control me, damn Zoe I loved you with everything in me, and all you did was hurt me." "So ya gaan ta tell me dat he doesn't hurt ya, because mi know he does." That's different." "How is dat different, di same ting ya ran away from mi for he's doing ta yuh." "He thought I was cheating on him with you." "And why would he tink dat," asked Zoe. "Because someone was calling him telling him that you were trying to get me back, and that's why he's been doing what he's been doing." "Dat doesn't make any since, why would someone tell him dat." "Um, I don't know." "Who told him dis," asked Zoe. "It doesn't matter, what matter is that were going to work on our marriage that's all that matters to me." "Wat if mi doesn't want him around mi kids," asked Zoe. "Look, I'll make the same promise to you like I made with Janet and Jay, if." "Janet and Jay, Jay knows about ya having mi babies and didn't tell mi," asked Zoe as he put the now sleeping Z.J. in one of the crib that was set up on the side of the sofa. "Um, yes, he found out a week ago." Zoe started pacing the floor. "Mi don't get dis, how can mi best friend keep someting like dis from mi, especially when he knows," Zoe caught himself as he stops and looks into Sasha eyes. "Especially he knows what, that you've been looking for me," asked Sasha. "No, no mi stop looking for yuh a long time ago, mi figured if ya wanted mi yuh come ta mi, but mi can't believe Jay would keep dis from mi." Sasha was hurt when he said he stopped looking for her, but she didn't let it show. "Look, he wasn't going to keep it from you, he gave me a week to leave Roy, but when the week was up Roy and I talked and that's when he told me that someone was calling him telling him all those lies, Jay and Janet came to our home to get me and the babies and I told them that I wasn't going, I let them know that I was going to work on my marriage, I promised Janet and Jay that I'd call them everyday and if I didn't then they could tell you about the babies, and Jay said he wasn't going to betray you and that he was going to tell you that was two days ago, so I guess he doesn't know how to tell you because your friendship means a lot to him, and I don't want you blaming him, if you blame anyone blame me, because I asked him not to tell you." "Yuh would go through all of dis so mi want be in yuh life or mi kids life," asked Zoe heart sicken. Sasha turned her head so Zoe couldn't see the lonely tear that formed in her eyes. "Yes, I didn't want you apart of either of our lives," said Sasha. "Well mi gonna make it easy for yuh, for now on mi only want ta spend time wit mi kids, mi get mi boy ta picked dem up on di Friday and return dem on Sunday, mi will pay yuh child support, mi will give it ta B ta give ta yuh, otherwise yuh want hear or see mi, be happy wid yuh marriage," said Zoe as he leaned over and kissed Z.J. and then Zara on the forehead and was heading towards the door. Sasha put Zara in the other crib and step to Zoe. "Please Zoe, don't leave like this, I'm sorry for not telling you, but it's for the best after all your starting a family with Brittney, I didn't want to make things complicated, she's been wanting a chance with you for years now, I just wanted to see her happy and to see you happy." Zoe pulled Sasha to him and kissed her deeply on the mouth, pulling her closer to him he deepen the kiss using his tongue to taste her. Sasha felt his dick harden as he grinded to her making her moan in his mouth. Lifting up Sasha dress Zoe put two fingers in her wet pussy and thrust a couple of times and made her cum insistently on his finger. Putting his thumb over her clit he massage it sending her into another orgasm making her moan again as he kissed her and brand her soul with his name. Stepping back Zoe looks into Sasha eyes. "When yuh husband touches yuh or fucks yuh, mi want yuh ta tink of mi and how mi just made ya feel wid just mi finger, and mi will never be happy because mi will never have yuh," said Zoe as he walked out the house. Sasha was sitting in the chair when Roy came to check on her. "Mi didn't hear Zoe leave, are yuh okay," asked Roy. "Yeah I'm fine, Zoe and I talked and he wants to have the kids on the weekend, he want be picking them up he's going to have one of his friends to pick them up and bring them back," said Sasha. "Okay, wats wrong did he say sometings ta yuh, yuh seems upset." "He hates me, he hates me because I didn't tell him about our kids," said Sasha biting on her lower lips. "He'll be alright, he just needs time ta digest all of dis, its not everyday dat yuh find out dat yuh got two beautaful babies by a beautaful and sexy lady dat y'all never have," said Roy as he kissed Sasha on the lips. Kissing him back Sasha closed her eyes and Zoe face pops into her head.

Chapter 19

Jay and Zoe

Jay was pacing Zoe living room floor when he heard his car pull up. Walking over to the bar he poured a glass of Jamaica Rum and took it to the head. Shaking his head he tried to think of a way to tell Zoe about Sasha and the babies, he waited two days and was getting restless by the minutes. Zoe was his only true friend and he didn't want to lose him like he lost Janet. "Wats wrong wid yuh, ya look like yuh lost ya best friend," said Zoe as he walked over to the bar and poured himself a shot of Jamaica Rum also. "Um, Z, mi need ta talk ta ya, it's very important," said Jay as he went to sit on the sofa. "Speak," said Zoe hoping Jay was ready to be honest with him about the Sasha situation. "Um, mi found out sometings dat I didn't tell you at dat moment because I made a promise, but mi can't lose mi friendship wid ya so mi going ta tell ya, but mi don't know how yuh going ta take it," said Jay. "Mi listening, wat yuh got ta tell mi mon." "Sasha, when mi goes ta check on her, she wasn't only beaten, mi found out dat she had yuh seeds, and dats not all," said Jay. "Ya telling mi dat Sasha had babies by mi," asked Zoe playing along. "Yeah, but dats not it, she's married ta mi cousin." "Wat," shouted Zoe, not believing what he was hearing. "Yeah mon, mi sorry for not telling ya, but mi got someting else ta tell yuh." "Wait a blood clot minute, first ya tell mi someting dat mi already found out just a few minutes ago, mi know yuh knew about mi babies, but mi didn't know Roy is ya cousin, so talk and talk fast," said Zoe as he and Jay both began to pace the floor.

"Remember like six years ago, mi cousin was arrested for beating his girlfriend." "Don't tell mi." "Yeah mon, mi tried ta get Sasha ta leave, but she said she's going ta work on her marriage." "She tells mi di same ting," said Zoe as he down his drink. "Mi have ta tell yuh someting, but mi don't want ya ta do anyting crazy," said Jay sitting back down on the sofa. "Wat more is there ta tell." "Sasha told us dat Brittney was calling Roy telling him dat yuh and her were trying ta get back tagether, and dats the reason he was beating her." "Ya got ta be kidding mi right," said Zoe as he looks at Jay. "No mi not lying, dats why she's giving him another chance ta work on their marriage." Zoe was quiet for a long time and Jay didn't say a word. "So wat do ya wonna do," asked Jay. "Noting, since yuh know where Sha lives mi want ya ta pick up mi kids every Friday, dat way if he do anyting we will know, mi was gaan ta give money ta B, but mi will give it ta ya ta give ta Sha, as of right now mi not gaan ta interfere, if Sha wants ya cousin den she can have him, but if he harm mi kids he's dead," said Zoe. "Don't worry mi already warned him, and he knows mi not playing." "Good, now let's talk business." "Zoe, mi hope ya can forgive mi and know for now on mi will hold noting from ya again." "So Janet agreed dat mi should know about mi seeds," asked Zoe as he walked over and poured himself another drank. "Um, no, when mi told her dat mi was gaan ta tell yuh she broke up wid mi, but mi understand, she's worried dat ya going ta hurt SaSa, and now dat SaSa giving Roy another chance she even more worried." "She broke up wid ya for telling mi about mi seed." "Yeah, but its okay, she'll come around." "Well ta ease yuh mind tell her dat ya didn't tell mi, mi sure Sha already called and told her dat mi found out on mi own when mi went ta B house taday." "Na mi good, mi want run after her no matter how much mi Luvs her, if she Luvs mi den she gonna have ta learn dat mi friendship wat ya is more important den anyting, yuh was always there for mi, and mi want let noting come between dat," said Jay. "Mi glad ya mi friend, but ya more den dat, ya mi brother and mi will always be here for yuh." Zoe and Jay talked for a couple more hours then they decided to go to their club and enjoy the rest of the night. As they made there way to the VIP section Zoe cell phone kept vibrating and a number he didn't know kept showing up, so as he did the first ten times he sent it to voicemail. As they sat down their waitress for the night name Angie whom Zoe hired personally walked over and brought them a bottle of Cirsta and a bottle of Jamaican Rum, as she placed the items on the table she gave Zoe and Jay a wink as she walked back down the stairs. "If mi wasn't in luv, mi would've been tap dat," laughed Jay. "Mi know wat ya mean, mi don't tink dis was a good idea after all ta come here, to tempting," laughed Zoe as he poured drinks for him and Jay. "But business is good, we got a good crowd everyday and night," said Jay. Zoe was ready to speak when his cell phone vibrated again. "Mi don't know who dis number is, dem been calling mi all day," said Zoe. "Don't tell mi dat ya got dat many ooman dat ya don't remember ones number," laughed Jay again. "Na man, mi not seeing anyone, and mi haven't talked ta anyone in months." "Den answer and find out who it is," said Jay as he leaned over and poured himself another shot of Jamaica Rum. Zoe looks at him and smiles as he flip open his phone. "Speak." "What the hell is going on Zoe, I come home to find all my things in the streets, and the rental office manager telling me that you demanded to have a refund back on all the rent accusing me of stealing your money," asked Brittney. "Mi busy, go ta di nigga ya was wid di other day and tell him ta help ya," said Zoe leaving out that he knew it was Roy. "What are you talking about, Zoe, I love you, and I want to be with you," cried Brittney "Wat ya trying ta take mi for, mi saw yuh wid a nigga at the hotel." "It's not what it seems." "Save di bullshit it's over just be lucky dat ya still breathing," said Zoe. "What about our baby," said Brittney hoping that he didn't know she had a miscarriage? "Now ya pissing mi off, wat yuh take mi for, mi followed ya scandalous, trifling ass ta di hospital, mi know yuh lost mi seed, ya pussy wasn't worth having mi seed anyway," said Zoe. "You followed me," asked Brittney. "Yeah mi followed yuh, so now yuh have no reason ta call mi, like mi said call dat nigga yuh was wid and leave mi di hell alone, dis be ya last warning if yuh call mi again yuh will regret it," said Zoe as he hung up the phone. "Ya want believe she just tried ta run game on mi about di baby," said Zoe as he poured a shot and down it and poured another one and down that one also. "Cool down man, on di real ya know how yuh get when ya drink like dat," said Jay worried and concern for Zoe. "Mi should go and blow her brains out, she don't deserve ta live, bitches like her will always be Red Eye." "Mi know what ya mean, so do ya really want her dead, mi can call mi boys and she's be sleep," said Jay. "Na mi got other plans for her and Roy, mi saw dem tagether yesterday at di same hotel, and den he shows up at B house like everyting cool, promising not ta hurt Sha." "Mi know, mi got mi boy following him and taking pictures of dem tagether, if mi want SaSa ta leave him den mi gaan ta need lots of evidence," said Jay. "So ya weren't betraying mi after all," said Zoe. "Yuh mi blood and mi would never betray ya, mi just wanted ta find away on mi own ta get SaSa away from Roy without damaging our friendship." "Dats wats up, now lets sit back and enjoy di rest of di night, mi don't want ta tink about no one," said Zoe as he lean back in his seat. Jay cell phone started to ring letting him know it was Janet calling. "Let mi guess, Janet," said Zoe smiling. "Yeah, mi don't know wat ta say ta her." "Let mi," said Zoe as he grab Jay phone and answer it. "Speak." "Zoe, this is Janet am sorry I must have dialed the wrong number," said Janet confused. "Na yuh dialed di right number, mi just wanted ta tell ya dat mi boy is hurting and it's not good for business, and mi also wanted ta let ya know dat yuh don't have ta worry about mi bothering Sha, as of right now mi only gaan ta be part of mi kids life mi want interfere in her marriage," said Zoe. "Look Zoe I don't know you to judge you, but what I do know about you I don't like, Sasha is my sister and she didn't deserve to be treated the way she was by her grandmother and then by you and then Roy. Just to let you know when she left it took her all her will power not to go back to you, SaSa saw someting in you that I could never see, but then again raised the way she was raised you would no nothing but wicked love of the wicked minds," said Janet. "Janet mi know about mi babies Janet, mi found out when mi went ta check on B, it's cool and mi hope yuh can forgive mi for everything mi done ta Sha, mi really do luv her but mi not gaan ta interfere in her marriage, dats mi word ta ya now let mi get off di phone mi boy is mean mugging mi," joked Zoe as he handed Jay the phone. When Jay started talking on the phone Zoe walked out giving them some privacy.

Chapter 20

Zoe, Jalen and Sasha

As weeks passed Zoe was spending most of his time at the restaurant or club, it was a normal weekend and Jay, and Janet was out on the dance floor dancing when Zoe turned the corner and bumped into a true beauty. "I'm so sorry I was looking for my friends and wasn't paying attention on where I was going," said the beauty. "Na yuh fine, so are ya enjoying yuh self," asked Zoe as he looks into the female eyes. "Oh yes, this place is really nice, and the atmosphere is wonderful." "So can mi get yuh name." "Oh I'm sorry my name is Jalen." "Jalen, mi Zoe, and mi would love ta buy ya a drink and get ta know yuh better, dat if ya single," smiled Zoe. "Oh yes I'm single, like I said I'm here with my friends and we kind of lost each other." "Mi will walk wid ya ta find dem if yuh like and den mi will buy ya dat drank," said Zoe as he took Jalen hands and walked with her to find her friends. Across the room Brittney stayed in the dark and just looked at them. Zoe and Jalen met up with her friends at the bar and he told the bartender to give them whatever they wanted. Zoe and Jalen went to the booth in the back and that's where the both of them stayed talking until the club closed. Four months later Zoe was in a relationship with Jalen, but Sasha still had his heart and soul, but he was determined to put her out his head for today because today was his kids first birthday. Zoe was going all out buy stuff they wouldn't need until they was two or three years old. He was now picking up the kids and dropping them off and he noticed that one day Sasha had a bruised on her cheek, but as promised he didn't say anything about it, he just kissed his kids and left without saying a good-bye to Sasha. After everything Brittney did, Roy was still sleeping with her. Zoe boy Gunny was following Roy everyday and everyday he ends up at the same hotel that Zoe and Jay saw them at. Parking his car Zoe and Jalen got out and walked up the flight of stairs of Sasha and Roy home, when they rung the doorbell Sasha open the door and her heart crashed in her stomach. "Um, hey your early the party doesn't starts for a couple hours," said Sasha looking at Zoe. Damn he was handsome, his locks just the right length not to long and not to short, his chest looked bigger and more buff, Sasha caught herself as she heard her mother calling her name. "I'm sorry come in you must be Rhonda Zoe sister, it's nice to finally meet you," said Sasha ready to shake her hand. "Um, no Sasha," said Zoe calling her by her first name. Sasha looked at him because he always called her Sha. "Mi wants yuh ta meet mi girlfriend Jalen, Jalen dis is Sasha mi kid's madda," introduced Zoe. Sasha heart broke in a million pieces. "Girlfriend," Sasha asked in surprise. "Yes, Zoe and I've been dating for four months now and it's nice to finally meet you, and I must say you have two beautiful kids," said Jalen smiling. "Four months, kids, you been around my kids," asked Sasha now looking at the female more closely. 'Oh, my, she's beautiful,' thought Sasha. "Oh yes, I hope you don't mind, when Zoe told me that he had kids he arranged for me to meet them the following weekend and I must say he's a wonderful father, and he adores y'all babies," said Jalen as they walked into the living room. "Oh, um, please have a seat, um, can I offer you anything to drink," babbled Sasha as her head began to spin. "No were fine, were mi kids," asked Zoe as he studied Sasha. "Um they're in their bedroom, um hold on and I'll get them," said Sasha as she hurried out of the living room. When she reached her bedroom she closed and locked it and then she broke down and cried. After five minutes in self pity Sasha took deep breath after deep breath until she got her composer back wiped her tears and left out the room, she called her mom to help her get the kids ready and then they headed to the living room where Zoe and Jalen was ending a passionate kiss. "Dada," yelled Zara as she wiggled out of Sasha arms and ran over to where Zoe was sitting. Getting up Zoe got on his knees and picked her up and then when Z.J. called his name he bent down and picked him up also.

"Happy birthday daddy babies," said Zoe as he kisses them on the forehead. Susan saw the pain in her daughter eyes and excused them as she pulled Sasha in the kitchen. "Wats going on, mi thought yuh said yuh was over Zoe," asked Susan. "I thought I was mom, but every time I see him all the feeling I say I don't have surfaces." Susan hugs her tight and strong. "I'll get over it, I just have to get use to him dating, and being with someone else that's all," said Sasha as she steps from her mom and began to fills a container up with potato chips. "Well I'm proud of yuh Sasha, now let's get back out ta di party, and enjoy ourselves," said Susan picking up the food that they wrap earlier from off the counter. When they walked in the living room Zoe and Jalen was sitting on the floor playing with the kids while Betty set up the camcorder to tape the birthday party. Sasha went to the back porch and started the grill. When she began to put the meat on the grill Zoe and Jalen walked towards her. "Hey do you need any help," said Jalen smiling. "No, but thanks any way," said Sasha as she ignored Zoe stares. "I really like your home, did you do the gardening?" "Yes, I like working with my hands and it's relaxing," said Sasha really not wanting to have a conversation with the woman Zoe was sleeping with. "I know, I've been helping Zoe with his gardening, can you believe that he didn't know what a dandelion was," laughed Jalen. "Sasha, Janet's on the phone for you," said Betty. "Okay, am coming, excuse me," said Sasha as she walked around Jalen and then Zoe. When she got to the door her grandmother handed her the phone. "Hey girl where are you," asked Sasha. "Waiting for Jay slow tail, he's getting dress as we speak, I just called to see if you needed anything before we get there?" "Yeah, bring me a fat blunt and whatever kind of liquor you got," said Sasha seriously. "Hold on what's wrong?" "Everything, first Roy calls and tell me that he's going to be late and then Zoe shows up with his girlfriend, a girlfriend who's he been dating for four months and to top it off she's beautiful. Jay, not pretty or cute she's beautiful, so Jay I need a blunt and a shot quick fast and a hurry," said Sasha. "I'll be there in ten and just relax, tell your mom that you have an headache and that your going to lay down for a few, and I'll be there as soon as I can," said Janet. Sasha did just that, as she lay across the bed she thought of the first time she smoked a blunt, it was on the first day Jay came to pick up her babies to take them to Zoe. Sasha was all to pieces, she called Janet and she came with a blunt and a bottle of

Rum. Two puffs and a shot later she was relaxed and at ease, and after that she smoked every weekend when Jay came to get her babies, she never smoked when her babies was at home and this was the first, but she had to calm down and that was the only way she knew how. True to her words ten minute later Janet was knocking on Sasha door and when Sasha opened it Janet was pulling out a blunt and a bottle of Rum. "Girl what would I do without you, did you see her, isn't she beautiful," asked Sasha as she paced her bedroom. "Will you please chill, your beautiful, now let's go in your bathroom and smoke this your mom said she was coming up here to check on you if you wasn't down in ten minutes," said Janet as she walked towards the bathroom. "Jay what am I going to do, Roy isn't here and Zoe is here with his girlfriend, look at my hands they want stop shaking, and what happened to Brittney, the last time I talked to her she was with him and pregnant." Janet lit the blunt and pulled on it a couple times and then handed it to Sasha. "Here smoke and relax." Janet broke the seal on the Rum and then reached into her purse and pulled out two shot glasses. "Drink, don't worry about none of that shit, I'm sure Roy will be here shortly, and I don't know what happened with Brittney, I thought you knew about Jalen," said Janet taking the blunt and inhaling deep. "Hell no I didn't know about Jalen, and as far as Roy we haven't had sex in four months, and he has a woman perfume on his cloths when he comes home so I'm guessing that he's cheating, I can't believe this shit after everything he put me through now this." "Want me to stay the night, we haven't had a girl only night since you got married," asked Janet putting the blunt out. "You know what, what the hell I can ask my mom to watch the babies and then we can go out like old times," said Sasha feeling much better. "Now that's what I'm talking about, let's go downstairs for your mom come up here and kick our ass, here you can keep these in case you have another emergency and I can't make it here in time," joke Janet. "Funny, but thanks, I don't know what I'd do without a blunt and a shot of Rum, makes me want to stack up on them," laugh Sasha. When they got back downstairs Zoe was looking at Sasha as she talked to her mom and grandmother when she lifted her head he noticed her eyes was red like she has been crying. "Jalen mi be back mi need ta talk ta Sasha for a minute," said Zoe. "Okay, I'll be fine I'll talk to her mom or Jay," said Jalen as she kissed Zoe on the lips before he got up to leave.

Once he was outside he stood and watches Sasha for a minute and then approached her. "Sasha we need ta talk," said Zoe. Sasha turns her head sideways to look at him. "You can talk, while I finish cooking, can you pass me those burgers over there," asked Sasha relieved that her hands wasn't shaking anymore and that she wasn't' nerves anymore either. Zoe walked up to her and stood in front of her handed her the plate, leaning in he sniff her shirt and then stood up again. "When yuh start smoking ganja?" Sasha couldn't believe he had the nerves to ask her a question like that. "Excuse me?" "Don't play games, now answer mi." "Why is that any of your business Zoe," asked Sasha. "Its mi business when yuh get high on mi kids birthday party," shouted Zoe. "Our kids and lower your voice, beside don't stand here and act like you don't smoke, so what's the different if I smoke." "Di different is dat yuh here wid mi kids, and yuh better not be smoking around dem." "You know what I don't have time for this, and to answer your question yes I smoke, do I smoke everyday, no, do I smoke around my kids, hell no, and to let you know something else I started smoking and yes drinking when you came into the picture, how's that, is that enough information for you," said Sasha as she put the burgers on the grill and closed the lead. "Since you want to question me, where Brittney, I thought you were with her," asked Sasha. "Brittney is no longer in di picture mi wid Jalen." "You'll never change will you, you change females like you change your boxers, I should know," said Sasha as she picked up the tray of food that was already done, and walked into the house leaving Zoe standing there fuming. Zoe cursed himself as he walked into the house, he wasn't trying to pick an argument, he could tell she was upset when he first got there with Jalen, but then she disappears and when she came downstairs he saw her eyes and they was red so he thought she was crying until he smelled the weed when he came closer to her. Now he finds out that she's drinking and smoking. "Shit." When he got in the house he sat down beside Jalen an as always she kissed him on the lips and began to ran her hands down his thighs, when he turned back around to play with the babies he caught Sasha looking at them. "Shit." "What's wrong," asked Jalen as she leaned forwards to look at Zoe more clearly? "Oh um, mi got a crap in mi leg, I'll be right back mi gaan ta walk it out," lied Zoe. He was feeling Jalen, but he had to get Sasha out of his system. The stunt he pulled on Sasha when he ravished and fuddled her at her grandmother house was fucking with him hard, everything he did to Jalen, Sasha would always pop up in his head, just the littlest thing, a hug a kiss on the cheek, hell even a phone call to Jalen reminded him of Sasha. He no longer could take a hot shower because it reminded him of the sex he experience with Sasha, and to make things worst he couldn't take Jalen out to his favorite restaurant, because he took Sasha to all of them and whenever he went somewhere she was right there in his mind. Shaking his head Zoe felt hands on his shoulder and turn to find Jay smiling at him. "Wat's up mon?" "Wat's up, wat took yuh so long mi been here almost an hour," said Zoe as he took out a blunt and lit it. "Mi had ta go somewhere earlier, and it took mi longer than mi thought, wat's up Z ya acting strange," said Jay. "Its Sasha, we got inta an argument because mi find out she smoking, did ya know anyting about dis," asked Jay. "Yeah, Janet told mi, but she doesn't smoke everyday if dats wat yuh worried about, only on di weekends when yuh got di babies," said Jay. Zoe was quiet as he stood looking at the sky. "How do yuh tink she took yuh wid Jalen, she seems cool wid it." "Dats how mi found out she was smoking, when we got here mi could tell she was upset and den she went upstairs ta her bedroom, and den when yuh and Janet got here she been acting cool." "So wat's di problem," asked Jay. "Dats it, there is no problem, mi just need ta chill di hell out mi self, come on mi need ta get back in di house mi lied and told Jalen dat mi had a crap in mi leg," said Zoe as he flick the bud of the blunt. When they walked into the house everyone was standing around talking and having a good time listening to some reggae Sasha had playing. Zoe went and sat on the sofa when Zara crawled towards him and then lifting herself up she reached for him. "Hey princess, are ya having fun, mi got someting for yuh and yuh brother," said Zoe picking Zara up and then standing back up. "Why don't I go get their present, I'll be right back," said Jalen kissing Zoe on the lips again and then left out the house. Betty walked over to him and kissed him on the cheeks. "Wat's dat for," asked Zoe. "For everyting yuh did for mi, and for being a good dad ta mi great grandbabies." "Mi luv mi kids, so how do yuh feel." "Great, mi can't complain, but mi didn't know yuh had another girlfriend," said Betty. "Um, yeah, we've been dating bout four months now." "Well mi hope she makes yuh happy, even if mi hope dat yuh and Sasha get tagether," smiled Betty as she pat Zoe hands. "Here you go," said Jalen as she sat four big gift bags on the floor next to Zoe. "Thanks baby, yo B, can ya keep Jalen company until mi talk ta Sasha, mi want ta show her di toys in case we brought someting di same," said Zoe. "Sure mi tink she's in di kitchen getting di cakes." "Mi be back," said Zoe as he handed Zara over to Betty. When he got in the kitchen he saw Sasha swaying to the music as she took out the ice cream from the refrigerator. He still thought she was the most beautiful woman he's ever saw. "Sasha, mi sorry for di way mi act," said Zoe. Turning around Sasha looks up at him. "I didn't think I needed to tell you, I usually smoke when the kids are gone, but seeing." Sasha stops and turned back around getting the paper plates and cups out of the cabinet. "Seeing mi wid Jalen, mi knows it upset yuh, but it shouldn't, after all yuh married, where he is any ways." "Um, Roy had to work late, he should be here in a little while, and I wasn't upset because you have a girlfriend, shocked yes." "Look mi got some toys mi want ya ta look through, mi didn't know wat yuh brought and mi didn't want dem ta get di same ting." "Okay, just put them in the living room where the others are if we or anyone else got the same thing it's okay, I'll be in there in a few," said Sasha not trying to be near Zoe for to long. "Okay, do yuh need any help wid anyting?" "Sure, grab the cakes and I'll grab the plates, cups and ice cream," said Sasha. Zoe was about to say something when Roy came in the kitchen door. "Hey sexy, sorry mi late wat's up Zoe," said Roy as he kissed Sasha on the cheeks. "Wat's up mon, mi gaan ta take di cakes in di dinning room," said Zoe picking up the cakes and left out the kitchen. "Wat's wid him, wat ya was talking bout," asked Roy. "If you were here then you'd know," mumble Sasha. "Wat yuh say?" "Nothing, he brought some toys and wanted me to look over them, it's that what you're wearing," asked Sasha, as she looked at Roy in a wrinkled shirt and work pants. "Nuh mi gaan ta go take a shower, mi be back down in a few." Sasha grab the plates, cups, and ice cream and headed to dinning room where saw Jalen kissing Zoe again. Janet came up behind her and gave her a hug. "They'll be gone soon, and then we're going out a have some fun, I've told Jay and he wants us to go to there club, do you think Roy would want to go," said Janet. "You know what, I really don't care if he wants to or not, I'll just be happy when this party is over." Sasha mom walked up to her and Janet and they talked until Roy came downstairs, then everyone sung happy birthday to the Zara and Z.J. Then everyone sat around and ate cake and ice cream and talked. When the party was dying down Sasha asked her mom if she could watch the babies why she went out, and she happily agreed. Roy wasn't too happy that Sasha was going out, but he didn't say anything, he was going to have to have a talk with her when they were alone. "Okay everyone it's time to open the presents," said Betty as she walked over and picked up Zara. Sasha went and picked up Zoe Jr. and walked in the front room and sat on the sofa beside her grandmother. Zoe and Jalen took a seat on the love seat while Jay and Janet sat at the bar. Roy went and sat on the arm of the sofa where Sasha was at and Susan took pictures of each present the kids received. Sasha notice Roy leaving out of the room talking on his phone, but didn't pay any attention to him, but to her kids. "Come here we need ta talk," said Roy as he pulled Sasha upstairs not even ten minutes after she was done opening the presents. "What's wrong," asked Sasha as Roy closed the bedroom door behind them. "Mi have ta go ta D.C. mi just got a call di water pump burst, and dem want us ta fix it right away, mi should be back in two or three days, mi will call yuh ta let yuh know," said Roy as he put some cloths in his traveling bag. "You got to be kidding me, you just got here can't someone else go," asked Sasha. "Mi di boss, wat it would look like if mi send someone else ta do mi job." "Fine, just fine, can you answer a question for me?" "Wat is it." "When are you going to spend some time with me, either you're at work or out of town, hell we haven't had sex in months, is there someone else, are you cheating on me," asked Sasha as she looks into Roy eyes. "Look mi don't have time for dis, mi not cheating just working, have fun wid Janet an mi will call yuh later ta let yuh know when mi will be home," said Roy as he zipped his bag and then he kissed Sasha on the forehead an headed out the bedroom door. Sasha was sitting on the bed when she heard Roy cell phone ring. She walked over and picked it up just as Roy came back into the room. "Hello," said Sasha as she answered the phone. Click the phone hung up in her ear. "Why di hell is yuh answering mi phone," yelled Roy as the snatches the phone out of Sasha hand. Sasha looks at him dumbfounded. "Oh is alright for you to answer my phone, and to check my phone, but it's a problem when I answer yours, you know what I'm through with you and your shit, whoever the bitch is she can have you," said Sasha as she headed towards the door. Roy was behind her and slammed it shut so hard that it shocked the walls. Grabbing her by the neck he pinned her against the door. "Don't try mi Sasha, mi haven't beat ya ass in a while, but yuh pushing yuh luck now don't vex mi, now mi going ta work and mi will be back when mi get back," said Roy as he released her and walked out the bedroom. A few minutes later Susan, Betty, and Janet came upstairs to check on her. "Wat's going on," asked Susan. "Its okay mom, we just had an argument that went to far," said Sasha. Betty walked up to her and checked her from head to toe. "He grab ya by di neck, no need in lying mi see di mark, has he been hitting yuh and yuh not telling us," asked Betty. "Momma Fill, um NaNa no he hasn't been hitting me, am just tired of being home by myself all the time, either he's at work or he has to go out of town." "And since him gwan outta town yuh and mi great babies can come ta di house and stay, its no use in ya being here alone," said Betty. "Okay, we'll come to your house and stay," said Sasha relieved that she wasn't going to be sitting in the house. "Look everything is going to be okay SaSa, we're here for you," said Janet. "Yes we are, now don't let him spoil ya day, come on downstairs and lets have some fun," said Susan. "Mom I want to talk to Janet for a minute, we'll be down there in a few," said Sasha. When her mom and grandma left Sasha closed and locked the door, then she walked over to her dresser and took out the blunt and Rum. "Okay talk," said Janet. "You know what I'm not even going to dwell on Roy, fuck him, we're going out, and we're going to have so much fun," said Sasha as she lit and then puff on the blunt, she then open the Rum and took a big sip. When she was relaxed she handed Janet the blunt. "Since we're up here get ya'll things, we can stay at the townhouse in Newport News tonight, its right down the street from the club," said Janet. "Okay I'll do that, I'm going to pack the babies things first, I already know what I'm wearing," Sasha said with a devilish smile. "Okay I'll let everyone know you'll be down in a few," said Janet as she headed out the door. Sasha knew exactly the dress she was going to wear. She purchased it at Patrick Henry Mall at the Wet Seal store, it was a red fitted skirt set that came above her legs, and shirt was bare back, and the material was so thin that you could actually see through it if you look long enough. Sasha went and took out a weeks worth of clothes for the babies and packed everything she would need for the couple of days she would be staying at her grandmothers. She decided to take a shower at Janet since she was changing there. When she got downstairs everyone was still talking. “Okay, I have the baby’s things ready, and I’m staying at NaNa house, because what’s the use of coming back here and be alone, so are you ready,” asked Sasha. “Hell yeah, you know am ready, now baby go and let Zoe know we’re ready to leave,” said Janet. “Oh Zoe still here, I thought he was gone by now,” said Sasha. “Naw he’s outside talking to Jalen,” said Janet. “Well if everyone’s ready we can leave,” said Sasha as Zoe and Jalen walks in the front door. “Hey we’re about to go,” said Sasha grabbing the baby bags and handing them to Betty. “Oh, um we’re about ta leave also, mi just came ta give mi babies a kiss good night,” said Zoe looking at Sasha and no one else. “Thanks for coming and drive safely,” said Sasha as Zoe leans in and kisses Zara and then Z.J. on the forehead while inhaling her scent. “Mi will, good night everyone and B, make sure yuh call mi tamorrow mi need ta talk ta yuh,” said Zoe as he and Jalen left out of the house. “What do you and Zoe has to talk about,” asked Sasha. “Mi don’t know I guess I’ll find out tomorrow,” smiled Betty. “I bet you will find out tomorrow,” smiled Sasha as they all headed out the door.

Chapter 21

Sasha and Zoe

Sasha took her a shower and got dress in a matter of no time, she flipped her hair that was now again shoulder length and added a little lip-gloss and make-up and was ready, when she got downstairs her and Jay talked while they waited for Janet to finish getting dress. “Do yuh want someting ta drink,” asked Jay as he walked over to the bar. “No am fine,” said Sasha as she got up and paced the floor. “Jay, I’m leaving Roy,” said Sasha out of the blue as she stopped in front of him. “Wat do yuh mean by yuh leaving him.” “I’m going to file for divorce.” “Wat made yuh change yuh mind about giving yuh marriage a chance?” “He’s cheating.” Jay was quiet as he down his shot of Jamaica Rum. “So why yuh telling mi,” asked Jay. “You were right and I was wrong, you knew all alone that this marriage wasn’t going to work, and I should’ve listened to you.” “SaSa mi only wanted yuh and yuh babies ta be safe, di only reason Roy hasn’t hit yuh is because he knew mi will kill him, but if yuh really gaan ta leave him den mi behind yuh and just call mi if yuh need any help,” said Jay. “Thanks Jay, now what’s taking your girlfriend so long,” joked Sasha. “She’s yuh best friend, mi will go see wat’s she’s doing, mi be back in a minute,” said Jay as he went up the stairs. Sasha blew out a sigh as decided she wanted that drink after all, so she went over to the bar and poured her a glass of Jamaica Rum, and down it. Ten minutes later Janet and Jay came down the stairs. “Oh my god, you’re stunning,” said Sasha and meant it. Janet was wearing a baby blue Wet Seal dress that clung to her like a second skin; the back was open showing off her dragon tattoo. "Me no you, that dress is banging, "said Janet. "Thanks, and how did you know I was wearing mines," said Sasha. "Cause I saw that devilish ass smile you gave me," laughed Janet. "You know me so well," said Sasha as they looped arms. "Mi differently gaan ta make sure mi take mi gun, ya two are gaan ta get someone kilt gaan out like dat," smiled Jay. "Well let's get going, I've already packed a bag for me so I'm ready," said Janet. "Well let's roll," said Jay as he took Janet and then Sasha hands and headed out the door. When they arrived at the club it was packed. "Oh I'm differently going to have some fun tonight," said Sasha. "Don't get to carried away, yuh still married," said Jay. "What you mean still married," asked Janet. "I'll talk to you later about that, right now we're going to have some fun," said Sasha as she got out of the car. When they walked in all eyes was on them. Zoe was just sitting down in the VIP section when he saw them walk in and his dick insistently got hard from the sight of Sasha. "Wat di hell is she doing here," said Zoe out loud. He watches as they headed towards the bar. "So wat do ya ladies want ta drink," asked Jay. "We'll have what ever you get for us, we're going on the dance floor," said Janet as she grabs Sasha by the hand and heads for the dance floor. "Come ta di VIP section when ya done, mi going up there," said Jay as he shook his head and order drinks for them. As Sasha and Janet dance to the music guys began to dance with them and Sasha was surprised that Jay didn't come and snatch Janet off the floor. "Girl is you crazy, you're not scared that Jay will trip," asked Sasha. "SaSa, Jay knows I love and want only him, hell he dances with other females to, we just understand each other," said Janet. "Damn I wish I had a relationship like that, Jay's a lucky man to have you Jay, and I mean it from the bottom of my heart." 'Girl Roy will come around, he just needs to be reminded that you're everything he needs." "Well its to late I'm going to divorce him, he's cheating so he can have her, as of tonight I'm going to get drunk have fun, and I'm not even going to think about Roy, matter of fact who is Roy," said Sasha as she turns around and starts dancing with a dark skin guy. "Your wild," yelled Janet, as she looks at her friend freak a dude on the dance floor. Jay made his way to the VIP section and was surprised to see Zoe. "Wat's up mon, mi didn't know yuh was gaan ta be here," said Jay as he put the drinks on the table. "Mi had ta get out of di house,

Jalen been pressuring mi about sex again, and mi don't know how much longer mi gaan ta be a gentleman," said Zoe. "Don't tell mi dat yuh haven't had sex wid her since yuh been tagether." "Den mi won't." Jay fell out laughing. "Mon, yuh want mi ta believe dat ya not sexing Jalen, wat's up wid dat," Jay said still laughing. Zoe nodded his head towards the dance floor. "Her." Jay stops laughing when he saw the seriousness on Zoe face. "Wat yuh mean her, wat do SaSa has ta do wid yuh not sexing Jalen." "Every time mi want ta sex Jalen, Sasha pops in mi head and den mi can't go through wid it, mi haven't had sex since Brittney, and mi about ta blow," said Zoe as he gulp down his one out of five shots Jay just noticing on the table. "Damn mon, dat's deep, so wat ya gaan ta do?" "Mi honestly don't know," said Zoe. Janet and Sasha walked into the area where Jay and Zoe were. "Hey Z, I didn't know you was going to be here," said Janet as she walks up and gave him a hug. "Hey, mi didn't know yuh was gaan ta be here either, wat's up Sha." "Oh now I'm Sha. Nigga's for ya," said Sasha as she picked up one of the shots on the table and down it. Zoe looks at Jay and Janet and then backs at Sasha. "Oh that's my song, come on Jay lets go back and dance some more," said Sasha ignoring Zoe stare. "Oh no, I'm going to sit for a minute, my feet is killing me," said Janet as she sat beside Jay on the two setter and put both her feet on his lap. "Okay, I'm going to remember that when you're song comes on," said Sasha as she left and went back on the dance floor. As Sasha danced to 'I Wayne' song 'Forgive' a light skin guy approached her. "Can I join you?" "Yes you can," said Sasha as she grinds up to him dancing real slow to the music. "You're beautiful, what's your name," asked the guy. "Sasha and what's your?" "Demetri, but everyone calls me D for short." "That's what's up D." Sasha and D danced through two songs and than D told her he'd be back and walked towards the bathroom. When 'Beres Hammond and Buju Banton' song 'My Woman Now' came on Sasha had her eyes closed when she felt strong arms circling her waist. Opening her eyes she stared at Zoe. "Dance," said Zoe. "No, I don't want to dance with you, your in a relationship and I'm married remember." Zoe ignores her, as he pressed her closer to him grinding harder. Taking his hands he ran them up her back and then down lower. "Yuh bewitch mi Sha, mi got ta touch yuh, fuck dat mi have ta have yuh," said Zoe as he pulls Sasha off the dance floor and into his office which was towards the back. Soon as they got in the office Zoe closed and locked the door and pulled Sasha to him. Taking her mouth Zoe kissed her as if his life depended on it. "Mi got ta have yuh right now," said Zoe as he raises Sasha dress up ripping off her panties. Bending down he kisses her stomach and then out of nowhere he lifts her up and began to eat her pussy, sucking, and biting. Sasha came insistently. Working her pussy in his mouth, Sasha didn't know if it was the alcohol or the lack of sex, but she couldn't stop herself. Putting her down Zoe kisses her letting her taste herself. Sasha was quiet as he walked her towards the sofa. As she stood before him she began to unbuckling Zoe pants. When his pant was around his ankles, Sasha unbuckled his shirt and kissed him from his neck down to his thighs and when she was on her knees she took his dick out and massage his length as she took the tip in her mouth and sucked tasting this juice. "Sha, oh my Jah," said Zoe as Sasha deep throated him at that moment. Bobbing her head she only could take so much of Zoe in her mouth but she liked how he called her name when she was pleasing him. Zoe couldn't take it anymore he had to have Sasha so he pulls his dick out making a pop sound, and lifts Sasha up. Laying her on the sofa Zoe kicks off his shoes and then his pant. Lifting up her dress he pulled it over her head and threw it on the floor. Leaning back he raised her legs in the air she wraps them around his waist as he entered her slowly feeding her inch by inch. When he heard her intake of breath he smiled a wicked smile. "So yuh miss mi dick," asked Zoe as he pumped in and out of Sasha wetness. "Yes I missed your dick," said Sasha as she came long and hard with in seconds. "Tell mi whose pussy is tis." "Yours, this is your pussy," said Sasha as Zoe fucks her harder and faster. "Yuh put a spell on mi Sha; mi can't get yuh out mi head." Sasha kissed Zoe on the lips and worked her pussy to him. Pulling out Zoe turned her over and entered her from behind. "Oh my god Z, dat's it fuck dis pussy," said Sasha as Zoe hit her G-spot making her bit into the sofa arm to drown out her cries. "Mi luv yuh Sha, mi luv ya so much, tell mi yuh luv mi." "Mi luv yuh Zoe, mi always luv yuh," said Sasha in her Caribbean accent. Zoe couldn't take it anymore as he thrust in and out of her faster and faster. "Mi cumin Sha," shouted Zoe as he filled Sasha up with his seeds. "Mi cumin ta," cried out Sasha as she came so hard her body began to shake from the orgasm. They both fell on the sofa. A few minutes' later Sasha looks into Zoe eyes, her breath caught in her chest as all the feeling she had for Zoe surfaced once again. "I'm divorcing Roy," said Sasha as she turns her head. Zoe didn't know if he was suppose to be happy or pissed off. "I just thought you wanted to know," said Sasha as she got up and walked over to retrieve her dress and ruin thongs. Seeing that Zoe had a bathroom Sasha went inside and closed the door. Walking in further, she noticed that Zoe had a shower so she cut it on and got in. As she listened to the music that was playing from the club she couldn't believe that she just had sex with Zoe inside his club. A few minutes later Sasha felt Zoe hands on her back as he got in the shower with her. "Mi hasn't had a hot shower in so long mi forgot how it feels," smiled Zoe. "Why haven't yuh had a hot shower?" "Because mi always tink about yuh when mi get in, mi haven't been able ta do a lot of tings since yuh been gaan." Sasha was quiet as Zoe massages her back and then began to caress her ass. "Mi wants yuh again," said Zoe as he kissed Sasha back and then her neck. She moaned and turned to look at him. "Mi want yuh ta, now take mi," said Sasha. Lifting her up Zoe pinned her against the bathroom tile and enters her slowly, when he was deep inside of her he rotated his hip making her cry out his name. Pumping faster and then slower Sasha came over and over again. "Damn mi miss mi dick," said Sasha as she threw her pussy to meet Zoe's thrusts. In and out and out and in Zoe made love to Sasha in the shower and when he was ready to cum, he took Sasha mouth and kissed her deeply. They both came together calling out each other name in each other's mouth as they rode to ecstasy. When they got out of the shower Sasha hair was a done deal, all the curls was gone and her hair was soaked. "What are we going to tell Janet and Jay," said Sasha. "Nothing, by now dem already figured out wat we been doing," said Zoe as he kissed Sasha neck. Sasha heard her cell phone ringing so she hurried up to get it. "Hello." "Where di fuck yuh been, mi been calling yuh ass for two hour," shouted Roy. "I'm with Janet and Jay, where are you," asked Sasha looking at Zoe in the mirror. "Mi just got ta D.C. mi calling ta let yuh know mi gaan ta be gaan longer den mi thought, di pipes were set wrong an dem need dem fix a.s.a.p." said Roy. Sasha was quiet as she took in what Roy just said to her. "Um, okay I'll stay at my grandmother house until you get back," said Sasha. "Yuh better answer di damn phone di next time mi call yuh, we're gaan ta have a talk when mi get home," said Roy as he hung up the phone. "So wat did he want," asked Zoe not liking that Sasha was still married to Roy when he just finished sexing her. "Oh he was telling me that he's going to be gone longer then he thought, its better this way, while he's gone I can go and handle everything with the lawyers." "So yuh really gaan ta divorce him?" "Yes, he's cheating on me, the only problem is that I don't have any evidence," said Sasha. "If yuh had di evidence den wat would happen." "The divorce would be settled faster, we sign an agreement, something like and annulment but if either one of us cheat then we'd get a divorce and leave what we came into the marriage with, but whoever he's cheating with I hope they be happy together, I'm ready to start over and start fresh," said Sasha. "Wat about us," asked Zoe. Sasha turns and looks into Zoe eyes. "Not now Zoe, I got to handle this situation first, plus you're in a relationship." "And mi can get out of di relationship." Sasha was quiet. "Look at mi Sha." When she turned around Zoe pulls her to him. "Mi wants ta know right here and right now, do yuh luv mi," asked Zoe. "Yes, I love you, but." "There's no buts mi luv yuh and mi want us tagether, mi will break up wid Jalen tanight, and when yuh get yuh divorce we gaan ta be tagether." "I'm scare Zoe, and I don't want to rush just to get hurt all over again," said Sasha as tears felled from her eyes. "Look at mi, mi swears to Jah dat mi will never hurt yuh again, mi will give yuh time, but di question is do yuh want dis, do yuh want ta be wid mi Sha." "Yes, I want to be with you and only you Zoe. I've loved you with my whole heart and am still loving you," said Sasha as she kissed Zoe on the lips. "Good now it's settled, after yuh get yuh divorce we're gaan ta be tagether, now let's go before Jay and Janet sends out a search party for us," said Zoe as he finished getting dressed. Sasha made due the best way she could after all her things was sitting on the seat in the VIP section, she knew there was no hope for her hair, and so she took out a rubber band and put it in a ponytail. When they walked into the area where Jay and Janet were suppose to be they were both shocked and surprised to see Jalen sitting at the table instead. "There you go, I thought I had to come search for you," said Jalen as she walked towards Zoe and kissed him on the lips. "Jalen wat yuh doing here," asked Zoe as he saw the hurt on Sasha face. "Silly I came to surprise you, I know you'd be busy earlier that's why I didn't come with you, I didn't want to come and crowd over you, you didn't tell me that Sasha was going to be here, if I'd known that I've would've came when you did," said Jalen now looking at Sasha. "Zoe didn't know I'd be here," said Sasha recovering faster then she thought. "Oh is that so, so where were the two of you, I've been here for an hour myself, Jay said you guys was talking, but when I knocked on your office you didn't answer," said Jalen. "Why didn't yuh just call mi phone, yuh know mi don't answer mi door for no one," said Zoe getting irritated with Jalen. "I did, but it put me through to your voicemail, but any ways are you coming to my house when you're finished here," asked Jalen. Zoe looks at Sasha as she down two shots back to back. "Um, yeah, mi be there later tanight," said Zoe as he watch Sasha passes him heading to the dance floor. "Sha wait a minute, we need ta finish our conversation," said Zoe, not wanting her to be mad with him or for her to dance with another man. "Look we can finish another time, I'm going to find Janet and Jay, nice seeing you Jalen," said Sasha as she left and headed to the dance floor where she found Janet and Jay freaking each other on the dance floor. "Where the hell you been, and where the hell is Zoe, Jalen is here," said Janet. "We know," said Sasha as she began to dance to the music. When Red Rat song 'Tight Up Skirt' came on Sasha, Janet and Jay had all eyes on them as they all dance to the music, they was having so much fun that they didn't see Zoe standing in front of them taking pictures of them. "Dis is differently gaanin' on mi web," said Zoe over the music. "Yeah mon, mi knows wat ya mean." Jay said as he grabs Janet and kisses her long and hard. Sasha burst out laughing. "Go get a room," she jokes as they all started laughing. When Gregory Isaac 'Night Nurse' song came on Zoe pulled Sasha to him and they started to dance to the music she thought he was only going to dance through one song but when Akon 'Bartender Reggae mix' came one he still held her close to him and she had to say that he was a good dancer. "Yuh see how yuh make mi feel," said Zoe as he presses harder against Sasha so she could feel his erection. "You make me feel the same way," said Sasha as she laid her head on his shoulder. "Where's Jalen at?" "She went home, mi going ta tell her tanight dat is over, mi want ta make tings wid yuh right." "I know, but I was wondering if you could hold off from breaking up with her, I can't let people know we're you know, and if word gets out that you've broken up with her Roy will get suspicious and I'm trying to handle everything while he claims to be out of town," said Sasha. "Okay, but mi have ta be honest wid yuh, she been pressuring mi ta have sex wid her, mi haven't because yuh always in mi head, but if mi go ta her house mi know wat she gaan ta want," said Zoe. "Be honest with me, do you have feeling for her," asked Sasha. "Yes, but there not as strong as mi feeling for yuh, mi like her but mi luv yuh." "So what are you going to do?" "Mi not gaan ta do anyting mi not gaan ta go, mi call her and tell her dat mi have ta go some where early in di morning." "Are you sure you want this, I don't want you to have any regrets later on wishing you'd had stayed with Jalen." "Mi knows mi heart and yuh have it, mi want have no regrets mi luv yuh and want only yuh." "I'll understand if you do, we're not together, and she is your girlfriend, I don't know maybe I'm asking too much of you, but all I know is I can't wait for me to be divorce from Roy and start a life with you and our kids." "Mi to," said Zoe. When they turned they saw Jay wave them over to the VIP section so he lead Sasha off the dance floor and headed towards them. They sat and talked for a while and before they knew it, it was time to close down the club. Sasha and Janet waited for Zoe and Jay they had to get some paper work out the office, and as they sat and talked they didn't see the figure standing at the door looking at them. Zoe wanted Sasha to ride with him, but thought better of it, but they all ended up at Janet townhouse. "Can I get y'all something to drink," asked Janet as she walked into the kitchen? "Can I get a water bottle if you have any," asked Sasha. "Yeah mi takes a water bottle ta," said Zoe. Janet brought them a water bottle and they all sat and talked for a long time, when they looked at the clock it was going on four o'clock in the morning. "Look am beat, since it's late Zoe your more than welcome to stay, am sure SaSa will show you where everything is, so good night," said Janet as she pulled Jay up from the sofa. "Yeah mon, mi sees ya in di mawning," said Jay as he followed Janet up the stairs. "So where do mi sleep," said Zoe looking at Sasha. "Where do you want to sleep," asked Sasha. "Don't play games, yuh know where mi want ta be," said Zoe as he pulls Sasha up off the sofa. Sasha leads him to the guest room on the other side of the house and when she closed the door Zoe pulled Sasha in his arms and kissed her softly on the lips. "Mi need ta talk ta yuh," said Zoe as he looks in her eyes. "Okay what's wrong?" "Mi wat ta tell yuh dat mi sorry for hurting ya di last time we were tagether," said Zoe. "Look that's behind us and I forgive you." "Mi need for yuh ta understand wat mi was gaanin' through in order for mi ta accept dat yuh forgive mi," said Zoe. "Okay I'm listening." "Mi family has a history of aggressive tendencies, when someting anger us we black out and we tink di one who's anger us is actually there in person, when mi hurt yuh mi thought yuh was Nancy, I know it isn't right ta hit female, but when mi in dat stage mi not know wat I was doing, mi never meant ta hurt ya." "So do you still, um you know when you get angry." "No I've been seeing a Therapy for almost two years now. I gotten control of mi anger and knows how ta control mi temper." "I'm very proud of you Zoe," said Sasha. "Come here," said Zoe. Sasha walks up to him and he kisses her deep. "Mi luv you so much and when yuh left yuh took a big part of mi," said Zoe. "I did, what I took," asked Sasha smiling. "Mi heart, its been wid yuh di whole time, it wouldn't let mi move on, even when mi thought mi would never see yuh again, mi heart wouldn't let mi move on," said Zoe. "Well I guess you had mines as well, because no matter how much I fought the love I had for you, you was always with me, even when I hated you I loved you and when I was afraid of you I loved you, crazy right," asked Sasha. "Not as crazy as you makes mi, mi luv yuh Sha." "Mi luv ya ta, now lets get some sleep, I have to get our kids in the morning," said Sasha smiling. "Mi know yuh not gaan ta do mi like dis, mi want be able ta touch yuh di way mi want, and believe mi, mi want ta touch yuh everyday," smiled Zoe. "Well show mi how much ya want ta touch mi," said Sasha as she lies on the bed. Lifting her in his arms Zoe took her over to the bed and laid her down; taking off her thongs for a second time, Zoe hurried and took off all his clothes and then taking off the rest of Sasha's. When they was both naked Zoe pull Sasha to him and sucked on her breast one at a time, sliding his right hand he fuddled Sasha pussy and like the last time she came insistently. Using his left hand Zoe caresses Sasha breast as he made his way down further down. Spreading her legs further apart Zoe dived in given Sasha head as she screamed out his name. As Zoe sucked nibbled and teased Sasha pussy he felt his heart swell with love. Lifting his head he kisses Sasha long and hard as then out of nowhere Sasha flips him on and put his dick inside of her and she gave him the ride of his life. Popping her pussy on his dick head she teased him by not going all the way down and then she'd drop down hard making him call out her name. In a slow motion Sasha went up and down and up and down on Zoe dick that he thought he would bust any second, but holding on Zoe grabs Sasha ass and together they found a rhythm that take took them on a further journal where ecstasy shook them to their bones. When they both came at the same time their heart connected and their soul became one. Zoe and Sasha felled asleep with no worries about their future or the pass. Down the hall Janet and Jay were getting undress and when they both were completely naked Janet pushes Jay on the bed. Crawling towards him Janet takes his dick in her hands and massages it softly. Taking him in her mouth she deep throated him making him call out her name. When Jay couldn't take anymore he lifts Janet up and lays her on the bed. When he entered her he held her close to him, as he work her nice and slow. "Mi luv yuh Janet," said Jay. "I love you to Jason," said Janet as she worked her body with Jay. Jay turned her over and kissed her on the back all the way down to her ass, licking and then biting. Jay gave Janet pleasure she didn't know existed. Turning her back over Jay enters Janet again and spreading her legs eagle style as he deep stroked her making her cum with each stroke. "Mi cumin baby," said Jay as he pulled Janet closer to him and thrust a couple more times filling her up with his seeds. Still pumping in and out of her, Janet came long and hard as she kissed Jay's lips. Jay rolled over bringing Janet with him. "Mi luv yuh, and mi want yuh ta be mi wife," said Jay as he sat up and grabs his pant. Reaching inside the pockets he took out a small black box. Janet sat up in the bed and looks into his eyes. Opening the box Janet heart skip a beat as she saw the five karats platinum engagement ring. "Will yuh marry mi," asked Jay as he got down on the floor on one knee. "Yes, oh yes, yes I'll marry you," cried Janet as she flew into Jay's arms, as he put the ring on her fingers he kissed her deeply. Jay picked her up and laid her on the bed. "Mi will do everyting ta make yuh happy." "You already have Jason, right now am the happiest person on earth," said Janet as she kissed him softly on the lips. Pulling her in his arms Janet and Jay fell asleep in each other arms.

Chapter 22

Sasha

The next morning Sasha called her mom to let her know that she was on her way, but her mom assured her that the babies was fine and for her to enjoy time with Janet. "Mi was wondering if Zoe coming here ta get da babies, mi didn't want him ta go all di way ta Richmond when dem over here," said Susan. "Um, Zoe is here at Janet's, we'll be there shortly, mom call if you need anything," said Sasha. "Baby, we're fine, now have fun and don't yuh call unless it's an emergency," said Susan as she hung up the phone. "Well my mom is watching the babies, so what do you guys want to do to day," asked Sasha. "How about if we go to the movies, we haven't been to the movies in years," said Janet getting excited. "What do you guys want to do, is a movie cool with y'all," asked Sasha. "Mi cool wid it," said Jay. "Mi cool wid it also, so wat time do it start," asked Zoe. "There's a six o'clock and nine o'clock showing which one is do you guys want to go see," asked Sasha. Everyone agreed to the six o'clock showing then they could go out and grab something to eat. "SaSa I have something to tell you," said Janet as she pulled Jay up to stand beside her. "What's wrong?" asked Sasha. "Nothings wrong, last night Jay asked me to marry him and I said yes," said Janet as she showed Sasha and Zoe her engagement ring. "Oh my god, congratulation," said Sasha as she got up and hugs Janet and kissed her on the cheek. "Are you really happy," asked Janet. "Girl hell yeah I'm happy for you, you deserve it, and I know Jay will take good care of you," said Sasha. "Congratulations mon, mi wishes yuh lots of happiness," said Zoe as he went and hug Jay. "Thanks mon." "So when is the big day," asked Sasha. "We haven't gotten that far, but you'll be the first to know," smiled Janet. At that moment Sasha phone rung. Looking at the caller I.D. she excused herself and went to answer it. "Hello." "Where yuh at, mi called yuh last night and yuh not answer," said Roy. "Hello to you to, I stay the night at Janet, where are you," asked Janet. "Still in D.C. mi want be back for another couple days, and when mi call yuh better answer di fucking phone," said Roy. "Anything else," asked Sasha. "Wat di fuck do yuh mean anyting else, we gaan ta have a long talk when mi get home, yuh beginning ta talk slick and mi not gaan ta have dat," said Roy. "Look Roy I'm sorry, I'm just a little tired, but when you call I'll make sure I'll answer it, now I have to go because the babies are crying," Sasha lied. "Make sure yuh answer di phone when mi call, yuh better not be hanging around Zoe, if so tell him mi said ta go snuff under his girlfriend and not mi wife," said Roy as he hung up the phone. Sasha hung up the phone and when she turned around she bumped into Zoe. "Not you to," said Sasha as she looks into Zoe eyes. Leaning forwards Zoe kisses her gently on the lips. "Mi not worried about him, mi already knows mi have yuh heart like yuh have mines," smiled Zoe as he pulled Sasha in his arms. "Good, because I'm calling my lawyer and I'm going to tell her to draw up the divorce, I want out of this marriage quick fast and in a hurry," smiled Sasha. "Dat makes two of us, now let's go take a long hot shower and get ready." Everyone agreed to A law-biding citizen with Jamie Foxx. Zoe cell phone rung so much during the movie that he decided to cut it off and when the movie was over he had thirty messages from Jalen. He only listened to three and when she started cursing him out he deleted the rest not wanting to hear them. Sasha turned her phone off also and when she checked her voicemail Roy had left her two voicemail also, after she listen to him threaten to beat her and show her who's the boss she deleted it not know what she was going to deal with when he got home. "Are yuh okay," asked Zoe. "Yeah, he's pissed because I missed his call, look I love you, but I have to call him back so he want come home and fight me, I have to keep shit smooth until I get these divorce paper straight, and you need to call Jalen if we want this relationship to work we got to keep both of them happy, or everything will blow up in our faces," said Sasha. "Mi know but I just want yuh, yuh better hurry up wid dem papers, mi don't want yuh wid Roy, just di thought of him touching yuh vex mi," said Zoe. "How do you think I feel knowing that you're going to be with Jalen, and first thing in the morning I'm call my lawyer to let her know to start drawing the paper work, oh shit I forgot I had to take her some paperwork," said Sasha. "Can yuh take dem ta her another time?" "Not if I want this divorce over with, it's the bank statement and other paperwork she needs." "Mi can take yuh home ta get it." "No, I'll see if Janet can go with me, I have to get our kids some more clothes anyway, but I'll call you when I get back, and if your free tomorrow maybe we can take the babies out to the park, I'll see if my mom and Momma Fill want to go." "Don't yuh mean NaNa, and I love that idea, but yuh better hurry up it's already getting late, but yuh better call mi when yuh get there and when yuh get back," said Zoe as he looks into Sasha eyes. "I will now come on so I can see if Janet can ride with me home." When they walked up to Janet and Jay they were ending a passionate kiss. "Sorry to interrupt, but I have to steal Janet away for a few, I have to go home and get some paperwork for tomorrow and I forgot them at home," said Sasha. "Sure, Jay has some paperwork he has to do at the club any ways, so are you ready," asked Janet. "Yep, I'll call you when we get there," said Sasha. "Mi be waiting," said Zoe as he kissed Sasha on the lips. "Now hurry, mi be at di club wid Jay." Janet kissed Jay on the lips and then they headed out to Janet's car. When they got in the car Sasha leaned back in the seat and took a deep breathe. "Girl I can't believe that you're getting married, am so excited, so did you call your mom yet," asked Sasha. "Yep, and she's happy, she's already getting the invitations in order and she's said she was calling her very own caters to do the wedding," said Janet. "Well I better be the matron of honor," smiled Sasha as they headed down I-64. "I wouldn't have it any other way, now let's hurry up so we can get back, and spend sometime with my god babies," said Janet. When Sasha and Janet was coming up to the house they saw Roy and another car parked in front of the house and heard slow music coming from the house. "What the hell is he doing here, he said he was in D.C. and who the hell car is that," said Sasha as she sat up in her seat. "I'll park around the corner that way he want see my car," said Janet as she parked her car around the corner and then they got out of the car and headed towards the house. Taking out her house keys Sasha opens the door and they walked in. "What the hell," asked Janet as they saw clothes throw all over the house, bottles of wines and candles that melted to the holder. Three plates that looked like steak and fruits was sitting on the kitchen table. Rose petals were all over the floor and soft slow song was coming from upstairs. "I know this motherfucker don't have some bitches in here," said Sasha as she ran up the stairs. What she saw caused her to throw up so she ran to the bathroom and did just that. "It's okay, so what are you going to do," whispered Janet. Standing up Sasha wipes her mouth with the back of her hands and walks out of the bathroom. When she got to the bedroom door this time she took out her cell phone she hit the camcorder and video Roy. "Dat's it fuck dat pussy Craig," said Roy as he watched the man fucked Brittney while Brittney sucked his dick. Thrusting faster and harder Craig fucked Brittney until he came long and hard. "Come here Brittney turn around so mi can fuck dat ass of ya," said Roy as Brittney got up and turns around. When she was in position Roy stuck his dick in her ass as Brittney began to pump fast. "Oh daddy dat's it fuck dis ass, now tell me that my ass is better then Sasha," said Brittney as she pumps harder on Roy dick. "Ya ass is way better den Sasha," said Roy. Brittney reached over and took Craig dick in her mouth and began to suck on it long and hard until it was hard again. "Yeah that's it, suck this dick," said Craig as Brittney deep throated him, when Brittney couldn't take it any more she pushed away from both men. "Now I want to watch the two of you fuck," said Brittney as she got up and began to fuddle Roy dick. Sasha couldn't believe her eyes as the man bends over and Roy enters him raw. "Ahhhh," cried out Craig as Roy pumped in and out of him. "Dat's it take dis dick," said Roy as he pumped faster. Brittney walked up to them and placed her leg on Roy shoulders so he could eat her, while he thrust in and out of Craig. When Roy felt he was ready to cum he pulled out of Craig and lifts Brittney up and put her on the bed. "Ride mi dick," said Roy as he position Brittney so she could ride him. When she was comfortable, Craig went behind her, and entered her in the ass. When Roy was ready to cum Sasha cell phone rung, and she quickly hit the snooze button on the side as Roy paused looking around. Sasha looks at Janet as Roy tried to get up off the bed. "What's wrong, where you going," asked Brittney. "Mi thought mi heard someting, did yuh hear anyting," asked Roy. "No," said Brittney and Craig in unison. Stepping back Sasha hit save on her phone as she and Janet rushed out of the house. When she got outside she threw up again on the front of her neighbor's lawn. "Oh my god Jay, oh my god," cried Sasha as she leaned against Janet car. Janet was quiet as she looks at her best friend. "He's gay, oh my god Jay, Roy is gay and he's fucking a man." "Damn SaSa, am sorry." Janet went and gave Sasha a big hug and opens the car door for her. "Come on we got to get the hell out of here," said Janet as she shut the passenger door and ran around to the other side and got in. Looking at Sasha she was about to say something when her cell started to ring. "Hello." "Where yuh at, Zoe said Sha didn't answer her phone we got worried when yuh didn't call," said Jay. "Um, hey we're on our way back right now." "Did she get di paper work she was looking for?" "Um, no we'll talk about it when we get back, we'll meet you at the club when we get outside I'll call you so you can meet us." "Is everyting alright, is dat SaSa crying," asked Jason. Janet was quiet as she looks over to her best friend. "Look trust me we're all right, we just um, we'll talk to you when we get there, I'll call you as soon as we get there," said Janet not wanting to tell what they just witness. "Okay, mi be waiting for yuh, mi love yuh." "I love you to," said Janet as she hung up the phone. Sasha was still quiet as they rode down the street and Janet was worried about her. "SaSsa what are you going to do?" "Get tested in the morning, from the looks of things this wasn't his first time sleeping with Craig and Brittney." "Are you going to tell Zoe about this?" "I have to we had sex last night without no protection, oh god Jay I can't believe this, how can he do this to me," cried Sasha. "Its okay I'm here with you and I'm not going anywhere." Sasha and Janet was quiet as they drove the two hour drive back to Newport News. When they was almost to the club Janet startled Sasha. "SaSa we're almost there, I'm going to call Jay and let them know, so they'll can be outside waiting for us." "No, um can you take me to Momma Fill, um I don't want to be around no one, but my babies and I'll call you tomorrow." "What about Zoe, you know he'll come to your grandma's house if you don't show up at the club." "I'll call him and let him know that I'll talk to him tomorrow, now you go to your man and have fun, I'll be okay." When Janet let Sasha out her cell phone rung again and she answer without scanning the number. "Hello." It's not over, I will have you again and soon, you can bet your life on that," said

Ed. Janet hung up the phone and leaned on the steering wheel. "Damn if it ain't one thing it's another," said Janet as she pulled in the main highway and headed towards the club. Ed lay in his bed and watched as his wife Pamela walked into the bedroom a few minutes later. He hated her ever since she had the abortion. "Why are you looking at me like that," asked Pam taking off her earring. Ed got off the bed and walked up to her. "You know what I want," said Ed as he drop his pants. Pamela knew he didn't love her but she was willing to make there marriage work so she forgot the other earring and took Ed in her mouth. As Pamela deep throated him and taking all of him in her mouth she almost passed out when she heard him screamed Janet name as he exploded in her mouth. Pulling up his pants Ed zip his pants and left out of the bedroom. That would have to hold him off until he had the real Janet mouth wrap around his dick; thought Ed as he walked out the house and got into his car and driving away from the house and to the bitch of a wife that was there.

Chapter 23

Sasha

Betty was sitting on the sofa drinking a cup of coffee the next morning when Sasha came in the living room. "Good morning baby." "Good morning, did the babies wake you?" "No, but ya husband and Zoe did, Roy called bout an hour ago looking for yuh, mi tell him dat yuh was sleep, he said he'd call yuh later, Zoe said ta tell yuh ta call him also." Sasha was quiet as she looks into space. "Wat's di matter yuh look sick gurl, is someting wrong?" "No am fine, look can you watch the babies for me, I have an appointment that I forgot about it shouldn't take that long." "Yuh know mi will, gwan and don't rush back Roy said he be here later on taday ta take us out ta eat, ya mom went out ta di store she should be here in a little while." "Okay, if Roy gets here before I get back can you call me?" "Okay, so if Zoe comes by do yuh want mi ta tell him ta wait also, he said he needed ta talk ta yuh." "No, um I'll call him while am headed to the meeting, maybe we'll met up and talk then." "Okay baby, gwan and take care of ya business, di babies will be alright." Sasha went back in her old bedroom and took out an outfit and then she went and took a hot shower, when she finished she saw her mom on the sofa talking on the phone. Walking over she kissed her mom on the cheeks as she headed out the front door. Thirty minutes later she was sitting in the parking lot of her doctor office. She couldn't hold back the tears as they ran down her face, trying to get her bearing her emotion won and she broke down and cried. Twenty minutes later she jumped when her cell phone rung. Looking at the caller I.D. she answers it. "Hello." "Hello, where are ya at mi been calling ya phone all morning, why yuh not call mi back," said Zoe. "Um Zoe, I need you to meet me at my doctor office, I'll explain everything when you get here," said Sasha as she gave Zoe the address. "Mi be there in thirty minutes," said Zoe as he hung up the phone. Sasha walked into the doctor office and signs her name and then she took a seat, ten minutes later her doctor came out and sat beside her. "Hey Sasha what brings you here, your appointment isn't until another week are you sick or something?" "Um can we talk some where private?" "Sure, follow me." When they were inside the doctor office Sasha cleared her voice. "Um Mrs. Pat I found out that my husband is cheating on me, and um me and um someone else needs to take an HIV test," said Sasha. "Okay, when do you want to take the test?" "Right now, um I caught my husband sleeping with um a female last night, um we haven't had sex in almost four months, but I just want to be safe then sorry," explain Sasha. "Oh am so sorry, well when do your friend want to take the test?" "Um he's on his way here, but I haven't told him yet on why I'm here, I'm going to tell him once he gets here, and thanks for squeezing me in." "No problem go have a seat in the lobby and when your friend arrives you can use the conference room across the hall to talk to him, and when y'all is finished let the front desk know and then we'll do those testes," said Doctor Pat as she got up from her desk. When Sasha went to the lobby Zoe was pacing the lobby floor. As he walked towards her he could tell something wasn't right. "Wat happen is someting wrong wid our babies?" "No, the babies are fine, um I need to tell you someting and I don't want you to get upset or angry, and if you do don't fight me, or hit me," said Sasha. "Wat are yuh talking about, mi will never hurt yuh again, now tell mi wat's wrong." Sasha pulled Zoe into the conference room and closed the door. "I asked you to come here because I found out that Zoe is cheating on me, um we need to take an HIV test Zoe." Zoe was quiet as he looks into Sasha eyes. "Mi knows Roy is cheating on yuh." "What do you mean you know Roy is cheating on me?" "Look it doesn't matter, we're gaan ta be tagether when yuh divorce him, unless yuh change ya mind," said Zoe. "Hold the fuck on and don't try and change the subject Zoe; what the hell do you mean that you know he's cheating on me." "Look when Brittney and mi was tagether mi saw dem at a motel tagether, dats why mi not wid her. Yuh said dat yuh didn't want mi and dat yuh wanted ya marriage ta work so mi not tell yuh, mi thought he would leave her alone after Jay tell mi dat she was di one lying on yuh bout us." "You knew this whole time," asked Sasha. "Yes, mi didn't want yuh ta tink mi was lying ta try and break up ya marriage so mi didn't tell yuh," explain Zoe. Sasha went and sat on one of the chairs in the office. "God, if it was only that simple I wouldn't care." Sasha took out her cell phone and pushed a couple buttons and then handed the phone to Zoe. "Wat di blood clot is dis," shouted Zoe not believing his eyes. Sasha didn't say a word as Zoe felled in the seat beside her. "Oh my Jah, mi will kill his batty bwoy ass," said Zoe as he got up and began to leave out of the office. "No wait Zoe, I can't let him know that I found out what he's been doing, I feel the same way you do but he's not worth it. Zoe, Roy can not know about any of this." "Wat di hell do yuh mean he can't know about any of dis?" "I'm going to handle this and make it work in my favor, but at lease we found out before it was to late now do you see why we have to take the test?" "Yeah, damn Sha mi didn't know if mi knew mi would have told yuh or killed him miself." "I know, now come on my doctor squeezed us in so we better hurry," said Sasha as she got up. "Mi luv yuh Sha," said Zoe. "I know, and I love you to Zoe." "So dis don't change anyting between us, we still gaan ta be tagether?" "Um, look we'll talk about this later, come on." Sasha looks into Zoe eyes and saw the disappointment in his eyes. "Wat do yuh mean we'll talk about dis later, wat are yuh not telling mi?" "Um nothing, we'll just talk later that's all," said Sasha as she hurried out of the conference room. Sasha doctor explained the test to them and that the results would be back in two to three weeks and gave them both a number to call to get the results. When they was outside the doctor office Zoe pulled Sasha in his arms and kissed her long and hard. "Come home wid mi, we need ta finish talking." "No I have to go see my lawyer and then get the babies, I'll call you later." "Promise," asked Zoe. "Yes." "Okay, mi be waiting for ya call," said Zoe as he kissed Sasha and went and got in his car. When he was gone Sasha called her lawyer to let her know she was on her way. When she got there she sat no longer then five minutes before her lawyer Mrs. Rose came out to greet her. "Hey how are you doing?" "I'm fine, um I know I suppose to have brought you the paperwork, but um I need to speak and show you something in private."

"Sure follow me to my office." When they got to Mrs. Rose office she closed the door as Sasha took out her cell phone; hitting a couple of buttons she hands the phone to Mrs. Rose. "Oh my, did you witness this?" "Yes last night, I forgot the paperwork you needed and went home to get them only to walk in on that." "So what do you want to do now?" "I want out as soon as possible, he can have the house and everything in the bank account, but I just want out." "Okay, I'll get the paperwork done right away give me a couple days to get in touch with you and I'll need for you to e-mail me that recording just in case he don't sign the papers, we can use it as the get out of an marriage card, believe me don't any man what to be labeled as being gay in the courts eyes, but I'll just download it to be on the safe side and then we'll go from there." "That's fine with me; I'll be going out of town today so please call me on my cell." Sasha e-mailed the recording to Mrs. Roses while she was still in the office and when Mrs. Rose let her know that she got it Sasha stood up ready to leave. "Okay is there anything else you need while you're here?" "No, I just want out of this marriage, I'll talk to you later," said Sasha as she picks up her purse and walked to the door. "Alright then, call me if I don't get in touch with you in a week, with what you just gave me it shouldn't take that long for a judge to rule in our favor." "Okay one week," said Sasha as she walked out the office. When Sasha got in her car her cell phone rung and she saw Roy number on the screen, sending it to voicemail she started her car and headed to her grandmother house. When she arrived she saw Roy and Zoe car parked in the driveway and felt her stomach sink. As she parked she didn't hear any arguing so she walked in the house and found Zoe on the living room floor playing with the babies. "Hey, I didn't know you were coming here." "Mi wanted ta spend sometime wid mi kids, mi want ta take dem out unless yuh got other plans," said Zoe. Roy walked into the living room with a big smile on his face. "Hey baby, where yuh been, mi called yuh on ya phone, and yuh not answer." "Oh um I had a meeting with a client while I was here, I thought you was in D.C.?" "Mi left early, ya right mi need ta spend more time wid yuh; mi gave di job over ta Craig." "Craig who's he?" "Mi hired him a couple months ago, mi can trust dat he do a good job." Flash back of the night before flashed in Sasha head and she hurried and ran to the bathroom and threw up. "Are yuh alright," asked Roy looking at Sasha strange when he walked into the bathroom. "Yes, I think it's was the food I ate earlier," lied Sasha as she went over to the sink and rinse her mouth. Roy reached for her and Sasha backs up from his reach. "Um look Roy I don't feel good and I want to lay down, I have another meeting in the morning so me and the babies are going to stay here tonight and I'll be home as soon as I'm finished," said Sasha as she walked back into the living room. "Mi wanted ta take yuh and Momma Fill out ta eat, and we need ta talk?" "We can talk when I get home, right now I just want to lay down and hope my stomach feel better in the morning but if Momma, um NaNa and mom wants to go and have dinner with you that's fine," said Sasha as she saw her mom and grandmother walk into the living room. "Oh we're gaan ta have ta pass, Zoe brought us something from Misty, you can stay if you like," said Susan as she went and picked up Zara. "Um dat's okay mi take y'all out another time, well mi hope yuh feel better and mi will call yuh later on ta check on yuh," said Roy as he tried to kiss Sasha on the lips, she moves her head and he kissed her on the cheeks instead. "I don't want you to get sick just in case I got the stomach virus," said Sasha, as Roy looks at her strange again. "Okay, well mi will call yuh and mi luv yuh," said Roy as he headed out the door. Sasha didn't say anything, and when he paused he turned, and looks at her again. "Did yuh hear mi?" "Um, no what did you say?" "Mi said mi luv yuh." "Me to, I really need to lay down, mom can you watch the babies when Zoe leaves, I think the food I ate earlier is bothering my stomach and I need to rest," said Sasha walking out of the living room. "Sure baby, I'll make you some soup and bring it up to you, now go rest," said Susan as she walked the now heated Roy to the door. Sasha went to her old bedroom and shut the door. She walked over to her purse and took out her phone and cut it off and then she took out her ipod and put the ear phones in her ears pushed play and laid on the bed listening to some reggae music. She knew she had to leave and she had to do it tonight. She knew she had to tell her mom and grandmom what happened, but she didn't know how to tell them that Roy was gay or bisexual and she didn't want to see or be around Zoe, she had to clear her head and decide her future without any interfering. An hour later there was a knock on the door and Sasha mom walked in carrying a tray with soup and crackers on it. "Thanks mom, you didn't have to go through the trouble, I feel much better now." "It's no problem, mi want ta do it, and mi have someting ta tell yuh." "Okay, what's wrong are you and Momma Fill okay," asked Sasha. "Oh yes we're fine, I just wanted ta know how would yuh feel about meeting Allen?" "I'm fine with it; as long as he makes you happy then I'm happy." "So if he came yuh would meet him?" "Of course, why wouldn't I, after all he's my step- father," smiled Sasha. Susan took a deep breath and hugs Sasha real tight. "Thank you so much." "Mom, I need to tell you something," said Sasha as she cut off the ipod. "Okay, what's wrong Sasha?" "Last night I found Roy having sex with Brittney and um." "You what," shouted Susan. "Shh, mom please listens to me." Shaking her head Susan went and sat on the bed by Sasha. "Um I saw Roy having sex with Brittney and um, a man." "Oh Jah Sasha, oh Jah," said Susan in disbelief. "I recorded it and took it to my lawyer today, now Zoe do know about this, but um, I'm leaving mom, not for long but until this marriage is over with, I know if I stay here then Roy and Zoe will both be coming and I really need sometime to myself and think this thing through. Um, Zoe and I we was trying to get back together, but after this with Roy, mom I'm scared to try again with Zoe." Susan put the tray on the floor and then she held Sasha as they both cried. "Dis is all mi faults," cried Susan. "Mi should never have left yuh, mi should've been here for yuh and mi choose drugs over mi own daughter and mi is so sorry for it Sasha, mi well do whatever yuh want mi ta do, mi will be right behind yuh," said Susan as she kissed Sasha forehead. Lifting her head Sasha looks into her mother eyes. "I don't blame you or anyone for the mistakes I've made in my life. I ran away from Zoe because he was abusive and I turn and married a man who I thought loved me only to find out that he was worse, not only was he abusive but he was a control freak, and to top it off he's sleeping not with a woman, but a woman and a man, now how is that your fault?" "It's mi fault because mi should've been here ta teach yuh wid luv is, and what luv is like, if mi was here den yuh wouldn't have been abuse and cheated on because mi would've been here ta teach yuh and ta protect yuh like a madda suppose ta," said Susan. "Mom look, this is not your fault I have put the past in the past and I want you to do the same thing, we're here and we're starting over with no past, I love you mom and what I'm going through is not your fault." Susan was quiet as Sasha got off the bed and paced the floor. Standing up Susan stands in front of her and places her hands on Sasha shoulders to stop her. "Mi will help yuh, Allen has a townhouse in New York dat he's not using, mi will call him and let him know dat yuh and mi grandbabies are coming up there and dat yuh will be staying for a while, mi will stay here, but mi knows Allen will take good care of yuh and mi grandbabies." "You sure he want mind, I can go somewhere else mom," said Sasha. "Mi sure, after all he is ya step- father," smiled Susan. They talked for a few and then Susan went to call Allen. Sasha looks at the clock and it was only going on seven o'clock when she heard another knock on the door. When she opens then door Zoe was standing on the other side holding both babies. "We thought yuh might want some company," said Zoe as he hands over the giggling Zara. "Hey princess how's mommy babies," asked Sasha as she walked back into the bedroom. "She missed her mommy." Sasha moved the tray and sat on the bed sitting Zara on her lap, and Zoe did the same thing with Z.J. "Mi want ta know wat yuh decided about us," asked Zoe looking at Sasha. "Look, I can't right now, I need sometime, and when I know I'll let you know, but right now I really don't know." "So ya telling mi, dat yuh not gaan ta be wid mi because of wat he did?" "Look Zoe all I know is that I love you, there's no doubt in my mind about that, but what I just found out about Roy it makes me wonder if I'm rushing into another relationship with you, I just don't want to get hurt anymore and right now all I need is a little time with no pressure from you or Roy." Zoe leans back on the bed and laid Z.J. on his chest. "Mi will not pressure yuh, if yuh need time den yuh got it, mi bout ta leave, call later," said Zoe as he kissed the sleeping Z.J. on the forehead and laid him on the bed. Sitting up he leaned over and kissed Zara on the forehead and kissed Sasha softly on the lips and left out of the room. When Sasha heard the car pull away her mother walked in and sat on the bed beside her. "Allen said it okay for yuh ta stay at his townhouse, here's di address and the direction, when will yuh be leaving," asked Susan. "In a little while, I have to pack our things and then I'll be heading out." "Okay, I'll help yuh, mom is gaan ta Bingo so she want be back no time soon," said Susan. "Bingo, when did she start going to Bingo?" "Since mi took her and she won an thousand dollars on di first night, she's hooked," laughed Susan. Sasha and her mom packed up her and the baby's things and was walking out the door when the house phone rung. Susan walked over and answered it. "Hello." "Hey is Sasha still sleep, mi called her phone, but she not answering," said Roy. "Oh hey Roy, yeah her stomach is still bothering her, but I'll tell her that you called." "Oh um, okay, mi will call her later ta check on her," said Roy as he hung up the phone. Sasha and Susan put the babies and their things in the car. Susan hugs Sasha and kisses her on her cheeks. "It'll be okay, call mi when yuh get there and den mi will call Allen so he can meet yuh there." "Thanks mom and can you tell Momma Fill, um NaNa what's going on, and tell her not to worry and that I'll be back real soon." "Mi will now galang and drive safe." Two hours later Sasha pulled in front of a beautiful brick townhouse with red rose's line in front of the house. As she got out a man came out of the house. He was about 6'1 and built, he had silver hair and a beard. His dark brown eyes sparkled when he approached Sasha. "Hello, you must be Sasha, am Allen and your mom been calling every hour to the hour checking to see if you made it safe," smiled Allen. "Oh shit, um sorry I forgot I turned off my phone, can you call her and let her know we made it," said Sasha as she went and open the car door and unhooked Zara car seat. "How about if I help you get the babies and then I'll call her for you." "Oh, um thanks and it's nice to finally met you, you've made my mom real happy." "Same to you, now let's get y'all inside. I stocked the refrigerator with everything you and the babies might need and whip up some curry chicken and white rice," said Allen as they headed towards the house each carrying a baby and a traveling bag and the babies crib. "Thanks, but you didn't have to go through all the trouble, I stop at a grocery store on my way here." "Look you're my family and I look out for my family, now if you need anything my number is on the refrigerator and I live about twenty minutes from here, am going to take these things upstairs for you while you get settled in, go and try some of my curry chicken, it's your mom recipe," said Allen as he took Sasha and the babies things upstairs. When he came back down Sasha was sitting at the table eating a bowl of curry chicken with rice while the babies crawled around the living room floor. "Now I can call your mother and let her know that your safe and getting settled in, don't forget to call me if you need anything and have a good night," said Allen as he walked towards the front door. "Thanks again Allen, and I'm happy that my mom found someone like you," said Sasha as she walked behind him and closed and locked the door. Sasha walked backed into the dinning area and picked up the bowl and put it inside the refrigerator and went and sat on the sofa and thought about her life and everything she been through as tears rolled down her face. Not wanting her kids to feel her emotions Sasha wipes her tears away and picks up the remote to the TV and turned the station to Bet and watched her favorite show The Game. Reaching in her purse she took out her cell phone and cuts it back on, her voicemail rung letting her know that she had messages and she dialed and enters her password and listen to first Roy asking her if she thought she was pregnant and that he'd be at Momma Fill in the morning to take her to the doctor to get checked out. Next there was a message from Zoe letting her know that he was coming to pick the babies up to give her sometime to herself. The next message was from Janet telling Sasha to call her, so Sasha hung up the phone and called her best friend. "Hey you, where are you and how your holding up," asked Janet. "I'm fine really, and I told Zoe and of course he flip but you want believe what he told me," said Sasha. "What?" "He said he knew Roy was cheating on me." "How did he know that?" "Apparently when Brittney and him was together he saw them at a motel and since I told him that I wanted be with Roy he decided not to tell me, because he thought I was going to accuse him of lying and trying to ruin my marriage, but after we talked we took an HIV test and the results should be back in a week or two, and after I left there I went to my lawyer and showed her the recording of Roy, she told me to e-mailed it to her for the records just in case if Roy doesn't want to sign then she can use it, she's going to call me in a week to let me know what's happening." "Well am happy that your ending it with Roy, and I'm happy that you had the nerves to tell Zoe or should I say show Zoe the recording, but any ways do you want to go out with me tonight, Jay wants to go out an celebrate." "Um Jay actually I'm out of town, I'll be back once this divorce is over with, I knew if I stayed at Momma Fill, Roy would come and I definitely didn't want to see him, and then there's Zoe even though he said he'd give me some time I just wanted to be alone, you know I needed some me time." "Yeah I know what you mean." "I'm going to call Zoe and Roy in the morning to let Roy know I'm divorcing him and to let Zoe know that it's not going to work." "What did Zoe do and what's not going to work?" "Nothing," said Sasha. "Nothing my ass, spill it SaSa." "It's that, um Zoe and I was going to try and work on a relationship but am scared Jay." "Scared of what?" "Am scared of his love; Jay am scared that if I gave Zoe and chance that he'll love me the way I want to be loved and I wouldn't know how to return it." "Did you tell him how you feel?" "No, it's like am eighteen all over again when I'm around him, I can't think straight and I get tongue twisted and he makes me feel all tingling inside." "What does your heart say?" "That's the problem, my heart says that I love this man and always will, but my mind is telling me to run and don't look back, and then my heart tells me to trust and forgive but most my heart is telling me to love and to fight for what we can have together, and then my mind tells me that he's going to hurt me, I don't know Jay." "Then I think you made the right choice to leave and have some you time, but just so you know am on Zoe side this time, because I've seen the love in his eyes for you and his kids. SaSa you have to tell Zoe how you feel, and I want you to be honest with him so you can be honest with yourself." "I will and thanks Jay, what would I do without you, and enough about me, what have you and your fiancé been doing," asked Sasha as she watch her kids play on the floor. "You know Jay, all he been doing is working and planning the wedding, but the reason I asked for you to call is because I have to tell you something." "Okay, what's up?" "Ed called me last night after I dropped you off." "Oh god, what did he say this time?" "He said he was going to have me and soon, I haven't told Jay yet only because I don't know what he'll do." "Jay you have to tell him, there's no telling what Ed might do." "I know I'm suppose to meet Jay later on at his house, I lied and told him that I have a client that I have to see in the morning so he told me to come to his house and stay." "Tell him Jay, call him and tell him right now, and then I want you to call the police and take out and harassment out against him hell give them the recording that you have," said Sasha as she began to pace the floor. "Okay I will now relax, I don't want you getting upset when your some where alone with my god babies, so I'll call Jay and tell him, and I'll call you later to let you know what's going on." "Okay, and Jay we're safe and I'll only be gone for a week or two and I'll make sure that I'll call you." "Okay, I love you SaSa, good night," said Janet. "I love you to and call and tell Jay." "I will," said Janet as she hung up the phone. Sasha called her mom next to let her know that she and the babies was all right, and her mom told her that Roy kept calling the house looking for her and so was Zoe. Sasha told her mom that she would call both Roy and Zoe in the morning and if they called to let them know. When Sasha flip closed her cell she saw that her kids were rubbing their eyes. "Okay beddy by for the two of you," said Sasha as she got up and picked up both of her kids. "Time to take y'all bath." As she made her way upstairs she saw that Allen put all of their things in the master bedroom, he even set up the baby's cribs. As she put the babies in their cribs she went and took out their nightclothes and then hers, when she finished she went to the bathroom and ran their bath water. Thirty minutes later both babies was asleep so Sasha went and took her bath and when she finished she lay in bed and was sleep insistently.

Chapter 24
Roy

Roy was sitting at the diner table the next morning fuming. He called Sasha all-night and only got her voicemail. He knew she wasn't with Zoe because he went to his club and saw him and his cousin there in VIP and he stayed there for a couple of hours watching him. He did notice that Zoe made a lot of phone calls while he was there, but he had Jalen with him so he couldn't have been calling Sasha. Roy left the club and then went to Betty house and he still didn't see Sasha car anywhere. "Where di hell is yuh at, yuh better not be cheating on mi or yuh gaan ta regret it," said Roy as he hit the table. As he got up to go into the kitchen his cell phone rung and he answered it without looking at the I.D. "Where di hell is yuh at," shouted Roy. "I'm where you left me, and when am I going to see you," asked Brittney. "Look mi will call yuh back later on." "What the fuck do you mean you'll call me back later on, I've been stuck in this fucking motel room for two days, and if you don't come and get me right now maybe I'll call that wife of yours and let her know what we've been doing for the last four months," shouted Brittney. Roy began to speak in his native language. "What the fuck did I tell you about speaking that shit, English motherfucker English, now what are you going to do?" "Mi be there after I get off work." "No you'll be here in a few minutes, don't try me Roy." "Don't yuh vex mi, mi marriage comes first." "Your marriage, if I call that bitch and tell her everything we been doing what marriage will you have then huh?" "If yuh call mi wife and tell her anything mi will kill yuh, now mi said mi will be there after mi get off work, and if yuh call Sasha it's over," said Roy as he flip shut his phone. "Dis bumbo clot is gaan ta make mi beat her ass," said Roy as he began to pace the floor after taking some deep breath. Roy went upstairs and took a shower as he thought of all the things he was doing without Sasha knowing. Brittney was a freak, and he was whip to a point where he actually excited to see her and see what she had plan for that day. After the sex with Craig, Roy didn't want to admit it but it felt good, but he knew he wasn't gay, but without Brittney knowing it him and Craig still fucked behind her back that's why he hired him. Brittney planned the sex theme they did and he was all too happy to assist. Once she brought in another female and they had a three-some. Roy was in heaven. Than it was the time she brought that big ass vibrator and wanted him to fuck her in the ass with it. Roy shook his head as he got out of the shower and got dress and headed to work. When he pulled on site he saw Craig standing outside his work trailer. "Hey, I called you last night, why you didn't answer," asked Craig as he followed Roy inside and shut and locked the door. "Mi was busy, wat can mi help yuh wid," smiled Roy. Dropping on his knees Craig unhooks Roy pants and takes out his dick and began to suck long and hard. "Damn dat feels good," moaned Roy as he pumped in and out of Craig mouth. Not able to take the sensation anymore Roy pulled Craig up and watches as Craig pulled down his pants then he bends over the desk knocking the paperwork on the floor. Entering Craig, Roy let his head fall back and closed his eyes as he thrust in and out of Craig. Roy imagine that it was Sasha as he took his anger out on Craig and went deeper and deeper until all his ten inches was inside of him. "Oh damn slow the fuck down man," cried Craig as Roy went deeper. "Yuh wanted di dick now shut di fuck up and take dis dick," said Roy, as he pumped harder then doing a circle motion and thrust harder again. "Damn baby slow down, we're the only one's here, take your time," pleaded Craig as Roy pumps a couple more time and then pull out and turned Craig around to nuts in his mouth. "Ah shit," said Roy as he pulls up his pants and went and sit behind his desk. "Now that's what I call a work out," laughed Craig. Just then Roy cell phone rung and he scanned the number, when he saw Sasha number his anger resurface. "Where di bumba clot yuh been, mi been calling yuh ass all night long," shouted Roy. "Well after today you don't have to worry about mi because it's over." "Yuh know before mi let yuh do dat mi will kill yuh first, now tell mi where di hell yuh been," asked Roy as he got up and pace the floor. Craig pulled his pants up and was ready to leave out of the trailer until Roy stops him. "Stay mi want be for a minute," said Roy as he winked at Craig. "Yes it will take only a minute to tell you that I've already filed for divorce, you can have the house and everything in the bank account." "So yuh gaan ta leave mi for someone else, so who is he?" "You got to be kidding me; you're accusing me of cheating on you." "Wat other reason is there for yuh ta try and divorce mi." "Okay you want some reason, I'll give you some reason and then I'm going to hang up and I never want to see or talk to you ever again, but are you ready for the reason Roy." "Mi doesn't want ta hear about mi hitting on yuh, mi haven't touched yuh in months." "True, but you also stop doing a lot of other things to me but mostly you stop loving me if you ever did. When was the last time we actually sat down and talked and listen to one another or went out to eat at a restaurant and enjoyed each other company, or hell even go to the movies to spend time with each other, but you know what that's not the reason why am divorcing you." "So if it's not any of dem, den why yuh are divorcing mi," asked Roy. "Because you're a cheater," said Sasha. Craig was rubbing Roy chest as the words soaked in. Pushing Craig hands away Roy went and looked out the trailer blinds and when he didn't see anything he walked back over and sat in the chair. "Mi cheat wat is yuh talking bout?" "Don't try and play me, I saw you with my own eyes, hell I even recorded you fucking a man and that stank ass Brittney in our home in our bed." Roy looks up at Craig and back down at the phone. "Yeah I thought that would shut you the fuck up. All this time you whipping my ass and you're a fucking batty bwoy, a faggot, and a ma'ama man." "Look mi not gay, mi can explain." "Explain what, that I married a fucking faggot. Do you know what I did yesterday before I saw you huh, I went and took an HIV test, and do you want to know why I threw up when I saw you? It's because the night before flashed in my head and it made me sick to my stomach." "Look, mi." "You what," asked Sasha. "Look mi will come ta Momma Fill house and we can talk." "Talk your lucky your still breathing, if I had the guts I'd kill you myself, but you're not worth it that's why I left town to get away from you until this shame of a marriage is over with." "Mi will never give yuh a divorce." "Oh you're going to give me a divorce or I'll let my lawyer show the court the video of you with Craig and Brittney." "Look we can talk dis over." "You got the over part right, sign the papers and don't call me ever again, my lawyer should be getting in contact with you in a week, if she calls me and tell me that you didn't sign I'll tell her to move forwards with the video and let the courts decide on who gets what," said Sasha as she hung up the phone. Craig went over to Roy and started to rub his shoulders and was shocked and surprised when Roy pushed him in the floor. "Don't fucking touch mi, wat di fuck have mi done," said Roy as he got off the chair and began to pace the floor. "What the hell is wrong with you," asked Craig as he got up. "My wife knows." "Oh." "Oh, is fucking right, mi fucked she recorded us." "What do you mean she recorded us?" "The other night when di three of us was tagether, when mi asked if yuh or Brittney heard anyting and y'all said no, she was there and she recorded us," said Roy. "So is that why you said you're not gay?" "Wat," asked Roy half listening. "You said that you weren't gay just a few minutes ago." "Look mi not gay, what we do is not gay, mi not penetrates in yuh." "Your kidding right, you think just because you don't nut inside of me that you're not gay?" "Look mi needs ta be alone, mi be back later," said Roy as he unlocked the door and walks out. Roy went to the house and went through all of Sasha things hoping to find anything to locate her. When he didn't find anything he got in his car and drove to Momma Fill house. When he got to the house he saw a couple men sitting on the porch playing spades and when he got closer he saw Susan and Betty sitting among them when he didn't see Sasha car he drove pass and went to Janet townhouse when he didn't see any cars he headed back home. When he pulled into his driveway his cell phone rung and he answered without scanning thinking it was Sasha. "Sasha mi sorry and mi love yuh, mi will never hurt yuh again," said Roy as he parked his car and got out. "Sasha, nigga you got it twisted calling me that bitch name, where the hell you at any ways," asked Brittney. "Brittney?" "Who the hell else do you think this is, where the hell are you, you suppose to have been here, you know how I hate waiting on motherfuckers, when your going to get me my car you been telling me that your going to buy me any ways," asked Brittney. "Look it's over and don't call mi ever again." "What the fuck you mean it's over?" "Sasha knows about us and Craig, her tinks mi gay and she's divorcing mi, and mi can't let dat happen, yuh was a mistake dis wasn't supposed ta happen." "Oh so now am a mistake, is our baby a mistake," said Brittney. "Baby, wat baby," asked Roy. "I'm pregnant," said Brittany. Roy was quiet as he opened his door and walked inside the house and sat on the sofa. "Wat did yuh say?" "I said am pregnant, but you know what you can have Sasha fuck you and her." "Look, mi be there later ta talk ta yuh, but right now mi have ta go," said Roy as he hung up the phone." Roy sat on the sofa for almost thirty minutes thinking of Sasha first and then Brittney and the baby she claimed she was carrying. 'Sasha mi will find yuh and when mi do, ya gaan ta regret it,' said Roy as he researched the house. When he came up with nothing again he went to their bedroom and sat on the bed when he's cell phone rung. Looking at the phone he smiled a wicked smile as he thought of a guaranteed way of finding Sasha. 'Mi got ya ass now,' said Roy as he got up and went into the bathroom and took a long hot shower. When he was finished he made two phone calls when he got the information that he needed he left out the house with a big smile on his face.

Chapter 25

Zoe

Zoe was still in bed when he heard his doorbell ring first and then continuous knocking at his front door, hesitant he got out of bed and walked down hall to open it only to find Jalen standing on the other side wearing a long black trench coat and a big smile on her face. "Good morning sleepy head, are you ready?" "Reddi, reddi for wat," asked Zoe. "Ready for this," said Jalen as she drops her coat and was naked underneath. "Wow, um." "The cat doesn't have your tongue yet," said Jalen as she and closes and locks the door behind her and walks further into the house. "So do you like?" "Um yes, but um like mi said mi have ta go ta a meeting," said Zoe as he backs up knocking over his lamp his mother gave him for Christmas last year. "I can tell you like what you see so what's stopping you from getting what you want," asked Jalen as she rubs up and down on Zoe semi- hard dick throw his boxer he forgot he had on. "Look, mi be back," said Zoe as he went down the hall and put on his robe. Jalen took that moment and put the crushed up pills in a cup and poured some Rum inside of it, her cousin told her that the pills worked fast and only last a couple of hour so she knew she had to move fast. When Zoe got back in the living room she was laying on the sofa drinking out of the cup and fuddling herself with a big smile on her face. "What's the problem Zoe, I know you're not gay, believe me I did my research on you, so how come you're playing hard to get?" "Wat do yuh mean yuh did ya research on mi." "I know for a fact that you love punany as you call it, and since you haven't been trying to get any of mines then I have a feeling that you're getting it from someone else," said Jalen as she put down her cup and got up and walked towards Zoe again. "Look it's not dat, mi got a lot on mi mind." "We been together for almost six months, and if it's not me then what's the problem?" Zoe walked over to the sofa and picked up Jalen cup and downed the rest of her drink, which was a habit of him doing since they've been dating and the reason Jalen sat it down. Zoe walked back to the bar and poured another shot of Rum and down that also. Trying to think of a way to get Jalen out of the house Zoe paced the living room floor and stop when Jalen was standing in front of him. Jalen took her hands and rubbed his now hard dick, and smiled. "So you do want me?" "Um," said Zoe as he tried to think of something to say. "What the fuck you mean um, either you do or you don't," said Jalen getting pissed. "Mi not in luv wid yuh," Zoe finally said. "But am in love with you, and am going to show you just how much I love you," said Jalen and with one quick move she had Zoe boxers down around his legs. As she got on her knees she took him in her mouth and began to suck nice and slow, she knew the pills was working by now. "Oh shit," said Zoe as Jalen deep throated him. Taking all of him in her mouth Jalen used her other hand and played with Zoe balls as began to rub them in a circle motion. Stepping back Zoe pulled Jalen up. "Mi can't do dis, go home now Jalen," said Zoe as he thought of a way of getting rid of Jalen. "What do you mean you can't do this, were a couple and of course we can do this," said Jalen walking towards him and kisses him on the mouth. As she made her way down his body Zoe tried to push her away again but failed as she felled back on her knees and gave him head again. 'Wat di hell is wrong wid mi,' Zoe said to him self as his mind began to get fuzzy and his body began to tingle and his dick grew harder. Shaking his head he looks up to see Jalen but he only saw Sasha. "Come get what you want," he heard a voice tell him as he was pulled to the sofa. When he was seated, Sasha image got on top of him and began to massage his now rock hard dick. Zoe shook his head again and looks up to find Sasha image straddling his lap. "Give me what I want," said Sasha image as she spread her legs and let her pussy covers his dick. Zoe body gave in to the sensation and his urge intensifies to the point that he couldn't take it anymore. Pushing Sasha down, Zoe spread her hips and lifted his hip up to get deep inside of her. As Sasha image rode up and down on Zoe dick he got harder with each stroke as he sat up and began to suck on her breast and squeezing them softly. “Shit Zoe that’s it, damn your dick is so big,” cried out Jalen as she bounced her pussy on Zoe dick taking more of him now. Zoe began to speak his language as he thrust faster. Not knowing what he was saying Jalen didn’t respond as Zoe worked her over in a five-minute orgasm. With long and steady strokes Zoe went deeper. “Oh that’s it daddy fuck this pussy,” cried Jalen as Zoe lifts his hip off the sofa and grabs her by the waist and thrust a couple of times and then he pulled out and flips her over on her stomach and with another quick thrust he enter Sasha image taking her breathe away. Zoe pulled Sasha hair and fucked her long and hard. “Oh Sasha, tell mi dat yuh luv mi in our language,” said Zoe as he thrust faster and harder. Jalen body tense when she her him call her Sasha and tried to push Zoe off of her. Zoe was thrusting faster and was about to come when he felt a smack on his face. “Get off, get the fuck off of me,” shouted Jalen as she pushed harder against Zoe chest. Shaking his head Zoe backed away from Jalen looking at her confused. “Wat di blood clot is going on Jalen,” asked Zoe as he tried to remember how he ended up having sex with Jalen when he was fucking Sasha. “Fuck that you just called me Sasha while we was having sex,” shouted Jalen as she reaches for her coat and put it on. “Mi called yuh Sasha because mi thought mi was having sex wid Sasha, wid di hell did yuh put in dat drank?” Jalen walked over and sat on the sofa. “Why, it doesn’t matter it didn’t work the way I planned,” said Jalen. “Wat di hell do yuh mean it didn’t work di way yuh planned,” shouted Zoe as he walked up to Jalen. “Look it was something my cousin gave me, it was suppose to arose us what else was I suppose to do I got tired of just kissing and grinding and going home with an wet ass and horny, five months Zoe, five months and we never had sex, and when we finally do you call me fucking Sasha, you wanted her the whole time we was together didn’t you?” Zoe walked over to the window and stared out at the morning clouds. “Sasha has noting ta do wid dis, yuh di one who drugged mi for mi ta sleep wid yuh not Sasha, look Jalen go home,” said Zoe. “Am not leaving until you let me know where I stand.” Before Zoe could answer her, his cell phone rung “Look mi got ta get dis, go home Jalen and mi will call yuh later,” said Zoe as he walked into the kitchen leaving Jalen sitting on the sofa. “Speak.” “Hey you, are you busy?” “Not for yuh, where are yuh," asked Zoe as he pulls his boxer up and tighten his robe around his waist. "Um, that's why I'm calling am out of town right now, and I'll be gone for a week or two." "So where are yuh, mi will come and spend some time wid yuh." "Um Zoe the reason I left is because I need sometime to think things through. I talked to Janet last night and she told me to be honest with you about my feelings so am going to tell you." "Okay." "Zoe I love you so much, but am scared." "Scared, scared of wat," asked Zoe giving Sasha his undivided attention. "Am scared that you might hurt me, and am scared that I'll want be able to love you the way you deserve to be loved." "Sasha." "No let me finish, all my life I've only known wicked love, no one ever loved me for anything, and I don't want our kids to be raise the way I've been raised." "Yuh know mi would never hurt yuh mi luv yuh and mi kids, mi would do anyting ta prove dat ta yuh." "I know, but." "No but, mi and yuh and our kids will be a family, now come home ta mi." "I really want to, but I'm not coming back until this marriage is over with, and I hope you understand?" "Mi understands, call mi later so we can talk, mi need ta tell yuh someting, but it can wait." "Okay, and I love you," said Sasha as she hung up the phone. When Zoe turned around Jalen was standing in the kitchen doorway. "So I guess I got my answer," said Jalen as she looks at Zoe. "Yes, mi didn't want yuh ta find out dis way, and mi sorry." "Yeah right, all y'all nigga's sorry when y'all ass get caught, but you know what I ain't mad at you, pay back is a bitch," said Jalen as she ran out the front door. Zoe went behind her but he was too late, because she was in her car and pulling out the driveway as he came out the house. Zoe came back inside and sat on the sofa and ran his hand down his face. 'Dis is not mi day,' said Zoe as he went upstairs and took a shower and got dress. Zoe knew he needed to clear his head and he knew he had to tell Sasha what happened, but first he had to tell the one person whom he trusted. "Yeah mon, mi need ta see yuh, like right now," said Zoe. "Meet mi at our spot in fifteen," said Jay and hung up the phone. When Zoe got to the park, Jay was the only one there sitting on the bench smoking a blunt. "Wat's up mon?" "Yuh want believe wat just happen," said Zoe as he lit a blunt. "Wat happen?" "Jalen came ta di house and she drug mi so mi will sleep wid her." "Yuh kidding right," said Jay as he inhales the smoke. "No mon, one minute mi telling her ta leave, and di next mi fucking her tinking she's Sasha." "Damn mon, yuh can pick some crazy ass females mon, so wat yuh gaan ta do?" "Mi have ta tell Sha, but wid everyting with Roy, mi just don't know how ta." "Wat's going on wid Roy?" "Damn mon, mi don't know how ta tell yuh dis, but ya cuz is a batty bwoy." "Yuh kidding right," asked Jay not believing what he heard. "Naw mon, Sha caught him in bed wid dat bitch Brittney and a dude name Craig." "Damn Zoe mon, mi didn't know, mi wonder why Janet didn't mention it to me, so how's SaSa taking it?" "Better den mi, we took a HIV test, but other wise she called mi and told mi dat she left town and want be back until di marriage is over, mi understand, but mi just want us ta be tagether." "Mi knows dat her and y'all babies mean everyting ta yuh, mi hope everyting works out." "Yeah mon Sha is divorcing him and now mi have ta tell her mi done fucked up again." "Look, just tell her she'll understand." "Mi hope so," said Zoe as he inhaled deeply.

Chapter 26

Janet

Janet was sitting on the sofa when Jay walked in round one in the evening. "Hey yuh, mi thought yuh had meetings taday?" "Um hey baby, can you come in here for a minute, I need to talk to you about something," said Janet and she twisted her hands together. Jason went over and sat on the sofa pulling Janet in his arms he kissed her long and hard. "Mi all ears," said Jay as he leaned back on the sofa and pulled Janet into his arms. "Um I need to tell you something, but I need for you to not get upset or angry, and I need for you to promise before I tell you," said Janet as she looks into Jay eyes. "Okay mi swear mi want get angry or upset, now tell mi wat's bothering mi wife." "Um last night before I came to the club I got a phone call." "A call from whom," asked Jay. "Ed." Janet felt Jay squeeze her arms and then felt them release just as quickly. "Wat di blood clot did he want?" "Um, he said he was going to have me and soon, I don't know what he means by it, but SaSa told me to tell you, because I was afraid of what you might do." Taking a deep breath Jay kissed Janet on the forehead. "Why yuh not tell mi sooner, mi suppose ta protect yuh, mi can't protect yuh when mi don't know wat di hell is going on." "Don't yell at me and don't curse at me." "Mi sorry, mi just don't want anyting ta happen ta yuh." "Am okay really, I went to the police station and give them the recording, and I press charges for him raping me and file for harassment against him, they're looking for him as we speak, I've sent the recording to his wife, father and his uncle who's the Mayor and believe me when I tell you that they're not at all happy." "Yuh still should've told mi," said Jay as he got up from the sofa and began to pace the floor. "I didn't what you to worry," said Janet as she steps in front of Jay circling his waist. "And I promise that if he calls or anything I'll let you know first, I just didn't want you to go do something and get in trouble he's not worth it." "Janet mi have ta tell yuh someting, and mi don't want yuh ta get upset or angry," said Jay as he step back to look into Janet eyes. "What's wrong?" "Mi had mi boys following yuh." "What do you mean you had your boys following me?" "Di first night when yuh tell mi wat dat blood clot did, mi had mi boys follow yuh ta make sure dat yuh got home safe, but Ed was following yuh so mi told dem ta keep watch and ta follow yuh where ever yuh go ta make sure dat yuh was safe," explain Jay. "Ed followed me home and you're just telling me this," said Janet as she stared into his eyes. "Yes, mi didn't want ta tell yuh because mi didn't want ta frighten yuh, um mi also got mi boys following Ed, just ta make sure dat he's not trying anyting." "Wow, I don't know if I should be angry with you or thank you." "Mi will understand if ya angry, but mi only did dis ta protect yuh noting more." "How can I possible be angry when you went out of your way to protect me, am just pissed that you kept this from me, and so you're telling me that Ed been following me since um, that night?" "Yes, but mi boys be watching him and if he tries anything he'll regret it, he knows ya being followed, but mi don't tink he knows dat he's being followed, mi hired mi cousin husband who's an detective ta follow him just in case tings went wrong." "Wrong like what?" "Dat's why mi hired him, now mi want yuh ta relax and don't yuh worry about him or anyting else," said Jay as he pulled Janet to him and kissed her on the lips. When they were sitting on the sofa Janet looked up at Jay. "Wat's wrong?" "I was thinking that since your boys are following Ed and they know where he is then we should call the police and let them know." "Okay, mi will call and check and see where dem at," said Jay as he reached for his phone. "Wat's good, Benny?" Jay ask as he sat down, and lean back on the sofa. "Wat's up J were in Virginia Beach sitting outside of a house he came ta bout two hour ago," said Benny. "Good, stay there mi just found out dat he called Jay again and threaten her, she wants ta call di police and have him arrested stay there until yuh see him in di police car," said Jay. "Hold on there's a black Cadillac pulling in di yard, now a woman and man is getting out, wat do yuh want mi ta do now?" "Give mi di address and were ganna let di police know where he's at." Benny gave Jay the address. "Mi will call yuh back, but don't leave unless he leaves," said Jay as he closed the phone. "What's wrong?" "He's in Virginia Beach and a black Cadillac just pulled up wid a woman and a man." "It has to be his father and wife; maybe they're there to talk to him so that he can turn himself in." "Mi don't know, but we need ta call di police and let them know where he is," said Jay as he took Janet hands. "I'll call and let them know," said Janet. When she reached for her cell it rang startling her. "I don't know this number then again it might be a client," said Janet as she pushed the send button. "Hello Your Dream Design Janet Day is speaking how can I help you?" "Um Janet this is Ed father James can I talk to you for a minute?" Janet looked at the phone and then at Jay. "Can you hold on for a minute," said Janet as she pushed the mute button on the phone not waiting for an answer. "It's Ed's father." "Wat do he wants," asked Jay. "I don't know do you think I should talk to him." "Just see what he wants, but mi suggest dat yuh record di conversation, ta be on di safe side," said Jay. "Okay." Janet hit the record button and unmutes the phone and put it on speaker so Jay could hear also. "Okay Mr. Gray how can I help you?" "Um, call me James after all we're not strangers or anything like that. Actually am here with Ed and I was wondering if um if we can talk and try and come to an reasonable understanding about the things your accusing Ed of doing." "Excuse me?" "Um, look I've talked to Ed and if you drop the charges against him, we made arrangement for him to leave the country and that he'll never contact you again." "You're kidding right?" "No am not. This is a difficult situation, am truly sorry for everything he's done to you and what you been going through, but let's be reasonable here; if you take this to court you're going to look like the jealous ex who just wants revenge because Ed broke off the engagement with you and married someone else. Ed told me that you agreed to meet him on the day in question and that you never said no when you'll was intimate he's not denying that he was intimate with you, he's denying that he rape you and his defense is that your doing this because he wouldn't leave his wife for you." "What?" "You're a young an beautiful young lady and I'm sorry for what my son did to you, but Janet we need for this situation to end immediately, am willing to write you a check for thirty thousand dollars if you just drop the charges against my son and forget that this ever happen." "Wat di blood clot," shouted Jay as he takes the phone out of Janet hands. "Hello, who's this," asked James nervously. "Dis is Janet fiancé' and if yuh tink she's gaan ta drop di charges and take ya money den yuh wrong, where mi from yuh son would be dead for wat he did, but we gaan ta let the police handle him, and mi advise yuh ta not ta call dis phone unless it's ta let us know dat ya son has been arrested for his crime," said Jay as he hung up the phone. "I can't believe this, I can't believe that he has the nerves to call and try and bribe me knowing what his son did," said Janet as she started to pace the floor. "Look come here and sit down, mi don't want yuh ta worry about anyting, mi gaan ta call di police and give dem di address and have him arrested, who was di officer yuh talked ta when yuh went down there," said Jay as he dialed 911 on his cell. "Bellco," said Janet. "Hello can mi speak ta office Bellco?" "What is this call in reference to?" "Mi got information about Ed Gray whereabouts." "Officer Bellco isn't on duty right now, but you can leave a message and he'll get in contact with you as soon as he comes in, please hold while I'll transfer you to his voicemail." Jay listened to the recording and when he heard the beep he gave the address where Ed was and hung up without leaving a name or number. Janet was in the kitchen making two sandwiches when Jay cell phone rung. "Speak." "Yeah mon, dis is crazy the woman and man who went inside di house just came running out, dem look scared." "Dem just called Janet and tried ta bribe her, look stay there and watch di house if he leaves call mi, but be careful mi have a feeling dat all hell is about ta break loose and a lot a blood is about ta be spread," said Jay as he hung up the phone. "Who was that," asked Janet as she brought two plates and sat them on the living room table. "Oh dat was Zoe, we suppose ta have met at di club, but mi told him dat mi catch up wid him later, come sit down and relax, we'll call di police later ta see wat's going on," said Jay as he pulled Janet close to him. Jay body tensed up and his heart began to pound fast as his pulse in his neck quickens and the same feeling he got when he was ready to kill was the same feeling he was feeling as he thought of Ed and what was to come.

Chapter 27

Sasha and Janet

Sasha was washing the little bite of dishes when her cell phone rung. She quickly ran over and answer it before it woke the Zoe and Zara, she been out of town for a whole week and only Zoe and Janet called to check on her and the babies. Her mom husband Allen stop by and check on her everyday to see if she needed anything, which she didn't and she figured her mom put him up to it, so she just went along, plus she was happy for the company. "Hello." "Hey girl, why haven't you called me," asked Janet. "I was but the babies and me went out and sight see and when I got back I was just tired, girl them kids got energy for days," laugh Sasha. "I know that's right I miss my godbabies, so when are you coming back?" "I was hoping for next week, but my lawyer said that she tried to get in touch with Roy, but he wasn't at home or at work for the last week, so she's going to go ahead and motion for the evidence to be part-take so know we have to go to court, she said she'll call me when she have everything in order, enough about me, what have you and your fiancé been doing, and what's up with the Ed situation?" "Jason and I are doing good, he been more protective of me since I told him what Ed said, but other wise were okay, but um about the Ed situation um, well I forgot to tell you that his dad called me last week and tried to bribe me, saying that he would pay me if I drop the charges, but not before he said that if I take this to court that I'll look like the jealous ex who's trying to get revenge because Ed left me and married someone else." "Get the fuck out of here; he said some shit like that for real." "Yep, but thank god I had him on speaker and then Jay got on and that's was that he haven't called me since." "So have you heard anything about Ed whereabouts?" "Nope Jay had his boy following him but when the police got there he wasn't in the house, so now no one knows where he is, Jay got his boy Hell Bent staying with me when he has to work, and even though I appreciate it, it's getting on my last nerves, I can't go shopping or no where unless he's with me, I was going to ditch him, but thought twice against it so now I just sit in the house and do nothing but work." "Girl it's better to be safe then sorry, there's no telling what Ed might do, hell am thinking about calling Zoe so he can come and be with the kids and me just in case Roy crazy ass come showing up no telling what's he's up to." "Well call him and tell him where you are, I haven't seen him in a while so I know he's worried about you." "I know, but I really need this time to get my head on straight if I want this relationship with Zoe to work, I don't want to compare him with Roy, and I don't want to jump ship when I get scared, hell my mom husband taught me some self defense moves so I know how to protect myself." "That's what's up, but you already know how to fight, don't forget we took boxing lesson together." "I know, but it's like when am scared I freeze, and even though my mind is telling me to hit or punch my body doesn't respond so I stand there and take there punches and blows." "Well it'll be all over and then you want have to worry about anything, now hurry up and get back home, girl I miss you so much." "Girl I miss you to, I tell you what, how about when I get back home I'll get my mom to baby-sit and we'll go out and have some fun, we can go to the movies, and then to the club, how does that sound?" "Fabulous girl, and on that note am going to go out and buy me that red Baby Phat outfit I saw at the Patrick Henry Mall with the purse and shoes that match," laughed Janet. "You know I saw a cute outfit on Broadway yesterday when we was sight seeing, I think I'll go back and get that," said Sasha. "Broadway, you better not tell me that you're in New York and without me." "Um," was all Sasha could say. "Oh hell no, where your at am coming where you at," laughed Janet. "Jay promise that you want tell Jay, if you do then Zoe will come looking for me and even though I might call him I want him to come when am ready." "Okay, okay I want tell him, but you better buy me an outfit." "Deal, now since you know where am at, my mom also knows where am at actually am at her husband Allen house." "So someone does know where you are?" "Yeah, but I didn't want you lying to Jay, so I didn't tell you and I hope you can forgive me." "Your forgiven girl, now how is my godbabies doing?" "Jay they gotten so big it's a shame and they're walking real well." "That's what's up; you better hurry up and get home." "I'll be back before you know it." The house doorbell rung and Sasha knew it was Allen coming to stop by to check on her and the babies. "Hey, hold on real quick; my mom husband is at the door." "Okay." Sasha sat her cell on the sofa and went and opens the door but on the other side stood Roy and the look on his face read murder. "How the hell did you find me," asked Sasha as she tried to close the door in his face. With one push the door flew open and Sasha fell to the floor. "Bitch do yuh really tink mi would let yuh leave mi di way yuh did," said Roy as he picked Sasha up by the neck and tossed her in the living room. "Roy please leave, someone will be here in a few minutes to check on me," said Sasha as she tried to get off the floor. "Oh ya talking bout dat nigga yuh been fucking, mi took care of him yuh don't have ta worry about him coming here anymore," said Roy as he looks around the house. Sasha took that time to get off the floor and ran across the room and picked up her cell phone. "Jay, Roy's here, help," cried Sasha as she felt Roy hands pulling her by the hair. "SaSa, SaSa," cried Janet as she heard blows coming through the phone. Hanging up she pushed the number two in her phone and Jay answer on the first ring. "Wat's up beautaful." "It's SaSa, I was talking to her and then someone knocked on the door and she thought it was her mom husband but it's Roy and then all I heard was him beating on her, oh my god Jason, Roy there and he's going to kill her, we got to go help her," cried Janet. "Slow down Janet, where is she?" "New York, she's at her mom husband house, she thought it was him at the door, but its Roy he's going to kill her," cried Janet. "Look mi have ta find Zoe, when mi find him mi will call yuh back, use di house phone and just keep calling SaSa, do yuh know anyone who knows where she is?" "She said her mom knows where she is, I'll call and let them know, Jay please don't let anything happen to her," said Janet as tears felled down her face. "Mi will try mi best now call her mom and let dem know wat's going on, maybe dem know someone who can help, mi be there in ten minutes." "Okay," said Janet as she hung up the phone. Janet called

Betty house and Susan answer on the third ring. "Susan this is Janet, Roy's with Sasha, and she needs our help," cried Janet. "Wat do yuh mean Roy's wid Sasha, dat's not possible." "I was talking to her and she thought it was your husband at the door but it was Roy, can you call your husband and see if he can go over there and check on her?" "Yes, yes mi will call ya back in a few minutes," said Susan as she hung up the phone. Janet was pacing the kitchen floor when Jay got home and when she saw him she ran into his arms. "Where's Zoe," asked Janet as she steps back looking for Zoe to be behind Jay. "Mi thinks he's at a meeting, mi left him a message, but mi will call him again and try and get in touch wid him, did yuh call Sasha mom?" "Yes she's going to call me back in a few minutes, and SaSa not answering her phone what are we going to do Jay, she's way in New York, how the hell can we help her when she's that far away?" "Don't worry, mi called mi cousins, and dem standing post until mi gets the address for dem." "How the hell did he find her?" "Mi don't know, but her mom needs ta hurry and call so we can make moves," said Jay as he dialed Zoe number again. Janet and Jay were waiting for Susan to call them back when they heard a lot of commotion in the living room, they both thought it was Zoe so they hurried to the living room, but when they went out to see what was going on they came face to face with Ed holding two guns in his hands. "Oh my god," cried out Janet and the next thing she heard was gunfire. Before she knew it Jay was standing in front of her shielding her, but she felt a sharp pain in her left shoulder before Jay push her out of the way as the bullets hit him in his chest and shoulders as well, and the next thing she knew blackness claimed her.

Chapter 28

Zoe

Zoe was walking out of his Therapy office when his phone rung. "Speak." "Zoe thank Jah yuh answer di phone, its Sasha," cried Susan. "Wat's wrong?" "Janet called and said dat Roy was at di house wid Sasha, mi called Sasha and mi husband and dem not answering, and den mi call Janet back and now she's not answering, Zoe wat mi gaan ta do?" "Where is Sha?" "New York, at mi husband house," said Susan. "Look give mi a minute ta find out wat's going on, push comes ta shove mi got people in New York who can go and check on Sha, so don't worry, keep calling both ya husband and Sasha and mi get back wid yuh as soon as mi can." "Thanks Zoe, hurry, and call mi back," said Susan as she hung up the phone. Rushing to his car Zoe called Jay phone and when he didn't get an answer he knew something was wrong. As Zoe, was heading out of the parking lot his cell rung. "Speak." "Boss, shit is gwan'in down, Jay been shot and his girl ex took her," explain Gunny. "Wat," shouted Zoe as he almost ran off the road. "Yeah mon, Jay just told mi dat yuh called, and ta call yuh back; he's ready for war mon." "Damn, this can't be happening, mi just found out dat Sasha in trouble, tell Jay mi on di way and ta saddle up," said Zoe as he closed his phone. Zoe went home first and when he pulled in his yard he couldn't believe his eyes. "Wat di blood clot do yuh want," shouted Zoe as he got out of his car. "I need some money, and since you got it." Taking his gun out of his back pants Zoe shot in the air and then pointed the gun to Brittney head. "Look yuh bumba clot, yuh got no minutes ta get di blood clot from mi house or mi will kill yuh." Backing up Brittney looks at Zoe and then at her fingernail. "So it's like that and I was going to give you some information on your baby momma," said Brittney as she turned around to leave. Taking the butt of the gun Zoe hit Brittney on the head and when she felled to the ground Zoe pointed the gun to her head. "Yuh got five second ta tell mi wat yuh know or mi will kill yuh." "Shot then." POW, Zoe shot Brittney in the hand and then pointed the gun to her head. "Four second." "Uh, you shot me," cried Brittney. "Three." "I've been following Roy to New York and he been watching Sasha and then earlier today I followed him and he went to this man house and he beat him telling him to stay away from his wife," cried Brittney as the blood gushed out of her hand. "Wat man," asked Zoe. "I don't know, everyday a man goes to the house and stay for an hour and then he leaves, Roy followed him home and then went back to the house and watched to see if Sasha went anywhere, and when she don't he goes to the motel down the street until the next morning." "Where's he now?" "In New York I guess, I left right after he beat that man up, hell he probable killed him he wasn't moving when I ran away from the house." "Shit." "Look I'm sorry, am really sorry," said Brittney as she tried to stand to leave. "Where do yuh tink yuh going?" "I told you what you wanted to know, I have to go to the hospital." "Ya not gwan'in anywhere, how long is it ta get ta di house where Sasha at from here?" "I don't know about two hours." "And yuh know how ta get there?" "Why?" "Because yuh gaan ta take mi and if yuh don't then mi gaan ta shot yuh in di head, den yuh want have ta worry about no hospital." Brittney was quiet as Zoe pointed the gun at her head again. "Choice," said Zoe staring down at her. "Damn, look Zoe I need to go to the hospital my hand is bleeding pretty badly." "Let's go," said Zoe as he pulled Brittney by the arm off the ground and pulled her inside the house, when he was inside he pushed a button and began to talk on the phone. Ten minutes later Hell Bent, Smokey, Killer, and Herb walked into the house with same man who was going to abort her now dead baby. Speaking in his language he said something and then the man went over to Brittney and examined her hand. "Clean." "Good fix it so we can leave," said Zoe as he pushed another number on his phone. "Tell Jay, mi be there in ten, and ta be ready," said Zoe as he hung up the phone, when he turned around the man was putting bandage on Brittney hands. "Done," said the man as he started collecting his things. "Good let's bounce we need ta hurry and get shit moving." Breaking all traffic law Zoe got to Jay house exactly ten minutes, as he walked into the house he saw Jay sitting on the sofa with his hands over his face. "Wat di hell happen here mon," asked Zoe as he gave Jay a hug. "Mi don't know, Jay called mi and said dat Sasha was in trouble and mi rushed here ta try and help, mi guess mi forgot ta lock mi doors, we heard loud noise and thought it was yuh, but it was Ed mi couldn't do noting mon he just started shooting and when mi went down Janet felled, mi don't know if she was shot or anyting," said Jay as he took a deep breathe. "Look, mi got ta help Sasha, and Brittney gaan ta show mi where she's at, but if yuh need mi here den mi will stay." "Naw yuh go and take care of mi cousin, give mi di address and mi will call mi other cousin and dem can watch di house for yuh until yuh get there." "Good, mi have ta make sure dat Sha and mi kids are okay mi will call yuh when mi get di address," said Zoe as he began ta pace the floor. "Go handle yuh business, mi waiting for Jay mom's ta call mi back, she said Jay phone has a tracking device on it, once we know where she's at den we can make a move." "Tracking device, that's how he knows where Sasha's at," said Zoe as he stops and looks at Jay. "Damn mon." "How are you holding up mon?" "Mi good, pissed but good, mi had a feeling dat something was gaan ta go down so mi was ready wid di vest he still caught mi on the shoulder but mi good, but he caught mi off guard when he came here, but when mi find his batty bwoy ass he dead yuh know?" "Same for mi, mi gaan ta kill Roy ass if he touches Sha or mi kids." "Go; call mi when yuh get there." Jay said as he stood up to hug Zoe. When Zoe got outside Brittney was smiling in Smokey face as he approached the car. "Hell Bent and Herb will ride wid mi, Smokey and Killer she can ride wid ya'll if she tries anyting shoot her," said Zoe as he got in his car started his it and pulled off not waiting for a respond. Twenty minutes later Susan called and told him that Sasha and her husband still wasn't answering their phone. Zoe didn't want to tell her what Brittney said so he just asked her for both address for Sasha and her husband and told her that he'd go and check on them. When he got off the phone he called Jay and gave him the address so he could call his cousins so they could go and check on Susan husband and to be at the house when he gets there. Two hours and fifteen minutes later Zoe spotted Sasha car outside of a townhouse and took in a deep breathe. Parking down the street Zoe, Hell Bent, Herb got out of the car and met Smokey and Killer. "Mi gaan ta leave ya here wid her, if she tries anyting kill her, if she does anyting kill her," said Zoe as he walked away from the car. As they were walking towards the house a car parked a little ways flashed there lights so Zoe, Hell Bent, and Herb walked over to the car. "Yeah mon mi Kilts and dis is mi boy Hellium, yuh must be Zoe?" "Yeah mon, thanks for ya help, do yuh know if dem still in di house or not?" "Dem inside, mi walked by and heard some music and babies crying, but dat's bout it, so wat do yuh want ta do?" "Mi ready ta go get mi babies and mi wife," said Zoe as pulled out his gun and clocked it back. "Den let's move, mi got mi boys around di back already," said Kilts. "Den let's do dis," said Zoe as they headed towards the house. When they got outside the door Kilts chirp his boy and told him that they was ready and then he took out a device and used it to open the front door. Zoe went in first as he searched the living room and when he saw his babies sitting on the floor he ran over to them and kissed them on the forehead, when he was sure that they wasn't harm he handed them to Herb and once when they was out the house he ran upstairs to find Sasha. As Zoe approached the first bedroom he heard music and then a popping sounds coming from the bedroom and couldn't believe his eyes as he saw Sasha handcuffed to the bed naked while Roy beat her with a thick leather belt. As Roy was ready to bring the belt down on Sasha bruised and battered body Zoe charged in the room tackling Roy to the floor, and for the first time in a year Zoe blacked out. A few minutes later Kilts and Hell Bent rushed into the room and saw Zoe beating Roy in the head with the butt of the gun and ran over and pulled Zoe off Roy lifeless body. Zoe stood up and looked around the room and when he was focus he took a deep breath and went to the bed and looked down at Sasha. Taking off his coat he covered her battered body and sat on the side of the bed. "Sha, can yuh hear mi," asked Zoe as he touched Sasha cheeks. When she mumbles something Zoe was happy that she wasn't dead. "Sha, its okay, mi here," said Zoe. "Roy, Roy." Zoe looked over at Roy body and then caresses Sasha face. "Yuh don't have ta worry bout him anymore, stay still until mi find di keys ta get di cuffs off yuh." "Roy, Roy has them, what, what if he comes back, oh god Zoe our babies, our babies he said he killed our babies," cried Sasha. "Dem fine, just relax." Hell Bent searched Roy pockets and when he found the keys he tossed them to Zoe. When Sasha was release from the cuffs Zoe help her sit up in the bed, looking around he found some sweat pants and a top and handed them to Sasha as he motion for Hell Bent and Kilts to move Roy's body so Sasha couldn't see it, then they left out the room. Zoe cell rung and he looked at the caller I.D. and saw that it was Jay and walked out of the bedroom so Sasha couldn't hear and answered it. "Wats gwan on, have yuh found Jay yet?" "Yeah mon, he took her ta di same house he was at, mi and mi boys are on di way now, have yuh found SaSa yet?" "Yeah mon, she's wid mi right now, but Roy beat her pretty badly, mi own di way ta yuh once mi found out about her mom's husband, ya cousin sent his boys ta check on him." "That's wat's up call me when yuh get here," said Jay and hung up the phone. When Zoe walked back in the room Sasha was sitting on the bed looking at the bloodstain on the floor. Zoe rushed over and tried to help her get dress, when she touched his hands to stop him she looked into his eyes and knew the answer to the unanswered question, as he was putting the rest of her clothes on the bedroom door burst open and there stood Allen with a black eye and busted lip, and Zoe could see he was okay. "Thank you God, am so sorry Sasha, I didn't know if you was alive or dead, that crazy motherfucker attacked me when I got home, are you okay," asked Allen as he rushed over and hug Sasha softly. Shaking her head Allen stood up and looks at Zoe. "I don't know who you are but I owe you and your friends my life, if you hadn't come when you did no telling what that motherfucker would have done." "Allen this is Zoe, Zoe this is my mom husband Allen," said Sasha as she tried to stand up." Allen reached over and shook Zoe hands. "It's nice to finally meet you, Sasha told me a lot about you." "Same here, but we need ta get going, do yuh want ta stay here or go wid mi," Zoe asked Sasha. "We're going with you." Zoe helped Sasha down the stairs and when she got outside she saw Brittney holding her daughter. With all her strength Sasha rushed over where she was and snatched Zara out of her arms and handed her to Zoe. "Don't you ever touch my kids again or I'll kill you, do you hear me," shouted Sasha. "Look." Before Brittney could say another word Sasha two pieced her knocking her down on the ground. "No bitch you look, look at me, you're the cause of this, you and your lies almost got me, and my babies killed," shouted Sasha trying to catch her breath. "Sha, she cool, she was di one who told mi wat Roy was going ta do," said Zoe as he tried to comfort Sasha. "She cool, do you know what she put me through, all her lies and her jealousy, look at me Zoe," cried Sasha as Zoe held her gently to his chest. "Sasha I'm so sorry," cried Brittney. "That you are, Zoe I need to get away from here," said Sasha as she limped to the car. Zoe looked at Brittney and then followed Sasha to his car. When they got in Allen rushed over to the car. "Hey I just talked to your mom and assured her that you're fine, but like always she wants you to call her right now," smiled Allen. "Oh my God Janet," said Sasha as she held her heart. "Wat's wrong," asked Zoe. "I just got a feeling that something's wrong with Janet, I have to call her and let her know that we're okay," said Sasha as she looked for her cellular phone. "Um, we can call her when we get there, right now just use mi phone and call ya mom," said Zoe as he looked at Sasha. "Okay, but I still have to call Jay; she must be so worried because I was talking to her when Roy showed up." Zoe was quiet as Sasha searched his face. "What you're not telling me is there something wrong with Jay?" Zoe was quiet as he thought of something to say and when he couldn't find anything he just stared at her. "Oh god, please tell me she's not hurt Zoe." "Mi really don't know, look relax yuh been through so much, mi worried about yuh and the bruises on ya body, mi need ta get yuh ta an hospital." "Fuck that, take me home so I can find out what's going on with Jay, if anything happens to her, I don't know what I'll do," cried Sasha. Zoe and Allen looked at each other as Zoe started the car and pulled off.

Chapter 29

Jay

When Jay got to the house he saw that he couldn't hide what he was about to do, so he looked over to Gunny, Skillz, Razor and Danger. "We go in quick, shot if yuh have ta but either way mi not coming out unless mi got Jay," said Jay as he clocked back his gun. "We ready boss," said everyone in unison. When they got out of Jay SUV they ran to the house, and then Skillz used his skills, and pick the front door and with a matter of seconds they were inside the house. As they shut the door quietly they searched the downstairs area, when they were sure no one was downstairs they headed upstairs. They had just searched the second bedroom when they heard noise coming from down the hall and Jay heart stop beating when he walked closer and heard Ed moaning and grunting. As he pushed opened the bedroom door he nearly went crazy as he saw Ed thrusting in and out of the unconscience Janet. As he looked around the room he saw Ed gun laying on the pillow inches away from his reach. He noticed that Janet eyes was closed and she wasn't moving and the next thing Jay knew he took his gun and casually walked over to Ed and shot him in the head. When Ed felled still on Janet, Jay pushed him off her. After he put his gun in its hostler he looked at Janet more clearly he saw that she had a bandage on her shoulders and was bleeding badly. "She was shot, go get di car mi need ta get her ta di hospital," shouted Jay as he took off his jacket and put it on Janet naked body. When she was covered he picked her up and hurried downstairs. When he got to the car a neighbor was standing on the porch as he put Janet in the car and walked over to the driver side as Gunny, Skillz, Razor, and Danger got in the car and drove off. "Wipe di guns off and put dem in di safe in di back in di floor, Skillz know di code," said Jay as he looked in the rearview mirror. Jay hit the interstate and did an hundred miles per hour not stopping even when the police was following him, thirty minutes later and three police cars later he pulled up at Norfolk General Hospital and rushed to the passenger side and took Janet out. "Freeze, don't move," said a white police officer as he pointed his gun on them. Jay now pissed and not caring turn to the police officer. "Wat di blood clot can mi go if mi come ta di hospital, mi fiancée' been shot and either yuh shot mi or get di hell out of mi face," said Jay as he looked at the police, when the police officer didn't say anything Jay turned and rushed Janet into the hospital. "Mi need help mi fiancée' been shot," shouted Jay as the nurses and doctor rushed to help. When they put her on the stretcher Jay felt helpless as the nurse told him that he couldn't go in the back. When he went outside he saw the police officer searching his truck and looked around and saw his boys in handcuffs. "Wat di blood clot is gwan on," shouted Jay. "Put your hands where I can see them sir," said the same white cop. "For wat, wat's gwan on," asked Jay again. "You and your friends are being arrested for breaking and entering and for murder, I got a call on the radio describing your vehicle leaving a house where the neighbor hear a shot and saw a black male leaving out carrying a lady from the scene." "Okay, so ya just gaan to arrest us not knowing the facts," said Jay as he turned with his hands over his head. When the police officer put the handcuffs on Jay he sat on the curve with his boys. After searching the car the police officer came and stood in front of Jay. "Where's the gun at boy, I know you people shot that man and left him dead I know y'all nig." Another white cop came and pulled the other officer to the side and said a few words to him and then he walked back toward Jay and his boys. "I apologize for my action and if you wish to make and complaint my commanding officer is willing to take it for you," said the officer. Jay, Gunny, Razor, Skillz, and Danger looked at each other and then back at the officer. "Yuh good, we don't want ta press charges," said Jay. Wiping sweat from his forehead the officer walked passed the other officer as he approached Jay and his boys. "Good evening gentlemen, am officer Smith, if you can please forgive my fellow officer he had no right to say what he said, if you can please tell me what exactly is going on maybe I can help you," said Officer Smith. "Look mi friends didn't have anyting ta do wid any of dis, it was mi alone. My fiancée' was kidnapped at mi house by her ex boyfriend Ed Gray." "Your fiancée is the woman you just brought in," asked the police officer. "Yes, mi found out where she was so mi went, mi broke into di house, but mi glad because mi saw him raping mi fiancée while he had a gun pointed ta her head. So mi made di decision and shot him first before he shot her and mi again, and mi gun is in mi vest under my coat," said Jay. The officer patted Jay down and when he came to his gun he removed it and step back. "What do you mean shot again," asked the officer as he looked at the gun and checked it to see if it was loaded. "He broke into mi house earlier and shot mi fiancée and mi," said Jay indicating his right shoulder. "Do you mind," asked the police as he checked Jay shoulder? "My God your not lying, son you need to be seen as well you're bleeding through your bandages," said the officer as he began to take Jay's handcuffs off. "No sir mi needs ta know if mi wife is okay, dats di only ting mi need right now." "Well am releasing you and your friends, but advise you not to leave the state until we resolves everything and I hope everything goes well with your fiancée," said the police officer as he motion for the other cop to release the others. "Thanks sir mi hope so," said Jay as he waited for his boys to be release then them all went into the hospital to wait on any news about Janet. His cell rung and when he looked at the screen he saw Zoe number. "Zoe mon, she was shot, mi at di hospital in Norfolk I know yuh got di issue wid SaSa but mi need yuh mon." "Say no more mi be there as soon as mi can we just passing Richmond, so hold tight, how are yuh," asked Zoe. "Mi good mon," said Jay. "Mi gotta make a quick stop, but mi be there." "Take care of yuh bizniz mon, mi be at di hospital," said Jay and hung up the phone. When he went and sat down his cell rung again and this time it was Janet's mother. "Hello." "Tell me that you found my baby, tell me that she's okay," cried Marcy. "She was shot, but mi got her ta di hospital, we're in Norfolk." "That bastard shot my baby, oh God," cried Marcy. When she settled down she took in a deep breathe. "I'm catching the next flight out. Jason?" "Yes." "Call me if they tell you anything about my baby, no matter what they say call me and let me know, and I'll be there as soon as possible." "Mi will, now don't worry she's gaan ta be okay." Marcy was silent as she hung up the phone. Jay sat back down in the chair and all of a sudden blackness claimed him. When he woke up Zoe was sitting in a chair beside the bed reading his chart. Looking around, Jay noticed that he was in a hospital room. "Wat happen," asked Jay as he tried to sit up on the bed. "Yuh got shot is wat happen, mon yuh scared di hell out of mi," said Zoe as he looked at his best friend. "My bad mon, but mi just wanted ta make sure dat Jay was alright, Jay, is she okay, did dem tell yuh anyting," asked Jay as he tried again and sat up in the bed swinging his legs to the side ready to stand up. "Mi haven't heard anyting yet," said Zoe as he pushed Jay back in the bed. "Where is she and wats taking dem so long ta let us know wats going on?" "She's still in surgery, and all mi know is dat she lost a lot of blood, now relax mon or yuh want be no good for her if dem keep yuh in here, ya need yuh strength." "Wat yuh doing wid mi chart," asked Jay as he looked at Zoe. "Just making sure noting else is wrong, yuh also lost a lot of blood, so dem probably will keep yuh over night ta make sure yuh blood pressure doesn't drop," said Zoe as he put Jay files back at the foot of the bed. "How are SaSa and the kids?" "Mi got Hell Bent ta take di babies ta B house, and Sasha good, got a couple of fracture ribs and a lot of bruises, but other wise she's okay." "Damn mon, how the hell did this happen ta us on di same day," asked Jay as he shook his head. "Mi don't know but mi glad dat Jah gave us another chance ta be wid dem, mi don't know wat mi would do if Sha or mi kids was dead, mi tink mi would have ended mi life wid dem," said Zoe. "Same here mon, same here," said Jay as he laid his head back on the pillow. "Look get some rest and mi be back in a while ta let yuh know wats up." "Tell Jay dat mi love her mon." "Believe mi she already knows, but mi will pass di message," smiled Zoe as he left the room. When he got in the hall he saw Sasha talking with a nurse and stop and watched her. When she turned she spotted him and ended her conversation with the nurse and walked towards him. "How's Jay?" "He's good asking about Janet." Sasha was quiet as tears felled from her eyes. "Wat's wrong Sha," asked Zoe with concern in his voice. "I hate this so much and I can't even be any help to our best friends because am a mess," said Sasha as she wipe the tears from her eyes. Zoe walked her back in the surgery waiting room and when she was seated he took a chair beside her, he was glad the waiting room wasn't as full as it was before now he could finally have a conversation with her without a whole lot of people around. Looking into her eyes Zoe took Sasha hands in his. "Look don't say dat, ya helping by being here, dem understand and mi know dat dem is happy dat ya and our babies are safe just like mi know dat yuh happy dat dem is safe," said Zoe as he gently pulled Sasha in his arms. "We don't know if Janet's okay, hell they want tell me anything. Why do people have to be so wicked? Why did he hurt her?" "Wicked minds, have wicked love Sha, when dem want someting but can't have, dem go about it the wrong way to get it, in dem mind dem not hurting anyone when dem is, mi know because mi had wicked love and a wicked mind." "So what, your saying that you don't have wicked love or mind anymore," asked Sasha as she looks into Zoe eyes. "Actually, some of my wickedness ended when yuh left mi, and when ya uncle pointed out dat mi was gwan about it di wrong way ta let yuh know dat mi luv yuh, and than some of my wickedness also ended when mi found out dat mi was a fadda. Sha mi can't promise dat mi will make yuh happy, or protect yuh, but mi can promise dat mi will try and ta always luv yuh and mi kids." "You already proved to me that you love us, you risk your life saving us, and for that I'll always love, respect, and cherish you." Before Zoe could say anything they heard a lot of commotion in the back and rushed over to the nurse station. "What's going on," asked Sasha? "Ma'am, please have a seat and I'll go and see what's going on," said the nurse as she got out and rushed to the back. Sasha and Zoe went back to the surgery waiting room and a few minutes later a doctor and a nurse came out. "Days family I'm Dr. Al-Sahim." "I'm Sasha Jones am Janet's sister how did the surgery go," asked Sasha. "I'm sorry Ms. Jones but she didn't make it, she lost too much blood," said the doctor. "What?" "We tried everything we could," said the doctor. "Oh my God, oh my God, she didn't make it, no," shouted Sasha as she fell to her knees. Zoe pulled her up and held her gently into his arms as she cried for the lost of her best friend. "Dr. Al-Sahim, we need you sir," said a young nurse rushing out of the surgery room. "Am sorry again for your lost," said Dr. Al-Sahim as he rushed to the back. Zoe walked Sasha back over to the waiting room and sat in a chair pulling Sasha in his lap and held her. "Oh Zoe she's gone, my best friend is gone, how do I tell her mom that she's gone how can I live when she's not," cried Sasha. "Look we will get through dis Sha, but mi need ta find a way ta tell Jay, mi don't tink he's gwan ta take this to well either," said Zoe as tears ran down his face. "Go and talk to Jay, I'll meet you there in a minute I have to find a way to tell Janet's mom that her only child is gone and then am going to have to call my mom and let them know also," said Sasha as she got off Zoe lap. "Do yuh want mi here wid yuh, mi can stay and be wid yuh while yuh tell dem." Shaking her head, Sasha wipes the tears from her eyes. "No I have to do this alone, just knowing you're here for me is giving me the strength to do this, I'll meet you in Jay's room when am finished," said Sasha as she kissed Zoe on the lips. "Sha, mi luv yuh," said Zoe. "Mi luv yuh ta," said Sasha as she walked towards the elevator. When Zoe entered Jay room Jay was trying to get off the bed. "Wat di hell is yuh doing," shouted Zoe as he rushed over to Jay and pushed him back on the bed. "Look mon, someting not right mi can feel it," said Jay as he sat back up on the bed. When Zoe didn't respond Jay stop and look up at him. "She's gwan isn't she," asked Jay. "Yeah mon, di doctor said she lost ta much blood," said Zoe. Without a word Jay started pulling out his IV in his arms and when Zoe came towards him he held out his hand to stop him. "No mon, mi need ta see her, mi need ta let her know dat mi will always luv her," said Jay as he got off the bed. All the monitors were beeping as nurses came rushing in the room. "Mr. Black, what's going on," asked the nurse as she looked at Jay and then to Zoe. "Mi got ta go, mi need ta see Janet," said Jay as he tried to steady his balance. "Please Mr. Black you have to relax, I'll page the doctor, and you can talk to him," said the nurse as she walked over and pressed the doctor button. "No mi need ta go now, where di hell is mi clothes," said Jay looking around the room. "Mr. Black, you've lost too much blood, and your arm is bleeding out, please relax." "Jay mon, if yuh want ta go see Jay den we go and see her," said Zoe as he walked over to the small closet and took out a hospital gown and handed it to Jay. When Jay had the gown secure he was headed out of the door when Sasha walked in. "What's going on, oh my god Jay your arm is bleeding out," said Sasha as she walked over to Jay and Zoe. "Jay wants to see Janet, and mi gwan." "Your going to what watch him die, look at him he can't even stand up by himself and you want to walk him all the way to the surgery room, no I don't think so, and Jay I know what your going through, but do you think Janet would want any harm done to you? If she saw you acting like this she would beat your head in, and I'm not about to lose another friend so I'll advise you to get back in that bed," said Sasha as tears fell down her face. "SaSa mi need ta let Jay know dat mi luv her," said Jay as he sat on the bed as tear of his own rolled down his face. "Don't you think she knows that, believe me if she didn't think you loved her she would never agreed to marring you. Jay, Janet loved you as much as you loved her, but she wouldn't want you to harm yourself, she would want you to get strong and love her memories," said Sasha as she went and sat beside Jay. "Mr. Black can we please take care of your arm, it's bleeding badly and we don't want anything to happen to you," said the nurse. "Yes please look after his arm," said Sasha. When the nurse was finished putting the bandages on Jay arm Dr. Al-Sahim walked into the room. "I'm so glad you're here, I need to speak to you about your sister," said Dr. Al-Sahim. "It's okay you can speak in front of everyone, this is my sister fiancé Jason Black, what about my sister," asked Sasha. "She's alive, we don't know how or what happen, but she's alive," smiled Dr. Al-Sahim. "What," everyone said in unison. "Ya telling us dat Janet is alive, dat she's not dead," asked Jay. "Yes, we just finished surgery, she'll be in ICU for a couple days so the nurses can watch her, but other wise she's fine." "Oh my God, oh my God, can we see her," asked Sasha. "Not at the moment, but as soon as she's in a room you can go sit with her." "Thank you, thank you so much, oh my God I have to call her mom and let her know," said Sasha as she reached inside her purse pulling out her cell phone. "Your welcome, Nurse Lean you page me." The nurse looks at Jay and then backs to the doctor. "No sir, I have everything under control sir, sorry for bothering you," said Nurse Lean. "Okay then I'll be in the office writing my report if you need me," said Dr. Al-Sahim as he left out of the room. Zoe walked over to Jay and touched him on the shoulder. "Are yuh okay mon?" "Yeah mon, mi is better den okay mi wife is alive mon, Jay is alive mon." "Mr. Black if you let me hook you back up to the IV's I'll take you to Ms. Day room in a wheelchair when they let you know she can receive visitors, but I can't let this gentleman or you to go by yourself sir," said Nurse Mathis. "Mi sorry mon, mi just want ta see Jay, mi good yuh can hook mi up ta wat ever yuh need ta hook mi up ta long as mi can see Jay," said Jay as he laid his head on the pillow. "Good, because you want be any good to your wife if the both of you is in ICU," smiled the nurse.

"Ya right, mi need ta be there for Jay." "Well am going to call her mom and everyone and let them know the news, will the two of you be okay if I leave you'll alone," said Sasha. "Yeah we'll be on our best behavior," said Zoe as he walked over to Sasha and kissed her on the lips. "Do yuh want mi ta go wid yuh?" "No, I want you to stay with Jay and make sure he behaves, I'll be back in a minute," said Sasha as she left out of the room. An hour later she was sitting in Janet's room holding her hands. "Jay, I love you so much, and the thought of you're not being here with me." Sasha took a deep breath and released it slowly. "You scared the hell out of me, you know that right, am so glad you're alright. Now I'm going to let you get some rest, but I'll be here in the morning maybe then your be up and talking, the doctor said you may not wake up right now because you lost so much blood, but I know you can hear me and I know you want leave me. I love you Jay and please come back to us," said Sasha as she kissed Janet on the cheeks. Sasha and Zoe stayed at the hospital a couple hours with Jay and then left to go to Betty house. Soon as she walked into the house her mom ran up to her and hugged her tight, when she cried out a little Susan let her go. "Mi sorry, mi forgot mi just so happy dat ya all right," said Susan. "I'm fine mom, just a little tired where my babies." "In di kitchen eating some grapes, do yuh want mi ta get dem for yuh?" "No, give me a minute and I'll be in there, I want to go and take a shower," said Sasha. "Okay, are yuh okay really?" "Yes mom I'm fine really," smiled Sasha as she walked towards the bathroom. "Mi be there in a few," said Zoe. When Sasha was in the bathroom Zoe took a seat on the sofa and blew a heavy breath. "Are yuh alright," asked Susan as she studies Zoe?" "Yeah, just worried about Sasha." "Wats wrong dat yuh worried bout her?" "She been through so much, and di thought of her losing Jay ate at mi, mi felt helpless." "Zoe, ya a good man, and mi glad dat it was yuh who was there for Sasha in her time of need and mi know dat she luvs yuh and dat yuh luv her, but what happen is over, ya all is safe and dats wats really matter, mi only can tell yuh ta look forwards and not back. Zoe wicked minds have wicked love and di out come is hurt and pain. Sasha had enough wickedness in her life and mi tink its time dat we as di people who luvs her needs ta show her how real luv is." Zoe was quiet as Susan words soaked in. "Mi want Sha ta marry mi." "Mi know, and all I want is for yuh ta promise dat yuh want hurt her or mi grandbabies." "Dats an promise I can keep, mi glad yuh back in her life also, look mi gotta go somewhere real quick, if Sha ask where mi at let her know dat mi be back real soon," said Zoe as he walked towards the door. "Okay, well am gwan ta go check on Sasha and let her know and to see if she needs anyting," said Susan as she also walked to the back. "Thanks Susan." "No, thank yuh." Zoe went to the jewelry store down the street and purchased a plaintuim engagement ring, when he was finished he called and talked to Jay and to his surprise the hospital put him and Janet in the same room. When he was sure that Jay was all right he headed back to Sasha grandmother house. When Zoe enters the room he saw Sasha and the babies asleep so he turned around to leave out the room. "Don't go." "Did I wake yuh?" "No I was just resting my eyes." When Sasha sat up she looked up to find Zoe staring at her. "What's wrong?" "Mi just tink, yuh di most beautaful woman mi ever known." "Stop lying I'm a mess but am, never mind." "Wat were yuh bout ta say?" "I was about to say that am blessed we're blessed. God has watched over all our love one and he beat the wickedness that was in our lives." Zoe was quiet as he studied Sasha. "Sha mi want ta ask yuh someting?" "Okay." "Will yuh marry mi," asked Zoe as he pulled out the engagement ring. Tears felled from Sasha eyes and Zoe didn't know if this was a good sign or a bad one. "Mi not pressuring yuh, mi just wants yuh ta know dat mi want us ta get married, mi want yuh ta be mi wife." "You don't have to pressure me, because I've been waiting for you to ask me to be your wife for the longest, and yes I'll marry you," said Sasha as she sat up and kissed Zoe softly on the lips. "Now mi di happiest man on di earth," smiled Zoe as he got on the bed. Sasha laid her head on his shoulder and closed her eyes and before she knew it they was both fast asleep.

Epilogue

A couple of months after the incident Roy body were found behind a gay bar in Richmond, so Sasha was granted with the divorce. She sold the house and everything in it. After a year of healing and dealing with everything that happened to them Sasha, Zoe, Janet, and Jason had the double wedding that they all wanted, and nine months later Sasha and Janet both gave birth to twin's boys and girls. Susan and her husband Allen moved to the Newport News area to be closer to Sasha and their grandbabies, and Betty Fills is more happier then she ever been to have all her family together again. Brittney hooked up with Smokey, but after a week of being with him she learned that in order to be happy you have know what true happiness is and that's what Smokey taught her, he made her feel like she was special and wanted, and he didn't hold her past against her. Even though Sasha her and aren't friends she did send them a wedding gift and when it wasn't sent back to her she had hope in to try and fix her relationship with Sasha. All in all Zoe and Sasha moved into a new home and started creating new memory for their future, with Janet and Jay for their next door neighbor...